AS HE READ THE NOTE, ART RODNEY'S KNEES WENT WEAK WITH FEAR CONFIRMED

Calculating thought faded out into pain and shock. His wife was gone. Not only gone, but rushing headlong into trouble.

Art made an effort to get back to calculation. To begin with, how far pregnant was she? Couldn't be more than ten weeks or so, he thought. He tried to remember when she had last had her menstrual week. She always checked, adjusted her contraceptive dosage then.

But it wasn't clear in his memory.

At least her belly hadn't begun to bulge. He was sure that he would have noticed that . . .

Love Conquers All

FRED SABERHAGEN

BAEN science fiction BOOKS

LOVE CONQUERS ALL

This is a work of fiction. All the characters and events portrayed in this book are fictional, and any resemblance to real people or incidents is purely coincidental.

A Baen Book

Baen Enterprises
8-10 W. 36th Street
New York, N.Y. 10018

First printing, April 1985

ISBN: 0-671-55953-2

Cover art by Susan Collins

Printed in the United States of America

Distributed by
SIMON & SCHUSTER
MASS MERCHANDISE SALES COMPANY
1230 Avenue of the Americas
New York, N.Y. 10020

And then, as the French book saith, the queen and Launcelot were together. And whether they were abed or at other manner of disports, me list not hereof make no mention, for love at that time was not as is nowadays.

—Sir Thomas Malory, *Le Morte d'Arthur*

ONE

Arthur Rodney walked through his little California house, calling his wife's name, but only the sound system answered him. The hidden sensors of the system marked Art's passage from room to room, and as he passed from one to another the music changed for him, the electronics of the system even blending each piece more or less smoothly into the next. Male voices in a muted roar offered a drinking ballad as he trod heavily past the open doorway of the party room; tranquilizing violins were trained upon his stomach as he traversed the kitchen. Even in this time of crisis his digestion was all right as usual, but somewhere inside him, even deeper than his stomach, the crisis had already settled. It was as if it were already known to him beyond a doubt what Rita's absence meant.

As soon as Art set foot in the children's room, where the two beds and a scattering of toys awaited him in a somehow ominous stillness, there came from the hidden speakers a cacophony of sounds that seemed metallic and inhuman but still bore a deliberate resemblance to a baby's cry. Little

Timmy and Paula were really too young for that teenage stuff, but Art and Rita had agreed to let them have it in their room, but never mind that now. There was no one in here either. Art heard the discordant metallic baby-cries cut off behind him the moment he went out.

In the master bedroom he encountered the music of heavy rattles, squalling electronics, pulse-beating drums, fit accompaniment for a wiggling, writhing dance that could find a fitting end only on the bed. But Art had no one here to dance with.

The wide bedroom window overlooked the neighbors' desert landscaping, complete with plastic iguana capable of eating real bugs, but little of the outside was visible because the glass had darkened itself almost to opacity against the direct force of the California sun. The sun was getting in anyway, reflecting blue and green through the modest depths of the indoor-outdoor swimming pool. By this water-mottled light, quivering in all the bedroom's many mirrors, Art came to the end of the first phase of his search for Rita. He saw that a small piece of white paper, folded, had been propped against the massage unit on his bedside table. He tossed his box of handcarved wooden Staunton chessmen rattling onto the large circular bed, set his digital tournament clock down gently, and picked up the note. It was in Rita's handwriting.

Darling, please believe that I love you as much as ever, but I have to go away for a time. The kids are both with me and will be okay. I really am pregnant again and Dr. Kuang says he has had to report my pregnancy to Family Planning. It's the law, as he says, and I guess I can't expect him not to report it. I will call you or write you soon so try not to worry.

Love, Rita

As he read the note, Art Rodney's knees went weak with fear confirmed, and he let himself sink down on the edge of the round bed. From there he glanced up at the ceiling mirror above him, but learned nothing from the sight of his own face. It was slightly pudgy, dark-bearded, pale and enigmatic in its shock. He looked down again at the note. He read it through again, once more, a third time, and then dropped it on the bed beside him.

Putting his weight on the bed had quickened the heartbeat of the sound system's drums, though if he began no rhythmic movements of his own within the next minute or so the system would switch to soothing, lulling music and in a little while he would be granted silence. He could of course reach out an arm and turn the thing off, but at the moment he felt too numb to make the effort.

Where to look for escape, or failing that for guidance? There were both flatscreen and holographic recordings within reach, and there were books, there on the short shelf built into the wall beside his bed. The hifi drums beat at him steadily. The words of Eros are those of the true heart. Art's arm was already reaching out, taking from the shelf a well-fingered gray volume with *Philosophy of Pleasure* lettered on the cover in a beautiful and lively pink. But when he had the book in hand he just sat there holding it unopened.

It was obvious that Rita had run off to her brother and his wife in Chicago. She would not have taken the children to leave them with anyone else, and it

seemed certain to Art that she was going to have
to leave them somewhere. Rita—there was no doubt
in her husband's mind about it now—meant to go
into hiding somewhere and bear an unwanted child.
Even though she'd probably have to put it up for
adoption later, secretly or otherwise. It was just
the kind of thing that sister-in-law Ann would en-
courage her to do; quite likely, thought Art, it was
Ann who had suggested the scheme to Rita in the
first place . . .

Calculating thought faded out into pain and
shock. His wife was gone. Not only gone, but rushing headlong into trouble.

Art made an effort to get back to calculation. To
begin with, how far pregnant was she? Couldn't be
more than ten weeks or so, he thought. He tried to
remember when she had last had her menstrual
week. She always checked, adjusted her contraceptive dosage then.

But it wasn't clear in his memory.

At least her belly hadn't begun to bulge. He was
sure that he would have noticed that . . .

So, it would be six months and more before she
bore the child, assuming she was able to hide out
that long and get away with it. If instead, as seemed
more likely, the BFP people caught up with her
and administered an abortion anyway, Rita was
probably going to have to serve at least a short jail
term afterward. That was the way it happened in
the cases that one read about. The next time her
husband saw her might well be during the course
of a conjugal visit . . . there would be, Art thought,
a legal requirement that he make a certain number of those . . . not that he wouldn't make as
many as they let him anyway . . .

Art found that he had opened the book at last.

There was some vague idea in his mind that he ought to be planning for the changes in his sex life that would be brought about by Rita's prolonged absence. Turn to Eros in time of trouble, and find . . .

After half a minute he realized what he was doing, threw the book aside, and went back again to re-reading the note, hoping without real hope to find some less terrible interpretation of its words. But, as he had known from the beginning, there was none to be found.

Pulling the phoneplate toward him on the bed-side table, Art started to punch out the home number of Ann and George Parr in Chicago. They had recently moved into a new house there—business was evidently good at George's karate school—and the new number was still fresh in Art's mind. He had looked it up for Rita last weekend, he recalled now, and there was another bit of evidence that she had gone—

Halfway through punching out the Parrs' number, Art hesitated and then hit the blankoff key. Rita had been gone only a few hours at most, and had probably not yet reached Chicago. Arguing with George would not be likely to do Art any good, since Ann would be the one most actively helping Rita—and arguing with Ann about anything was, in Art's experience, certain to be futile. And anyway it was not the kind of thing Art wanted to talk about over the phone. His best move would be not to call at all, but just to go straight after Rita and for her own good compel her to behave sensibly. And the sooner he caught up with her the better.

He reached again for the phoneplate, and this time tapped out the number of the Chess Director's Office, in the mid-California branch of the State

Bureau of Arts and Games. There was a wait, half a minute with evanescent rainbow static on the plate. Then a man's florid face appeared.

"Oh, hi, Art," the face said. "What's up?"

"Listen, Nick, I just called to say you'd better not pair me in for the first round of the Quarterly. I'm taking a little trip and I don't know if I'll be back in time."

"Second round?"

That would be the day after the first. Art hesitated. Something told him that when he got to Chicago matters might not be as simple as grabbing Rita by the hand and towing her away.

"Better not pair me in for the Quarterly at all."

"Oh, okay. Let me know about the August Monthly, hey?"

Somehow Nick sounded unreasonably casual about the whole thing. Art said: "Certainly I will. Go'th Eros."

" 'Bye."

For a moment Art continued to stare at the blank phone. In spite of his larger worries he found himself still irritated by the Chess Director's offhand manner. Bureau of Arts people were supposed to believe in the importance of what they were doing; a director of tournaments should at least show a little formal regret when a rated master withdrew from an event. But Nick had seemed as indifferent as a factory foreman checking attendance.

The thought of factories reminded Art that in courtesy he should call his own place of employment before he left. But the chime of an incoming call forestalled him. His finger hesitated over the LISTEN AND RECORD switch, but then he changed his mind and answered openly.

On the plate appeared the face of a young woman,

full-featured and of flawless skin. "May I speak to Ms. Rita Parr-Rodney, please? I'm Emma Lazenby of the Bureau of Family Planning."

Art knew an unpleasant contraction in his stomach. "I'm Rita's husband. She's not in the house right now. Ah, she's out shopping somewhere, I expect."

Ms. Lazenby smiled, a friendly smile that looked as if it could become sympathetic if and when the need arose. But not, perhaps, until then. "Actually the reason for my call concerns you too, Mr. Rodney, and your two children." There was perhaps just a slight emphasis on that penultimate word. "Will you ask Rita to call me back as soon as possible if she returns home during business hours? We're open till five. Or otherwise could she call me in the morning at her earliest convenience?"

"I will, yes, I'll tell her that."

"Thank you." And Ms. Lazenby blanked off.

Art sat on his bed clutching the phone. Maybe Dr. Kuang had smelled trouble coming, and had called in Family Planning right away, reporting Rita to them as a possible problem case. Art thought: Call back tomorrow, Ms. Lazenby, and you'll get some recorded message here, and no matter what recording I leave you'll still be suspicious that something's up. But call back two or three days from now, and I'll have a willing Rita here to talk to you, I promise you that. Maybe not all that willing, but ... or maybe you'll never have to call back again. Maybe in two or three days that Certificate of Abortion will already have reached your BFP computer banks.

What next? Oh yes, there was his job. Courtesy required that he do something about that. Art punched out the number of the Macrotron Electronics plant in San Bernardino, and then the personal extension number of Pete Kinelo, his boss in the test equipment engineering and maintenance department.

The plate showed first the Macrotron logo, and then the recorded image of a young woman who was coyly either nude or very nearly so, it being impossible at the moment to tell which because most of her lower body was concealed behind a receptionist's desk. Two small vases on the desk held rosebuds, one vase standing in front of each of her breasts, so that the nipples were just concealed.

"One moment please," the receptionist said, smiling pleasantly. "Your party has not yet answered her or his personal phone. We are continuing to page your party; thank you for waiting."

The music of *Swan Lake* began. Now the young woman affixed an electrostatically clinging sequin to each of her nipples, and then teasingly displayed a G-string and wriggled into it. Only then did she come up and out from behind her desk, writhing in an erotic dance. In another moment she was dancing along the shore of a lily pond, somewhere outdoors, and after that in and out of the curtain of a small waterfall.

Art waited impatiently, looking at his watch. There were several other calls that he really ought to make, now that he thought about it. Another chess club or two. But first the bank, to see how much cash was readily available, in other words how much Rita had already taken; fortunately he had come home today with the first prize for the Weekly in his pocket, and so he should at least be able to buy a ticket for Chicago. Second, he ought to call Transcontinental Transit, to see how soon he could get a seat on a tube train. That beat flying, as a rule, by avoiding weather problems ...

The dancing girl was suddenly replaced by the earnest face of Pete Kinelo. "Art?"

"Hello, Pete. I can take next week off too."

"Oh, good." Pete beamed through thick safety glasses; he must be right in the shop somewhere; yes, a robot moved behind him. "Then I can bring another substitute engineer in for a week. That'll put us in real good shape on personnel utilization. Say, there's nothing wrong, is there?"

"No, no. Ah, I've been winning quite a few prizes and I've got my nerve up. Maybe I'll try some of the big tournaments coming up around Chicago."

"Great. Fine. And Art—be sure and let me know if you're coming back week after next."

TWO

The transcontinental train, a string of sealed metal cylinders almost windowless and almost silent in its movement, hurtled eastward in frictionless balance through its buried tube, at a speed already supersonic and steadily increasing. An interplay of magnets in the tunnel and the train supported the cars and produced acceleration.

At the front of the interior of each passenger car, a holographic stage ran sollies. On the stage in the car where Art was riding, the life-sized, solid-looking images were enacting a drama set in Victorian England. That was the locale of a lot of fiction these days, and Art was bothered by it, even now when he had vaster problems to distract him.

The story currently on stage centered on the romantic pursuit of a prim London nursemaid by a young leftenant (in the play they pronounced it that way), freshly returned from Inja. Apparently there was no limit to what they could get away with showing nowadays. Almost every second or third shot, or so it seemed, was a long lingering closeup of the heroine, showing her swathed almost from chin to ankles in clothing that was not only loose-fitting but practically opaque. Only just enough of her skin and shape showed through to have kept the Bureau of Arts people from clamping down with an A rating. Doubtless the producer would argue that in real Victorian England *nothing* had showed through, but thank Eros that kind of evasion was not yet accepted by the Bureau and the courts. Ann, when Art met her in Chicago, would probably be wearing something like this heroine's costume. Rita wouldn't be, though. She had better not.

What should he say, what ought his very first words to be, when he caught up with her? Something firm and decisive, certainly. He loved her, but he wasn't going to stand for this. What kind of facial expression should he try to wear? Art thought over those questions for a while and then decided there was no use trying to plan for that moment in such detail. A lot would depend on circumstances, on what Rita's own attitude seemed to be.

Of course there would be no room for argument on terminating the pregnancy. That had to be done. He would be absolutely inflexible on that. Rita could be stubborn, as he well knew, but this time he would be more stubborn. Maybe if he had taken such a firm stand earlier, things would never have come to this.

Maybe. The trouble was that he could discern no single turning point where things had gone wrong. They had just somehow drifted into this trouble.

Of course, unplanned pregnancies did happen. There was really no shame in a woman's getting pregnant for the third time, or the thirteenth. The only shame was in not doing something about it.

Oh yes, pregnancies happened, all right. They had
certainly been happening to Rita, ever since Art
had known her.

Art had been teaching high school electronics
when they first met. Rita, eight years younger, had
been a student, though not in any of his classes.
There had been no more than a casual acquain-
tanceship between them until the first night of the
Senior Prom for Rita's graduating class. Art had
been one of the chaperones. The Prom had been
held aboard a tube-train, basically like this one,
only furnished differently. And that one of course
had been a local, chartered to keep running for a
couple of days in an underground loop around
mid-California.

In keeping with tradition, the Prom had been
the occasion for the graduates to break formally
and officially out of their own age-group for sexual
activity, and Rita had spent a good deal of time in
one of the beds with Art. Later, he had felt a little
guilty about such protracted distraction from his
chaperone's duties, for as it turned out there had
been some stargazing trouble in the baggage car—
well, it was regrettable, but in a large group it had
to be expected. That sort of thing had happened
before at Proms and dances, and would again.

A few weeks after the Prom Art had accidentally—
as he then thought—run into Rita at the school,
where some kind of one-day seminar about col-
leges was going on. Later, Art was to realize with a
warm glow that she had made a determined effort
to locate him and meet him on that day.

But that was later. At school, on the day of the
seminar, Rita in the course of casual-sounding conversation mentioned to him that she was pregnant.

"That's too bad," Art commiserated mildly. In general he disliked listening to people talk about their ailments.

"I think it must have happened at the Prom." Rita smiled at him, and brushed back her naturally blond, almost platinum hair, for which Art had a number of times, at intimate moments, declared his admiration. "Maybe it's a little present from you."

An odd, ill-mannered thing to say; the humor of youth, Art decided, from his eminence of nearly thirty. "I suppose it quite possibly is. The Prom was great fun, though, wasn't it? I hope your escort wasn't too put out with you for spending so much time with me."

"Great fun," Rita agreed, rather solemnly. "But now," she said, "it looks like I'm leaving my good old school days all behind. At least for a few years."

Art didn't get it. He was certain that Rita was too bright to just drop out and settle for Basic Income all her life. "Surely you're going on to junior college at least?"

"I was going to the university. But a pregnancy sort of changes everything. At least for me it does."

"Well ... surely you'll be all over that before the fall term starts? Are there complications?"

"In a sense I suppose there are. You could call it that. I'm going to have the baby, Art." On the first night of the Prom her calling him Mr. Rodney had stopped forever.

"You're *what?* I'm sorry, it's none of my business, of course, but ..." They were standing in a school corridor, an occasional student hurrying by.

"I'm going to bear the child. And raise it. If I can."

This calm determination was a side of Rita that

he had not seen before. Groping, mystified, and to his own surprise intrigued, he asked:

"But why?"

His evident mystification dampened her enthusiasm, if that was the right word for the bright, purposeful attitude with which Rita had brought up the subject. But her determination was intact. She said: "That's what my parents keep asking me, why. It's hard for me to explain to anyone. It's as if there were already a tiny baby inside me, depending on me. Though I can't even feel it moving yet, of course."

"Hormonal changes are proceeding early, I suppose," Art muttered, to be saying something. Why was she going on like this, telling him all about it? It was, as he had already said, none of his business—unless, he realized with a shattering silent flash, unless he wanted it to be.

His young adult life had been spent in trying a number of lifestyles, not including marriage. He had known vague dissatisfaction with them all. Certainly he knew plenty of married people who were dissatisfied with their lives too. But Art had not yet made that trial for himself, and it was perhaps getting to be time to seek and choose a wife. And he liked this young woman, liked her better each time he saw her.

He said: "I suppose your parents have pointed out to you that having a child already is bound to make things harder for you when the time comes when you want to get married. Not to mention the problems of raising a kid by yourself."

"I know, you're absolutely right." Rita frowned, as if to demonstrate that she was in the habit of considering big decisions thoughtfully. "I guess most men want to raise two kids that they think they might have fathered themselves."

Art couldn't argue with that. He felt that way himself—or rather he had always expected that he would feel that way when the time was ripe to play the role of father. You might as well accept the first two healthy ones that came and raise them as your own, even to the point of ignoring obvious postnatal indications that the biological father was someone else. And if some woman you knew socially had a kid that was especially strong or smart or handsome, why you might nurse a belief you were the sire. Conversely, if your wife gave birth to a child that seemed a little slow, or unattractive—or even one of the rare full-term infants that the BFP would not certify as developmentally human—you might convince yourself that someone else had fathered it.

But that was all still theory as far as Art was concerned. Right now the really pertinent question was: Would Rita Parr make him a good wife? From observing his married friends Art knew that you generally wound up spending a lot of time with a marriage partner, especially when you were trying to raise a child or two. And he had decided, based on observation, that frequent divorces and remarriages were not desirable—the fewer stepparents a kid had the better off the kid was—was the way he looked at it.

He said: "Rita, I wish I knew you better."

His wish was granted.

As if with some tacit understanding, from the day of that summer meeting in the school Rita and Art started going out together regularly. Art got to know Rita's parents, and her likeable brother George. Art had no close family locally available for her to get to know, which he supposed was some kind of an advantage.

He considered from every angle, or tried to, the idea of marrying her. On the few occasions when he did communicate with one of his own parents or steparents he hinted at the prospect of his coming marriage, and when he could detect any notable response at all it was always a mild glow of approval. That, of course, was as much as he could expect from any steparent or parent; it had been a long time since what Art did was of deep concern to any of them, or vice versa.

He and Rita were together frequently, sometimes more or less continuously for several months. Art became convinced that she wanted very much to marry him. What he himself wanted was harder for him to determine. They quarreled, and then made up. In the spring her Timmy was born and Art sent flowers to her at the hospital and a few days later came to pay her a visit at home.

Rita, sitting in a rocking chair in her bedroom as she nursed the baby, told Art: "You know, I still think he's yours. I have that feeling about him, and I'm glad."

Studying the small wizened face, still bearing its bruises from the violence of birth, Art could detect in it no resemblance to himself. But he realized that he was hoping to find a resemblance. Giving this hope some solitary thought a little later, he decided that it was enough to tip the balance.

A month later he and Rita, now legally and socially united by the bonds of matrimony, moved into a new apartment with little Tim.

*   *   *

After marriage, just as before, Art and Rita preferred to spend most of their free time in each other's company. He was relieved to find that things worked out that way. Rita continued to be his favorite sex partner, too. He found himself going weeks, once a whole month, without bedding anyone else. And, while he wasn't absolutely sure, he had the impression that Rita's sex life was even more intensely concentrated on him. Looking back, it occured to Art that perhaps he should have made a point of finding out. Such concentration of lust upon a single object was one of the danger signals that the popular psychologists of shows and newsprint tended to harp on, a sign that one's sexual attitudes might be warping in a dangerous direction.

He and Rita had been about two years married, quite happily for the most part, when she surprised him with the announcement that she was pregnant again. It was really a surprise, because they both been taking anti-fertility drugs. But, as Dr. Kuang explained, the drugs were not one hundred per cent certain. Anyway a pregnancy was of course no real problem; they had caught it quite early, and he could do a menstrual extraction right now in his office if they wished.

But no. Oh, no. Although Rita seemed as surprised as Art was by this pregnancy, and not as calm about it as she had been with her first one, she turned out to be if anything even more determined that this gravidity should produce a baby. To her, the fetus even in this early stage was already a person, a human life inside her belly, one of the family, though nameless and still of unknown sex. She felt she must protect this life. To Art it seemed that his wife felt as if someone had taken a real baby and stuffed it in there. As far as he could tell, Rita had not absorbed this opinion from any of the religious fringe groups or humanistic sects that still maintained it as official doctrine. She had somehow arrived at it by herself.

Naturally, since they were now married, Art saw even more of her during this pregnancy than during the previous one, and by now he was able to read her moods more easily and guess her thoughts. What he saw this time began to frighten him. The first time he had thought that she was merely being stubborn on the subject, acting in an immature, adolescent way. This time he saw her as in the grip of some enormous force, a force that was bent on using her as a tool for making babies. She refused even to discuss the possibility of getting an abortion. She even refused the amniotic tests that would have shown birth defects; whether or not some bureau of doctors certified developmental humanity, she said, it was and would be her baby still. Of course the chance of some gross dehumanizing defect was really too remote to worry about. But still. And if Art persisted in trying to argue with her about it, Rita quivered and suffered, in real emotional pain he was sure.

Well, Art had always hoped to have two children. And a lot of people said that it was more convenient if your kids were close to each other in age. They could play with and entertain each other, and you got the diapering and the other messier parts of the business over in a relatively short time, once and for all. So, since Rita was so determined to have this one, why not?

A couple of days after Paula was born, Art called Dr. Kuang to talk over the best means of insuring against yet another pregnancy. Frowning from the phoneplate, Dr. Kuang told him that Rita's psychological profile showed that surgical sterilization was definitely not indicated in her case. He would prescribe new medication. "And you say you and your wife are frequent sexual partners. So of course you should have a vasectomy yourself."

"I'll do that. Yes."

"And whenever she's with other male partners, she should choose sexual activities that can't possibly result in pregnancy."

"Right. Yes. Of course." Art thought, but did not say, that sex activities other than copulation were never much fun for his wife, and that she only chose them, or rather submitted to them now and then, out of politeness or from social pressure. That was also Rita's attitude about choosing partners other than himself.

So Art hastily went in for his vasectomy, and also went on new antifertility medication. In six months or so all the sperm now residing in his ductworks would presumably have had their chance and he would be permanently and completely sterile. Rita went on new medication too.

Art had done all he could, or so he thought. He loved his wife, and his two kids, fascinating babies. Often he didn't see as much of the three of them as he would have liked. He had switched from teaching electronics to working at it, landing a job at Macrotron; he had also begun to spend more time away from home, improving his chess rating and winning more prizes. And then one day he came home and found a note.

THREE

The suggestive dialogue of the pseudo-Victorian play nagged almost subliminally at Art's attention, pulling him away from the fruitless game of trying to guess how he might better have managed his life with Rita in the past. Intending to drown out the play with music or soothing sound effects of surf or waterfall, he looked for the set of earplug phones that should have been attached to his seat. To his disgust he found that one plug of the set was missing; its connector of steel-jacketed wire had been neatly severed by some vandal, who seemed to have gone to the trouble of using a cutting torch.

So he was not going to be able to avoid hearing the struggle of Phyllis and Rodney (respectively nursemaid and leftenant) against their mutual lust, a struggle in which Art was sure they would eventually be victorious. But at least nothing forced him to watch the repulsive sight. He could watch his fellow passengers instead. He could try to obtain something to read. Or he could turn his face to the small window beside his luxurious chair. In the buried tunnel, whose wall was practically against the outer surface of the window, there was of course nothing to be seen except advertisements, the kind called flickersigns. These were tens of kilometers long, lettered in glowing, elongated characters designed to be intelligible only to one hurtling past them at a distance of a few centimeters and a speed of hundreds of kilometers per hour.

Art was watching the passage of one such ad, without absorbing one iota of its meaning, when without warning the train was thrown into violent deceleration. It was braking at emergency rate from jet aircraft speeds, and the first touch of such inertial forces popped the airbags, normally packed away out of sight in front of each seat. Great plastic flowers bloomed, their multiple release coming with the sound of a single explosion. Art's body, in the first instant of sliding forward from his seat, was caught and held.

A second after the bags had bloomed, they were deflating, sagging into soft plastic detumescence, the people they had caught released to movement once again.

"Phyllis," said the sollie show leftenant's voice, loud and clear in the first breathless silence of alarm among the passengers, "Phyllis, I am not an animal, to hurl myself upon you."

Whatever Phyllis replied was drowned out in the rise of general commotion. The passengers around Art were exchanging exclamations, questions, and comments. As he rubbed his nose, stung by the blasting airbag, a woman seated across the aisle looked his way and asked him, almost pleadingly: "It must be just something wrong with the machinery, don't you think?"

Bracing one foot on the seat in front of him,

against the continuing heavy deceleration, Art tried to give the woman a reassuring nod. "Yes, it must be." But he recalled the missing earplug; the Transcon tubes were not immune to vandals, not any more at least. Therefore they were probably not immune to apes either, or to terrorists of one persuasion or another. Glancing at his watch, Art decided that at the moment the train was probably under Iowa somewhere.

Now the deceleration eased markedly. A look at the blur of tunnel wall and flickersign outside the window indicated that the train was now moving not much faster than an automobile.

As the train continued to slow toward a full stop, the holographic play was interrupted. A man's recorded voice, strong and confident, issued from the speakers on the momentarily empty stage. "Ladies and gentlemen, there is no cause for alarm." The voice paused, as some decision-making process, human or electrical, selected the next phrase. "A technical difficulty has arisen." Pause again. "To minimize your inconvenience until your trip can be resumed safely, you will shortly be conducted to the surface by human guides. Please remain seated. Remain seated after the train stops. Ladies and gentlemen—"

There was a glitch of noise, and abruptly a girl's tremulous voice added: "Rodney? I—I've always wanted a—a large family."

A moment later the image of Phyllis, as heavily garmented as ever, had reclaimed the stage. Facing her was Rodney, standing in such a way that his uniform's flat lack of any bulging codpiece could not very well be ignored.

By now the airbags were nothing but wrinkled draperies across the seats, discarded wadding on the floor. The passengers, who had been quieted momentarily by the recorded announcement, were now babbling louder than before, and some of them were standing up. The train's full stop, settling gently to material support on the tunnel's floor, did no more than make them wobble.

The woman across the aisle from Art was once more talking to him but he could not hear her in the general noise. Now she stood up and moved closer to Art, standing hovering over him. He unthinkingly took this as a social move and began to caress her hips, which were bare except for a G-string, but the woman gave only a perfunctory wriggle of response and in a moment he realized that her intent was not to approach him but to peer out of the little window beside his seat.

"Is that *water* in the tunnel?" the woman asked in a loud, clear voice, looking out. Other passengers took up her words and echoed them. Alarm began to mount.

Art took a turn at the window, trying to squint downward at a difficult angle along a concavity of dim concrete. The train nearly filled the tunnel from side to side and top to bottom. It was hard to see anything, but Art thought there was at least some wetness on the concrete wall.

"Yes, it was a Thug who strangled him," groaned a stage voice, that of a grayhaired senior officer in full dress, also of course sans codpiece. "But I am the one really responsible for my son's death."

And that, at last, was the last of the play. The phantoms vanished from the stage, as behind it, with a hiss and a clack, an emergency door in the front of the passenger car swung open. A man in a blue translucent uniform was coming through the door, directly onto the stage. Looking at first no

more real than Rodney or Phyllis, he wore a hard
blue helmet with a clear faceplate, and carried
some kind of pistol holstered at his belt. His stern
expression eased into a professional smile as soon
as a quick glance through the car assured him that
everything was peaceful here. Then he stepped down
briskly in front of the stage, making room for two
more men, similarly uniformed and armed, to
mount it from behind.

The man who had entered first was wearing
stripes on his sleeves, like those of a military
sergeant. Leaning casually on one of the front seats,
he now addressed the passengers in a loud but
friendly voice. "There's nothing to worry about,
folks. The company regrets the inconvenience. We're
going to have to ask you to walk a few steps through
the tunnel, that's all. Will you all form a single
line and move out this way, please, through the
front of the train?"

Eager as they all were to get out of confinement
in this watery tunnel and on their way again, the
sergeant had no trouble keeping the passengers
moving, a single file going past him and onto the
stage and over it. Meanwhile his two aides had
gone on to the rear of the car, presumably to
start evacuating people from the next car in that
direction.

"Nossir, there's no flood," the sergeant loudly
reassured a man who had mounted the stage ahead
of Art. "It's no more than a puddle. There've been
heavy rains. Keep moving, please. This way out."

A few people were burdened with enough luggage to make it a job for them to get up onto the
stage, and Art felt like offering a hand. But he
would have had to back up or push ahead in the

line to do so. Anyway the sergeant helped when necessary, and everything went on smoothly.

Art and his fellow passengers had to traverse two cars ahead of the one they had been riding in, surmounting a sollie stage in each, before an open door in the very front of the train allowed them to descend a short, steep, folding emergency stair into the semidarkness of the tunnel. From somewhere not far ahead, beyond the point where the line of passengers preceding Art vanished in the gloom, there came a sound of heavy splashing, as of wading, shuffling feet. And now Art could distinguish another watery noise, as of a minor waterfall. The tunnel seemed to slope downward gradually ahead of the train, so it was natural that the water, wherever it was coming from, would be deeper there.

A pebble's toss ahead of Art, one of Transcom's uniformed private police was shining a pocket flash about, and someone else was doing the same thing much farther on. The only other illumination in the tunnel was that which shone from inside the train, and from a dimly glowing line in the tunnel wall that stretched, bending and breaking, into the distance. It took Art a moment to realize that this was one of the elongated flickersign symbols.

Staying close to the vague form of the passenger ahead, he felt the water get deeper as he moved forward, until it sloshed about his ankles. Now in the glow of the flickersign he spotted the water leak, or at least one leak. From a small crack in the curved concrete up near the tunnel's top, a stream of a size to have come from a kitchen faucet was burbling down the concavity of the wall. But it did not appear that swimming was going to be necessary. Now, just ahead, another sergeant with another pocket flash was lighting the file of evacuees into a doorway in the tunnel's side. When Art neared the door he saw just beyond it a service stair ascending in a tight helix, with better light trickling down.

He climbed, on stairs wet from the feet of those who climbed ahead of him. It was a good thing there was nobody in a wheelchair. The light got better still, but it wasn't daylight yet. At a landing that Art hoped was near the top, but later proved to have been approximately halfway up, another policeman was stationed to urge them on.

"Step right up, folks. We'll see you safely across the river, then get you on another train. Sorry for the inconvenience. This way."

As if there were some other way. A black woman past middle age, gasping from the climb, wearing gigantic false breasts and an obvious merkin of false pubic hair beneath her transparent gown, stepped out of line to ask questions. "River? What river is this? Why were we stopped here, for sex' sake?"

"It's the Mississippi, lady," said the officer, politely gesturing her upward, then when she still delayed, taking her arm with easy firmness and propelling her along. "You're almost in Chicago. Don't be alarmed, we'll get you through in good shape."

The Mississippi. Still three hundred kilometers to go, Art estimated. As he climbed on, he could still hear the guide's voice from behind him: "Have to keep moving, folks. You're almost at the top. No telling how high the water'll come up these stairs if the tunnel should collapse down there. Step along please. Stay together at the top. If you should see a little light rioting on the surface, don't let it throw you. Just assemble where you're told, and we'll see you through."

Light rioting. People looked at each other. Art kept looking up. Presently he got an unmistakeable glimpse of sky. At the top, the stair delivered its stream of refugees into a graceful low concrete structure, open on three sides to the late summer afternoon. On more peaceful days it might serve as a picnic shelter, standing as it did in a half-wooded, parklike area. The near bank of the wide placid river was only a good stone's throw away, at the bottom of a broad, gentle grassy slope. The sun was lowering behind Art's back as he faced across the river toward a solid array of wooded bluffs that rose above the distant eastern shore.

In and around the concrete shelter lay a good many pieces of freshly splintered wood, that might very recently have formed its picnic tables and benches. Nearby a trash container lay on its side, meager contents scattered. But at the moment there were no rioters in sight. Some forty or fifty passengers, probably all who had preceded Art up from the tunnel, were standing with their luggage on the grass beside the shelter, like some motley levy of inducted troops about to begin their training. A single uniformed policeman stood casually in front of them, giving them something to look at at least, a focus of attention. Three more police, one a woman wearing inconspicuously on her collar what Art supposed was officer's insignia, were standing closer to Art inside the shelter. The helmet of one of these people was buzzing with distant messages. Standing with the three police was a shivering middle-aged civilian man who wore a translucent coverall and thick, clear, tough-looking boots with mud on them.

The officer looked up from her conversation with the others. A hundred meters or so away along the water's edge, some people were emerging at a run from the concealment of some trees. There were men and teenage boys, only a couple of women. They were all running to and fro like clowns in twos and threes and fours, whooping and waving. There were twenty or more of them altogether, and they might have been playing a game, or just scampering about in high good spirits. One man waved a festoon of what looked to Art like cables or plastic tubing.

The civilian man with the police was talking rapidly; with a little sideward glance he included Art in his audience, and went right on. "—so we had our boat in toward the west bank here, taking sediment samples, and just as I turned to say something to Carl, why pow, this rock went by my head and missed me by about a centimeter. And then I saw this mob running out on the bank and heard 'em yelling. Sex, once you hear a yell like that you know what it is the next time. It means a bunch of people have all gone ape. Carl had his helmet off, see, but he still had his diving suit on, and it must have looked almost opaque ... I dunno, maybe they thought we were from the monastery. I gunned the boat to get out from the shore, and then we must have hit something, a log or a piece of junk. Maybe someone fired something at us, I dunno. When I came up for air the mob was flinging more rocks. I ducked under and swam and waded, and came downstream here about half a kilometer and climbed out here when I saw the uniforms. Never saw what happened to Carl. Hope he managed to get his helmet on before he went under."

The people who had been capering along the

riverbank had disappeared back into the trees again, perhaps deterred by the sight of uniforms.

"Looks like they got her burning, finally," said one of the police, squinting to the north. There the west bank of the Mississippi mounted higher, in tree-clothed bluffs. Rooted somewhere among the trees atop the bluff, an ominously burgeoning growth of black smoke towered like the djinn of riot above the countryside.

"Must have been an old building," another policeman remarked.

"Did someone say it was a monastery?" Art put in. Violence and vandalism outraged him, no matter who the target.

"That's right," said the civilian man. "Order of St. Joseph, they called it. Not right for people to take the law into their own hands, but what can you expect? I live around here. The rumor's been going around that the monkeymonks up there've been carrying on some kind of experiments with abortion specimens. I don't mean scientific work, but creating some kind of monsters. Chastity, I don't believe everything I hear, but how do they expect people to take it when they're so mysterious?"

Experiments? Art didn't get it. It was his understanding that Christian monks, or at least the old antichoice faction among them, were against such experimentation on organisms they considered to be endowed with human rights even if unborn. Probably a garbled story, not that it couldn't have started a riot anyway.

All this time a continuing trickle of passengers, now mostly the gasping and the nearly lame, had been continuing to emerge from the nearby stairhead and straggle into place in their loose formation on the green. There were now about a hundred

of them above ground in all. Now the trickle had
slowed and it seemed that the end might be in
sight.

"Here comes a couple more refugees," the engineer remarked. Hiking across the inviting park,
from the direction opposite the smoke, came a
couple who evidently had been picnicking, for he
carried a red plastic picnic cooler and she a small
outdoors pack and a folded translucent blanket.

The young woman was a full-bodied brunette of
eighteen or twenty. The man, considerably older,
was somewhat flabby, in shorts, sandals, and a
broad-brimmed hat, and freshly sunburnt. As the
couple drew near, Art saw that what he had at
first taken for sunglasses on the woman's face were
really artificial eyes of what must be some advanced design. They might have been opaquely
dark sunglasses, except for the increased bulk of
the lenses and the frames, which around the eyes
were molded into tight contact with the skin. The
girl—there was something immature about her—
was neatly and modestly dressed in a sports bikni
of the latest style. Her translucent bra was extended in twin peaks by finger-long cones of pinkish nipple-colored plastic.

As the couple, obviously agitated, approached
the shelter, the river engineer called to them:
"Kinda rough out there, huh?"

The man blinked at him. "Yes," he said after a
moment. He looked at the police. "Can we join
you?"

"Sure. They get your boat too?"

"Yes," the man said after a moment. He appeared to be in slight shock, having to think over
even simple words before he understood them. The
girl had said nothing as yet, looking around ner-

vously, and staying close to her companion. Art
thought she was looking at him, but he could not
be sure, nor could he read her expression. The
artificial eyes functioned like a mask. Faint cat's-
eye gleams shone out from the depths of their dark
lenses, and the plastic frames were studded with
artificial jewels. Or could those stones possibly be
genuine?

"Sure, come along with us," said the woman
police officer, energized now by the appearance at
the stairhead of the last passenger, sitting in a
wheelchair (so there had been one after all) and
just now being heaved aboveground by a team of
puffing police. "Looks like we're all here now."
The officer looked at her troops. "Let's start getting these people over the water."

Art moved along with the two saved picnickers
to join the other evacuees. Just as the whole group
with its escort of police began to move, the brunette girl beside Art let out a sudden, choked cry,
and Art saw her begin to tremble. Following the
direction of her gaze, he beheld a new eruption of
rioters boiling out of the woods and cutting across
the passengers' path, with the evident intention of
intercepting them before they could reach the river.
Why the river? Coming downstream, halfway between the banks, was a large launch, starting to
turn in now to the west bank where a small dock
waited at the end of the passengers' present line of
march.

The march continued. The officer barked an order or two, and her blue-uniformed men, now about
a dozen strong, formed a single marching rank
between the people they were escorting and the
potential foe. There were twenty-five or thirty people in the mob approaching. Half a dozen or so

were women, and these were yelling the loudest.
Most of the men and boys wore the gaudily colored and oversized codpieces favored these days
among youth of the Basic Income class. One so
garbed, a large, florid young man with close set
eyes, came right up to the police line and peered
over uniformed shoulders at the shrinking sheep
behind, as if he were bent on choosing one for
slaughter.

"Any triplet priests in there?" the florid one
demanded. "Any sublimatin' vivisectionists? We
got one already, but there's some more experiments we'd like to try."

He seemed on the point of trying to push his
way through protective line, and one of the bigger
police shoved him roughly back. When the youth
demonstrated anger at this treatment he found
himself looking at a drawn handgun.

"We're just passing through, bigmouth," the policeman told him. "Now you just pull your sublimatin' jaw out of the way and let us pass."

There were no firearms visible among the rioters,
and indeed Art could not see that they carried
weapons of any kind. The sight of the gun knocked
them back almost like a physical force. Keeping
within reach of each other like the cells of some
multiple organism, moving together as if under
the control of a single mind, they fell into retreat.

We got one already. The words echoed in Art's
mind. But maybe they were only brag and bluff.

The passengers with their convoy of police moved
on unmolested toward the dock, which was now
only about a hundred meters off. The immediate
threat apparently was over, but the girl with artificial eyes, walking beside Art, continued to breathe
as if she were on the verge of hysteria. Her escort

on her other side held her by the arm and kept
speaking to her in a low voice, perhaps forestalling
a screaming fit.

Now in the infested woods nearby another out-
break of shouting rose up, blended with the noises
of running feet trampling the undergrowth. The
girl moaned and moved away from the noise, leaning against Art like a frightened child. He put an
arm around her—her waist was really slender—and
squeezed her in a polite caress. "My name's Art,
by the way. What's yours?"

"Rosamond. Rosamond Jamison. Oh!"

A scream had just come from somewhere in the
woods. To Art it sounded like the real thing.

The man on the other side of Rosamond was in
difficulty. Maybe he was getting sick. Some people
shat their pants in times like these. Now the victim stopped in his tracks, so fellow-refugees hurrying along behind him had trouble avoiding a
collision. The woman leading the police shouted at
him to move it, and he stumbled on. But he was
having trouble. Art saw his face, pasty with fear
under his new sunburn, as he handed Rosamond
the weighty-looking picnic cooler. She took it automatically and continued moving forward. Behind
her back, the man looked at Art and said: "Try
and look out for her, will you? See that she gets on
a train to Chicago?"

"Of course, I'll try to help. But what are you—?"

Muttering some last, unintelligible phrase over
his shoulder, the man was gone. Moving with unexpected strength and speed, he had pushed his way
through the police escort on the side of the column
toward the woods, and was running inland before
anyone else was fully aware of what he was about.

"Halt!" the officer shouted, when she caught on.

"Come back here! Don't be a sublimatin' fool!" The running figure did not pause.

The chaste fool, thought Art unbelievingly, squinting after the man. "What's your friend up to?" he demanded of Rosamond Jamison at his side.

"He . . . he . . . we had friends back there." The fleeing man was out of sight in the woods now. Rosamond, wrestling with her picnic cooler, faced forward again. The pace of the column had speeded up, and she was struggling to maintain it. In the rear shifts of volunteers were guiding and pushing the wheelchair along.

Art put a hand on the cooler's carrying grip. "Let me help you with that."

"Oh, thank you." But she seemed reluctant to let him take the weight. When he did so, however, they made better time.

The riverboat, which was moored at the dock by the time the column reached it, was some sort of sightseeing craft, evidently commandeered by the police for this occasion. With all the refugees aboard it was crowded, dangerously Art was sure, with people standing, sitting, and squatting on the deck between the rows of seats. Most of the police remained behind on shore, and as the boat pulled away from the dock Art saw them beginning to march in loose formation back up the slope toward the picnic shelter and its stairhead.

They were approaching the shore of Illinois, whose woods looked wilder and less parklike than those of Iowa just left behind. There was no dock in evidence, and whoever was at the controls of the boat simply brought it in near shore until it scraped bottom, then held it there in the swift current.

A voice, straining to be cheerful, made an announcement to the passengers. "Folks, we have to take the boat back across the river and pick up some more people from another eastbound train. Then we'll be getting you all on your way to Chicago very shortly. Get off the boat promptly, please, step right into the water there, it's not very deep." A couple of police hopped off, standing knee-deep in the current to demonstrate. A couple of the more eager or anxious passengers followed. Soon there was a regular disembarkation. Plenty of volunteers rallied around the wheelchair again, with grins and jokes, to carry it ashore safely. People were sometimes marvelous.

The muddy but solid shore was only a few steps away. Once on solid ground most of the passengers began gravitating inland, despite urgings by their guides to wait, as if in spite of everything there might be another handy tube terminal right at hand. Art and Rosamond drifted along with the slow migration, stopped when it stopped. Thirty or forty meters uphill, a narrow unpaved road paralleled the river, but traffic at the moment was nonexistent. Beyond the road and a wire fence, the tree-covered bluffs rose up unpromisingly. The passengers who had probed the farthest in that direction soon came back with unhopeful reports. No one knew where the point of access to the eastbound tunnel might be. There was apparently no place to go, and nothing to do but wait as they had been told.

Art and Rosamond, having the cooler to carry and both of them lacking any desire for an aimless hike, remained somewhat behind most of the other passengers as the group drifted up to hang around the otherwise empty road. The two of them sat on a grassy bank where the sun, now lowering over Iowa, still shone brightly. Rosamond was quiet now, and seemed less fearful, though she was still looking intently back over the river.

"He'll probably come over in the next boatload," Art offered, trying to comfort. "He's probably all right and they'll be able to pick him up and bring him along."

She turned to him and reached across the cooler to tickle the palm of his hand. She smiled at him beneath her enigmatic eyes. "I think I would enjoy some sex right about now."

"Of course." And they spent an enjoyable ten minutes at it, with Art's paper shirt spread over the rough grass beneath their bodies. Afterward as they lay together relaxing Rosamond began to shiver; the sun was so low now that it had lost its heat, and a cool breeze had come up. Presently she sat up and pulled on her bikni again, but of course it was too small to provide any real warmth. Art picked up the paper shirt, now noticeably wrinkled and soiled, and held it out. "Afraid this is the best I can offer you. There doesn't seem to be a clothing vendor anywhere around."

"You'll be cold, won't you?"

"I'm a little fat." He stood up and adjusted his codpiece and his transparent trousers. "I guess that helps to keep one warm."

Rosamond pulled on the shirt, and then sat down in the grass again with her legs crossed, legs and feet tucked in completely under the garment so that it fell around her like a small tent. The shadow of a bush fell over her now and in the dulled light the shirt was practically opaque, and she was concealed and shapeless from the neck down. Now it was Art's turn to shiver slightly, and his shiver was not caused entirely by the cold. Unwholesome thoughts had come unbidden to his mind. He controlled himself, however, and like a gentleman looked away.

Whenever you thought you had the temptation to repression squelched, it popped up again with a new ploy. He had given his shirt to the poor girl because she was really shivering. It was natural that in her effort to keep warm she should sit down in such a position. Neither of them had calculated the effects of fading light. But maybe if her legs were warmer she wouldn't have to sit that way.

He cleared his throat. "Want my trousers?" he asked. It was incidental, Art told himself, it was not important in this emergency, that removing his trousers would mean taking off his codpiece too, and this would mean stripping his detumescent body of its proper sexual emphasis.

Rosamond appeared not to find anything wrong, suggestive of sublimation, in his offer, but she declined it all the same. "No, this is fine. Thank you. You've been a wonderful help, Art. I hope I can repay you some day."

He slew a mosquito on his bare shoulder. The river before them was beginning to reproduce a sunset. Around them on the grassy part of the riverbank a number of the other stranded passengers had also come together in pairs or larger groups and were embracing or resting between embraces. The presence of these others made real impropriety unthinkable and helped Art put temptation from his mind.

There were more boats in the river now, police or other official craft of some kind, and their searchlights were beginning to play over the far bank.

Groups of people were still moving around over there. Some of them had improvised banners to carry, and rhythmic chants to sing. From where Art sat on the eastern bank the words of neither song nor sign could be distinguished, but the powerful tones of the chanting carried across the water.

FOUR

As the train began to slow for the Chicago terminal, Rosamond leaned across the seat arm and snuggled once more against Art's shoulder, while one of her hands, like some small animal seeking shelter, strayed inside his tattered shirt. "Art, are you sure you can't take the time to meet Daddy tonight? I know he's going to want to thank you for helping me."

"I wish I could, but I'm really anxious to catch up with my family." Of course he hadn't told her that they had run away, or why. He glanced at his watch. It was nearly midnight. "Some other time."

"You be sure and call me while you're in Chicago. I mean it." She dug out a pen and a piece of paper from the pouch attached to the seatback in front of her, and scribbled a number, using the top of the picnic cooler as a desk. When Art's fingers touched the plastic top, in reaching to pick up the paper, it felt as cold as ice. Like Rosamond's eyeframes, the cooler was perhaps more expensive than it appeared at first sight. Whatever picnic remnants were inside it much be frozen solid; she hadn't

suggested during the protracted journey that there
was any food available.

The train ride came to an end at last. Rose
insisted on carrying the cooler off the train herself.
As Art emerged from the tube car into the station's
vast cheerful cave of ceramic tile and warm light,
he turned to say goodbye to Rose, and saw with
surprise that she was already gone. He caught a
glimpse of her through the crowd, being met and
welcomed by a couple of well-dressed men. Strange
girl. But he forgot about her quickly enough in
looking for what he needed next. There it was, a
huge electronic display outlining the city's public
transportation system.

It was late enough for traffic to be light, and the
taxi Art had chosen as the probable fastest means
of transport made good speed through the well-
illuminated streets. Still, Art kept shifting restlessly in his seat, and pulling at his beard impatiently. He could not escape the feeling now, so
close to his goal, that minutes counted, that even
now Rita might be taking some irretraceable step
toward an illegal parturition. The feeling was
irrational, no doubt; any actual birth would of
course have to be months away. But Art was sure
there was a federal law against even *conspiring* to
commit illegal parturition. Midwifery, as the news
media usually called it. Art didn't know exactly
how far one could go in that direction without
running afoul of the law. He didn't know exactly
what the law said. It was one of those things he
hadn't wanted to learn about, probably because
all along he had been subconsciously afraid that
someday it was going to menace Rita and him.

How could she do such a thing, get herself and
him too into this kind of trouble? In her note she

had said that she still loved him. She had used the word twice. But that wasn't really the question, or the problem. He knew his wife, and she was perfectly capable of doing this thing, loving him or not.

Cruising easily through the radar-assisted signals at one intersection after another, the cab driver turned in his seat and glanced back at Art through the bulletproof partition. Through the intercom speaker the driver's voice asked: "Someone meeting you?"

"Yes." Art stretched the truth. "At the block entrance. It's a block of townhouses."

The cabbie faced forward again without answering. Art had just killed his hopes of collecting an easy bodyguard fee, in what the cabbie must know was a good neighborhood.

The street broadened, became an avenue. The cab was entering a section of the city that looked new, as if it had all recently been rebuilt. Under new streetlamps that closely simulated daylight, tall genengineered elms warmed their fine June leaves. Now, on each side of the wide, gently curving avenue were high stone walls, new-looking, windowless, smooth enough to be unscalable but still with enough irregularity in shape and texture to please the eye. The walls were two stories high or more, and Art knew that they must enclose townhouse blocks, about the size of the old city blocks they had replaced. The pedestrian entrances to the blocks, never more than one on each side, were narrow-mouthed and especially well-lighted. Inside each entrance, Art supposed, there would be a security guard watching from a protected booth. The vehicle entry ramps would be similarly protected; they curved down from the street to enter a subterranean level of each block.

The cab stopped presently, in front of one of the pedestrian entryways. Art put money into the slot in the bulletproof partition, got back a reasonable amount of change, and disembarked. He walked into the bright rocky tunnel of the block entry, through walls that looked as thick as those of some ancient castle—or even of a cave, perhaps.

Three meters in, the bright-lit narrow passage was blocked by a gate of steel grillwork, heavily functional despite its ornamentation of nymphs and cupids. In a booth built into the wall beside the gate sat a gray-haired, gray-uniformed man who looked out at Art through a small window of bulletproof glass. Around the guard were rows of controls, layers of video monitors. The man also had a pistol within easy reach. He eyed Art with alert suspicion, no doubt sharpened by the lateness of the hour.

"I want to visit George Parr," said Art into a panel microphone. "Would you tell him please that Art Rodney is here? It's important. He'll want to see me." He checked the time on his watch and began to wait, as the man in the booth began some process of communication.

Less than three minutes had passed before George came into view beyond the steel grillwork, which slid open at his arrival. He was smiling and holding out his big-knuckled hand. Aside from the callus pads over the base knuckles of forefinger and middle finger, there was nothing peculiar in the feel of George's hand, lethal weapon though it was supposed to be. And George was not really impressively built. Rather short, sturdy, but not bulging or rippling with muscle inside his transparent shirt.

His pale hair, almost the color of Rita's, was crewcut, shorter even than his neat goatee.

"How's it going, Art?" George didn't look upset about anything, but then Art could not recall that he ever had.

"Well, I'm upset, naturally. I want to talk to Rita right away."

"She's been here, but now she's gone again."

"What?"

"That's right. Come on in." With gentle pressure on Art's arm George steered him through the gate. Speaking to the microphone below the guard's window, George added: "My brother-in-law. He's going to be staying with us for a day or so." The guard did something to one of his screens, saving an image of Art already captured.

George pulled on Art's arm again. Art let himself be steered inside, though he wasn't at all sure about the duration of his stay. "Where is she now?" he asked impatiently. "Couldn't *you* have talked to her?"

George simply continued to smile in his likeable way. "Come on in and have a look at our new home. We can talk the whole situation over. It's not something that can be settled in a couple of words. Ann's fixing up a bed for you."

"All right." Art sighed, abandoning whatever hope he had left of somehow catching up with Rita tonight. Let Ann fix the bed. He was willing to bet she would never offer to share it with him, which was fine with Art. He would make polite gestures of desire toward her, whether or not she had the good manners to reciprocate, but in truth she aroused him not at all.

Another few meters of curving tunnel, and they had reached the interior of the block. It looked much

as Art had expected, but still he was impressed.
Most of the interior was a single open space, wide
and pleasant, green now with summer grass and
trees and shrubs. This central park was mostly in
darkness now, but it was surrounded by the lighted
windows and patios of the block's thirty or so
townhouses, which were all backed against the
block's encircling outer wall, and were probably
in some way integral with it.

Shaded lights on knee-high stands gently illuminated curved paths of flagstone paving that
branched off into the balmy night in several
directions. Crickets sang of summer and tranquility.
In spite of his worries Art found himself pausing,
soothed by the peaceful scene. He said: "Looks like
you have it pretty nice in here."

George pounced gratefully on this retreat to
banality. "I tell you, it makes me feel a lot easier
about the kids. There's even talk about getting our
own elementary school started right here in the
block." He gestured the direction that Art should
take and they walked on. Somewhere nearby, people playing stringed instruments were rehearsing
a melody, starting and stopping and trying again.
Somewhere else a wild party was in progress, but
its uproar came heavily muted from some deep
interior, and to the string musicians inside their
own house it must have been inaudible.

"Yes, very nice," said Art, following where George
led.

"We have our own emergency power generator,
too," said George. "In case vandals knock out the
city power or there's a breakdown. That's happened a couple of times in the last year."

"Good idea." Art's sandals scraped on the slight
unevenness of flagstones as they walked a pleasant

curve between the houses' vine- and bush-screened patios and the openness of the central park. Each house was surprisingly private behind its trellises or open-work wall or evergreens. Art wondered if Rita might be sheltering at the moment in some other one of these discreet dwellings, hidden by friendly conspiratorial neighbors until Ann could throw the persecuting husband off the track with some halfway plausible story. "Yes, this is a beautiful place."

"Costs an arm and a leg and a testicle too," said George, his voice now turning grim. "I don't think there's a family in the block who don't have two jobs, or one good one—I mean one *real* good one—or their own business. In fact I'm repressin' sure there isn't." Talking man-to-man, George would sometimes use strong language. In front of ladies, Art had noticed, he never did. George added: "I just hope we can keep up."

"How are things at the dojo?" Art asked, the subject of business having been raised. Then he turned his head at the unexpected sound of a splash, followed by a trill of feminine laughter. Way out in the middle of the common park the lights of a swimming pool glowed in the soft, safe darkness, and he saw the wet tan gleam of a biknied body. What were possibly the lights of a second pool were almost completely blocked off from view by intervening shrubbery.

"Oh, good enough, I guess," said George. "Here's our happy home." He walked behind a vine-covered trellis to a patio. Ann, as if she had heard them coming, was peering out with a hospitable smile from her doorway of white stone and Spanish-looking ironwork. Stalking across the Parrs' hedged-in patio on six thin metal legs, a knee-high electric bugkiller lured flying creatures to itself with a nervously flickering eye of yellow light and a whisper of supposedly attractive noises. It broke its whispering with zapping hiccups as some of its larger victims were ingested.

As Art had expected, Ann's dress was radical. Her skirt fell almost to her knees, and her blouse covered both breasts almost completely, leaving only a narrow strip of midriff bare. Both garments were somewhat loose-fitting and practically opaque. Also as expected, Ann's chin was lifted high in challenge, despite her smile of welcome. She would be glad to have Art stay for a day or two, he was sure, and argue with her; that would give her a chance to convert him. Ann's face was reasonably pretty, and her hair a curly brown. She was small and strong, like George, and her strength was even more subtle than his.

"Rita thought you might come after her, Art," she greeted him. "You didn't bring a bag? That's all right, there's a clothing vendor right here in the block. Of course you're staying with us, we have a spare room. My brother was here for a couple of days, but he moved out when Rita showed up." Ann shrugged away her sibling's behavior.

"Fred's here in Chicago too?"

"Yes. The day he finished high school he just had to apply for Basic Income, like a fool. Couldn't see going to college, or even trying to go. He wants George to give him a job, or so he says. Come and see your children, they're asleep."

Inside the townhouse the furnishings were rather sparse and disorderly, indicating that the Parrs were not yet really settled in. Evidently they had barely finished unpacking in their new house when one after another of their crazy relatives began to arrive from California. Following Ann across the great room, Art saw an electric fireplace. The floor here looked like real hardwood. He could well believe that only the prosperous lived in this block.

They climbed stairs. After gesturing for silence in a second floor hallway, Ann slid open a door. Art went into a darkened room to find Timmy and Paula curled up in their usual positions in the strange bed, child-bodies clothed in opaque pajamas like unopened flower buds all sheathed in leaves. Across the room in another bed were two small mounds that would be George Jr. and his younger brother Enoch. On the wall Art noticed a version of what he recognized as a traditional Christian statuette, depicting the putative founder of the sect fastened to a wooden cross. The figure was quite large for the room and the wall, and crudely but strongly carved in some pale wood. Art wondered if Fred might have done it.

"Don't wake them," Ann admonished, whispering, as Art bent over his own two children. "They're still worn out from traveling."

Art had not intended to touch them and risk a waking, but now he gave each one a kiss. They were not as deeply asleep as they had looked, for Paula reached up to tangle her baby fingers in his beard. Then, as if reassured, she slept again. Tim, almost three years older, murmured: "Daddy."

"Go to sleep," Daddy whispered. And Tim did so, for once.

Art walked downstairs again with Ann. "So," he commented, "Rita's gone into hiding somewhere. How long does she expect the children to stay here?"

"Art, you know we don't mind having them in the least. Husband George, where are you?"

"That wasn't what I asked."

"Black Russian?" asked George from below, appearing in the doorway of what was evidently the recreation room, holding a couple of plastic bottles in his hands.

"Thanks, I will," Art answered. Inside the rec room was a bar, and a second fireplace, with a tag marked INSTRUCTIONS still hanging from one andiron. Art sank down with a sigh upon a leather-like couch, and received from George a glass with ice cubes floating in a dark and powerful-looking fluid.

Ann had vanished, apparently to the kitchen, for already there drifted in sounds and smells suggesting the preparation of food. Art, famished, wasn't going to argue with that. From out there somewhere Ann's voice called: "How do you like our medieval fortress? I'm very happy with it. The kids have a safe place now."

"It's very nice," Art called back, downing his first swallow of Black Russian. I saw two swimming pools, didn't I?"

In a chair opposite the sofa George sat, or squatted, pulling up his sandaled feet and folding his legs in an effortless contortion. "The pool in the bushes is more Ann's than anybody else's. She's always wanted a nude pool available, and when the blockhouse corporation was being formed she kept standing up in meetings and demanding."

"Well, why shouldn't I?" Ann, smiling, was in the doorway already, pushing forward a serving cart laden with sandwiches and cups of soup. "You know me, Art."

He thought he did. While moving clutter from a small table to make room for some food, Art was treated to a good look at the covers of some of

Ann's radical magazines. The cover holograms featured startlingly shrouded bodies. Bold print that appeared to drift over the images promised that inside were articles of shocking frankness, detailing what every adult ought to know about the history of celibacy and the ancient, once-honorable techniques of self-control. On Ann's coffee table Art would have expected a more sophisticated obscenity than this. He thought that she was watching for his reaction to the magazines, and he resolutely determined to show none at all.

Art didn't care much for the idea of his kids staying here, but where else was he going to put them while he searched for Rita, assuming she didn't somehow reappear tonight? And Paula and Timmy were too young, he supposed, to be much affected by Ann's idea of morals, or her lack thereof. He liked to think of himself as fairly liberal, but this woman just had a dirty mind. It was as simple as that. He could imagine a man marooned in a long orbit with her, and Ann wearing long opaque coveralls continuously, refusing sex, refusing . . .

He had thought he was conjuring up that image as a private expression of his scorn, but somewhere in its ugly heart a kernel of attraction lay, which made Art angry when he realized it. Repulsive woman! He could feel sorry for George, who was a gentleman, except that George must have known what kind of woman he was marrying and George still seemed very well satisfied. George in his own quiet way was evidently pretty far out himself.

"You know, old girl," said George the squatting guru, "your ways are actually more old-fashioned than your opponents' are. You go back to the twentieth century. Or was it the nineteenth when everybody pretended to be chaste?"

Ann took a seat on the sofa next to Art, and gave Art a look intended to show comic exasperation with her husband. "I'm hungry," she said. "Let's eat. Oh, George, you know it's not what's new or what's old-fashioned. It's not whether people wear suits when they swim or not. It's *why* they wear them or go without."

"Ann." Art swallowed the last bite of his first sandwich, and set down his glass, which had somehow become empty. "Ann, where is Rita? Where did you send her?"

"Art, listen to me. I'm not going to tell you where she is, because I don't know."

"You don't know? Come on. When is she coming back to get the children? As soon as I leave?"

Ann, with maddening assurance, ignored the question. "Art, I suppose you realize that she's expecting the bureaucrats at Family Planning to make trouble for her."

"Of course I know that she's in Family Planning trouble. Why do you imagine I'm here?" If he hadn't had the drink, he would be shouting at Ann by now. "She left me a note, I know she's pregnant. I even had a call from the BFP before I left California." Art repeated as well as he could the few words of Ms. Lazenby's message.

Ann listened to him in sympathetic indignation, as if the BFP agents had broken down his door and beaten him. "Well, if and when our third one comes along—I take my pills and pray it never does, but if and when—I'm going to do just what Rita's doing."

"You have that right," affirmed George in a low voice.

Ann's eyes flashed over at her husband, glad of his support though not needing it. "No court or no doctor is going to murder one of mine, I don't care what the law says. And no one's going to make me call it unwanted, either. Not once I know that it's alive!"

Even soothed by food and drink, Art's nerves were still badly worn. His voice got louder. "Most people would say that you yourself have rather a murderous attitude toward the wanted people of the world. The ones who are alive right now, including all the babies. You're talking about adding to the crowding. Remember Calcutta. Remember Rio. Where will this year's cannibalism be?"

Geoge had begun on his cup of soup with apparent good appetite. Now he reached in between the disputants for some crackers. "Peace, brethren, peace, cistern," he said, smiling genuinely. "Art, how was your trip?"

"Oh, exciting." Art sat back and took an interest in his own soup. Arguing general principles with Ann was certain to wear him out and get him nowhere. Let the atmosphere cool off for a minute and then he would return to the subject of his wife. He began to tell the Parrs about his adventures on the journey.

The attack on the Christian monastery was naturally a shock to Ann, and Art let her see the real sympathy he felt for whatever victims there might have been. "I suppose we passengers should have stopped and demanded that the police do something for whoever it was screaming off in the woods. But I doubt they would have listened if we had. They were only Transcon's private police, and I suppose they had their orders, as they said."

Ann looked at him, wanly mystified. "But was

the monastery being attacked *because* it was a monastery? Or was it just apework? Or what?"

Art thought back. "I heard a couple of things that would indicate the former, I think. But there was more to it, I think. One man said something about the monks' performing experiments on some aborted fetuses—something that sounded ridiculous, about creating monsters."

For some reason that got home to Ann. She was sitting quite still now, shocked, perhaps even frightened. Art went on: "It *did* strike me as rather inconsistent for these monks, presumably as much opposed to abortion as you are, to be using biologically active fetuses in experiments. If that's really what they were doing. Of course, whatever they were really doing in the way of research, that's no excuse for violence, for mob action."

Ann and George were exchanging looks now. Then Ann brought her attention back to Art, and asked him: "Who was this girl that you said you helped?"

"Oh, her name was Rose something or other. Said she lived in Chicago. She was really terrified. I suppose she can hardly be blamed."

Ann's perturbation continued. "There doesn't seem to be any safety for anyone any more. I'm so glad we've got this place. Art, you and Rita should think about getting into a townhouse like this. I don't think California is any safer to live in than Illinois."

"Sure. I'll talk the housing situation over with Rita right away. As soon as you tell me where she is."

His voice was grimly determined enough to shake Ann back into her anger mode again. Her eyes brightened and her chin lifted. But before she could speak, George put out a preemptory hand. "Ann," was all he said. But, to Art's surprise, she closed her mouth.

George got to his feet, with a neat automatic untangling of his legs. He set down the empty soup cup that he had been turning round and round in his fingers for some time. "Art, I'm satisfied that Rita's in good hands."

"Then you know where she is. If you know, you're going to tell me."

"I didn't say I knew where she is. I do know my sister. I believe she knows what she's doing. Isn't that enough?"

"Not for me." Art was inflexible. "You knew she was trying to do something illegal, and dangerous, and wrong. You didn't try to stop her, did you?"

There was a pause that seemed long. Ann, evidently still considering herself commanded to silence, was biting her tongue. Her husband still held the floor, dominating the room without trying to, unconsciously rubbing his enlarged knuckles. "I know it's dangerous," George said unhappily. "She could go to jail for what she's doing. But she wants to do it. She made a free decision."

"What about me?" Art demanded. "Don't I have any say about how many children I have in my family?"

Ann's headshake snapped a decisive *No.* She came leaping out of the penalty box. "No. Not if it means killing."

"*Killing?* How can you call it . . . if I dig up an acorn, am I killing an oak tree?" But it was no use. He didn't want to argue with Ann, and anyway it would really be impossible. She lived in a reality so far from the generally accepted one that Art could see no place to start. At least he couldn't now, not after a day of strain and wife-chasing and rioting and Black Russians. Somewhere along the line George had refilled Art's glass, and now it was half empty again.

"I wish we could forget our differences," Art went on, lowering his voice. "Rita's welfare is the only thing I'm worried about right now. All else is secondary, as far as I'm concerned."

"We know that," said Ann with honest impulsive sympathy.

"Eventually I'll find her," Art insisted. "You know I'm going to find her and bring her home. You think I'll just let her drop out of my life for six or seven months? It's an insane scheme and I won't allow it . . . and what about the children, are they going to stay here for that length of time, while I search? Timmy should be starting kindergarten. In any case Family Planning will find her if I don't. Don't you suppose they can quickly track her down? Isn't there a law they could prosecute her under already, conspiracy to commit parturition?"

"Not without more evidence than her dropping out of sight for a few days," Ann said quickly. "Not without a lot more evidence than that."

Art blinked at her. He realized that he was somewhat groggy. "For a few days? I don't understand. What does she hope to accomplish by doing that?"

Ann fell silent again. George waved a hand and seemed about to speak, but then he only sat down again, staring into the dark and cheerless maw of his new fireplace.

"Will somebody tell me, please?"

"You see," Ann began slowly, "once nine calendar months have passed since conception, no doctor is allowed to put the baby to death, except for certain categories of deformity, without the direct petition of the mother or other next of kin. The Supreme Court was very clear on that several decades ago, and the decision still stands. And what does a conspiracy indictment matter to a mother who can save her baby's life?"

"But that's after nine months."

"Yes."

Art couldn't make any sense out of it. It was well after midnight, and they were all tired. He felt nearly dead. Eros, but Rita too must be tired this midnight, wherever she might be.

Ann said: "Art, your room is ready. And I'm so tired now. Can't we talk about it in the morning?" She was really asking him, not telling him.

"In the morning, then," Art said. "But never doubt that I'm going to find her and take her home."

FIVE

Fred Lohmann woke up with someone's smooth and slender arm thrown across his bare chest and someone's delicate breath snoring gently into his left ear. Where was he? Oh yeah. The YPP hotel, in Chicago. Yesterday he had checked out of the Parrs' plush new house, more or less urged on his way by his sister Ann, and anyway not anxious to get himself involved in whatever had brought George's sister Rita in weeping from California. Rita had looked pregnant, far enough along to show a little. And Fred seemed to recall that the Rodneys had two kids already.

Whatever Rita's trouble was, it was none of Fred's affair. He had big problems of his own, and important events were scheduled for today. First of all, this morning Fred as a newly independent and adult citizen was going to collect his first Basic Income check from Uncle Sam, the check covering the month that had passed since his graduation from high school in California. And that first BI check might well be his last; he sublimatin' well hoped it would be anyway, for this afternoon he was going to have a real workout with George, a test, and if things went well at the dojo he might be a jobholder by tomorrow. And that would prove a lot of people wrong, people who had yammered at him about going on to college.

Now, what about this sleeping arm that weighed so gently on his breathing? In a moment Fred remembered. Her name was Marjorie, and she too was a newcomer to Chicago, looking for a job. Last night the desk clerk at the Y had assigned her and Fred to adjoining rooms and the same bed. The atmosphere at the Young Persons' Playclub was certainly different from what it was at the Parrs'. George might get a chuckle out of it when Fred described it to him, and Ann would lift her chin and make a speech. Behind the front desk, down in the lobby, was a big sign reading PURE THOUGHTS ARE THE MARK OF A DIRTY MIND. And they were serious about it, too. They were really that old-fashioned here, with a house rule strictly requiring at least two people in every bed.

Marjorie was by all indications a conservative, well-brought-up, lascivious girl, quite willing to enjoy sex. But she had agreed with Fred last night that the sign was funny, and they had shared a little laugh about it. Things had worked out all right. He might have been paired with someone a lot less congenial.

Now Fred disentangled himself gently from Marjorie's naked body and got out of bed without awaking her. Half of the bed folded down from each side of the wall that separated his tiny room from hers, so that when it was time to go to bed the rooms were connected by an opening. Ingenious, Fred thought. Raising either side of the bed was enough to complete the wall and separate the

rooms, allowing both parties privacy for business
or social reasons.

After a quick visit to the alcove where his toilet
and shower were located, Fred came back to the
center of the small room. He studied his tall, muscular body critically in the wall mirror, and did a
few light exercises. Just loosening and testing a
little, making sure the knee and elbow joints moved
freely and with plenty of snap. He tensed his corru-
gated belly muscles and snapped his rocklike fist
at his solar plexus, leaving a small red mark on
the pale skin. He told himself he looked older than
eighteen; the beard was coming along okay. But
he hadn't really worked out in more than a week,
and though he tried not to admit it to himself he
was scared by the thought of this afternoon's pend-
ing test with George.

Would George take Fred's word for it that he
really had a brown belt ranking, or might George
call California to check, and catch him in a lie? Of
course the idea was to do really well in the workout,
show George some real good moves, so he wouldn't
bother to check up. He would hand Fred a brown
belt to wear, and put him to work instructing
novices. Starting today he, Fred, would work out
all he could, and in a few months he could start to
think about moving up to black . . .

Marjorie stirred in her sleep, as if she were getting ready to wake up. Fred hastened to get his
codpiece and shorts from the chair and pull them
on. She seemed like a nice girl, so Fred was treating her with respect; he didn't want to display to
her his unmannerly shriveled lack of arousal on
this nervous morning.

. . . all the same, though, you never knew. Some
guys Fred knew who had really been around said

that the nice girls like this one could really be the coldest chillers once they let themselves go. Looking down now at Marjorie's still-sleeping form, Fred could easily imagine it covered, blurred into sexlessness by opaque drapery. Without the padded bra that she had thrown off last night, her upper body was almost boyish, and it had been years since Fred had wanted a boy as partner in his bed.

He could picture Marjorie's eyes opening now, their clear and penetrating gaze (so he imagined them; last night he had not noticed) pushing lust aside, pushing inward through his body, seeking to touch *him* . . .

Fred gave himself a mental kick, and looked away from the sleeping girl. Not that he felt guilty. Twins, every normal guy had thoughts about chastity and sublimation, and enjoyed them, too. It was just that today Fred didn't want to get himself into an emotional state.

. . . still it was impossible not to notice how childlike Marjorie looked in her sleep. In his imagination Fred found himself putting a long, snowy, opaque gown around her . . . he kicked himself mentally again, and busied himself with getting dressed.

She woke up, turning and stretching, before he was quite ready to leave. He looked around at her and swallowed hard, for suddenly the clear-eyed gaze he thought he had imagined was quite real.

"Good morning—Margie. You don't mind if I call you by your first name?" He had forgotten what her last name was.

"No, I don't mind. Uh . . ."

"Fred. Fred Lohmann."

"Oh sure. Fred." She rolled onto her back, giving a routine wiggle of her hips. "I'm hot for your body this morning." Her tone made the invitation no more than a polite form.

"I'm burning too." His tone was even more casual than hers. "Too bad, but I gotta get an early start on some business today."

Her eyes seemed to chill, sending something like a sensation of real cold along Fred's back. She murmured softly: " 'What is a poor girl s'posed to do, when the guy she's with says he just won't screw?' " The verse from which the line came was common latrine doggerel, ancient and more than mildly dirty.

If ever Fred had heard encouragement, this was it. Basic Income could wait. Even karate could wait. "Well then, how about it, pal?" he asked boldly. "How about you and me just frosting things a few degrees?"

He had been too bold too soon. "Just don't rush it," Marjorie said crossly. In a moment, with a curving of her spine, she had become all sex again. Who could tell anything about women? She rolled out of bed on her side, into her own room, where she at once reached for a transparent robe.

"I'm sorry," Fred muttered, bending down to look at her through the bed-gap in the wall. "Don't get sore." Sublimation, was she going to complain to the management now? Would he be thrown out?

Somewhat mollified, she paused in the act of raising the bed between them. "Just don't rush things, okay?" Her eyes had lost their deep coldness, but at least she was smiling.

"I'll be around tonight!" Fred called through to her. He lifted his side of the bed-barrier into place, and gave it a jovial pat as it sealed him off.

An hour later, he had found his way to the nearest branch of the Social Security office and was standing in one of the several slow-moving lines. Having no permanent address since leaving California, he had arranged to have his first Basic Income check held for him in the Social Security data bank until he called at an office somewhere to pick it up. Most of the other people in line around him looked like the BI's he had seen in California, staring ahead and speaking little. They would be livelier when they got out of here. So would he.

The jobholders in the office sat on the other side of glass, or counters, snugly fortified behind their desks and counters and computer consoles. Or else they walked quickly by, trying to give the impression that they were up to something really important. Chastity, everyone knew that they just happened to be the ones who had some kind of political pull, or they'd be out here standing in line too. They seemed to have little regard for the people they were processing so slowly. Fred lit up a small cigar.

He swore under his breath. Now the window at the head of his line was being closed for some reason, and a man came to divide the line and lead its fragments to different windows.

"No smoking in here!" he snapped at Fred. He was a paunchy, waddling man who reminded Fred of a particularly unpleasant high school teacher he had still been suffering under only a few months ago. "No smoking, I said! Put it out at once or you'll have to leave the office."

"I got a right to my check," Fred muttered, but so weakly that it was doubtful if the officious man even heard him. At the same time Fred was crushing out his little cigar on the sole of his sandal, for he knew very well that he was never going to win an argument with the paunchy jobholder. Not in here, at least. Now if they ever met anywhere else . . .

Fidgeting and waiting, thinking vague and sullen thoughts, Fred centimetered forward with the line. At last he reached the window, gave his name and federal identity number, and held the tips of all ten of his fingers against a scanner-plate. After only a few seconds some papers emerged from a slot in front of the clerk who was processing Fred.

"Well, this is your first check, Fred. Do you have a permanent address to give us yet?"

"No. I'm staying at a Yipsie now."

"Which one? What's the address there?"

"Here in Chicago. The one on north State Street."

The clerk made a note on his computer input. Then he pulled more pieces of paper from beneath the counter. "Take these booklets, Fred. They'll tell you more about your rights and responsibilities under the Basic Income law. If you win more than five hundred dollars' prize money in any state or national lottery, or in any government-sponsored competition, in any one calendar month, *or* obtain gainful employment, *or* acquire ownership of more than fifty shares of corporate stock, you are required to notify us so that your Basic Income can be adjusted. There are penalties for failing to notify."

There was a little more that Fred was required to listen to. When at last they released him by handing over his check, he hurried from the office, dropping his booklets in the general direction of a trash receptacle as he went through the door. He'd notify them, all right. As soon as he moved up to jobholder, and the sooner he could tell them that, the better.

He had already decided that since he had such a good chance for a job, there was no use hoarding his money like a miser. A month of scrimp-along money could buy a few days and nights of real fun. After that . . . well, he'd have a job. Anyway, nobody starved.

Fred noticed a kind of gravitational pull that was leading him onto a particular slidewalk, one that would carry him in the direction of a certain run-down neighborhood he had noticed not far from the Yipsie. In a neighborhood like that he should be able to hit a coffeehouse bar or two. He could get some lunch there as well as anywhere. There was plenty of time before he was due to meet George at the dojo. And Fred wanted to see about getting hold of some gladrags, in case it turned out tonight that Marjorie was not just teasing but was really in a willing mood. If you went to the right place and asked the right person, a few dollars would always buy a pair of voluminous plastic cloaks, thin but stiff and perfectly opaque, folded together into a pocket-sized carton.

Art awoke with a start in the bed in the Parrs' guest room. Blind women with artificial eyes of diamond had just been chasing him through a forest. He sat up blinking, and looked at his watch, which informed him that it was a little after nine in the morning. He looked around.

On the barren tile floor in one corner of the sparsely furnished room lay a pair of men's translucent disposable trousers, apparently used and ready for the discard. Not anything that Art had brought with him, and in a BI style that neither he nor George would be likely to wear. Oh yes, of course, Ann's brother Fred had been staying here. Conceivably Fred would have some clue to Rita's present whereabouts, if Art could have an opportunity to question him. Art remembered Fred as a wild-looking adolescent, tall and awkward.

Before retiring Art had bought himself some disposable clothing from the block's vending machine. Now, after a quick shower and a beard-trim he dressed in fresh shorts and shirt. Still it was only a quarter after nine. While buttoning his shirt he stepped into the children's room and saw the four of them still sleeping. They must have been allowed to stay up late last night, playing together.

While meditating on parenthood he heard the doorchime from downstairs and went out into the hall to listen. Presently voices came drifting up, one Ann's, the other a man's voice Art did not recognize. From the upstairs hall he could make out only a stray word or two, not enough to indicate the subject of the conversation.

As soon as Art had finished dressing he went down, avoiding the room where the voices were, heading for the kitchen first. He was liable to feel sick unless he ate something as soon as he got up. Rita had kidded him from time to time on having morning sickness. Rita . . .

From a shelved box he took out a cinnamon-flavored protein bar, laced with vitamins and minerals. On the complex new stove he dialed himself coffee. Five minutes alone in the kitchen, while the low dialogue continued in another room, and Art had the indispensable minimum of breakfast aboard. Chewing on a toothmint, more or less ready to face the world, he walked out to see who Ann's visitor might be.

The low voices stopped at Art's entrance. The visitor was a lean, stooped man with thinning hair, wearing a conservative transparent business jacket above his shorts. He was standing just inside a door that had been closed last night, and that now, partly open, revealed the top of an access ramp to what must be a lower-level garage. The man looked up at Art with keen interest. Or perhaps he was only glad of any interruption.

Ann, her pretty chin a notch higher than usual, turned with arms folded from her stance of confrontation with the visitor. "Art, this gentleman claims he's a Mr. Hall, from Family Planning. George is out right now." Her tone managed to imply that George, if at home, would have beaten this probably fraudulent intruder to a pulp, and Art was welcome to do the same thing if he liked.

"My name *is* Hall, and I am from the Family Planning Office." The visitor had a determined voice, though not angry and certainly not flustered. (Aha, Ann, have you met your match at last?) His eyes were sharp. "I take it you're Arthur Rodney?"

"I am." Ann was looking at him encouragingly for once, but her gaze conveyed no useful information.

"I was hoping to run into you here, Mr. Rodney. Our California office has asked us to make a routine investigation into your wife's case."

"Her case? My wife hasn't broken any laws."

"That's fine! Then if you'll tell me where I can get in touch with her, we can clear all this up promptly and with as little inconvenience as possible for everyone."

The protein bar in Art's stomach had suddenly

gone lumpy. He supposed that criminals must have terrible chronic digestive problems. Or maybe they got used to it. He could think of nothing to say in reply, nothing to do but stand there like a fool and look guilty.

Hall's determined voice kept coming at him. "I understand, Mr. Rodney, that you did not accompany your wife to Chicago, but you followed her here?"

"I—yes, what of it?" Surely, thought Art, he had the right to refuse to answer these questions. The right to talk to a lawyer before answering. But once he refused to answer, and started bringing lawyers into it, then Hall's suspicions, possibly they were no more than suspicions now, would surely be confirmed.

"Mr. Rodney, is there some reason why you don't want to tell me where your wife is at the moment?"

"I don't know where she is." It was Ann's fault, and George's, and Rita's too, that he had to conduct this argument in ignorance. It was their own fault, not Art's, if he got them all into deeper trouble. Meanwhile he marveled greatly at how quickly the deadly pits could open beneath one's feet in the dull corridor of life.

"You don't know?" The interrogator's tone implied that Art had to be a fool or a knave, or both, to hope to get away with such an answer.

Art folded his arms, in unconscious imitation of Ann. "That's right."

Mr. Hall glanced toward Ann, who with her own arms folded was obviously quite ready for him. He appeared to stifle a faint sigh, and then turned back to Art. "Mr. Rodney, our California office has received medical testimony indicating that your wife is several months pregnant."

"Yes, I know about that."

"The first trimester must be nearly over. But we have no record that she's made any appointment with a physician to have this pregnancy terminated."

"I, ah, know nothing about that."

"Well, I'd like you to at least give me your opinion on the subject, Mr. Rodney. Do you think your wife is planning *not* to have this pregnancy terminated normally? Does she intend to carry it on to parturition?"

There was no way Art could admit the fact. "No, I don't think that," he had to say. Then he was forced to pause, for a nervous, choking swallow. Ann was just standing by, letting him flounder, confident that they had told him no secrets and so there were none he could betray. Triplets, but he hated her at the moment.

When he had his throat under proper control again he said: "I'm sure Rita means to have it terminated properly. She's, uh, probably just gone away by herself for a few days to think things over. You see ... our psychologist has recommended against her being sterilized. She always takes her medication, I'm sure there was just a chemical failure somewhere, I'm sure she didn't plan the pregnancy. Unless it was subconscious." There seemed to be news stories every day about apes who avoided legal punishment by pleading their subconscious compulsions. If they could do it, why couldn't Rita? Lay the groundwork now. But Art told himself that he was talking too much. And he shut up.

As soon as he quieted, however, Hall was after him again. "Mr. Rodney, is it like Rita to go off by herself for days at a time? When was the last time she made a similar disappearance?"

"I . . ." He was cornered. Once he started making up a string of lies, Hall would have them knotted around his neck in no time at all. "No, I can't say it's like her," Art said in desperation. "I tell you, I don't know where she is. If I knew where she was, I'd be with her right now."

Mr. Hall shuffled his feet, which were no doubt tired from standing, and glanced again at Ann, and sighed once more, more openly this time. "Mr. Rodney, will you walk with me back to my car?"

"There's no need for you to do that, Art," Ann put in.

"All right, Mr. Hall," Art said, since the alternative was to go along with Ann's instructions.

Ann was not going to argue with him, not in the face of the enemy. "I'll have some breakfast ready when you get back," she promised, holding the door. She gave Art a ritual kiss as he went out, but offered no kiss or caress to Hall, who in turn contented himself with a barely polite pelvic thrust in her direction.

Walking beside Art down the narrow ramp to the garage, with no one else about, Hall said quietly: "Mr. Rodney, I hope you don't think of us at Family Planning as being out to *get* your wife. Believe me, we want to help her. I think right now she's a woman who can use some help."

Art was silent. They emerged at the foot of the ramp into the well-lighted garage, which seemed to extend under most of the block. A variety of vehicles were berthed in a series of numbered, gate-protected stalls. Other sizable areas were stripe-marked for delivery vehicles and for visitors' parking.

At the moment there was still no one else in sight. Hall stopped, facing Art. "If I don't get a chance to talk to your wife, it's going to be awfully hard for her to stay out of trouble. And you yourself can be in trouble if you're deliberately withholding information. There is the federal conspiracy statute. We may not like the world in which all these laws are necessary, but it's the only world we have."

"I've been telling you the truth."

"Another thing," said Hall, very slowly resuming his walk in the direction of the visitors' parking area. "Giving birth is still a somewhat risky proposition at best—I'm sure you, as the father of two legitimate children, realize that as well as I do. And in some of these birth-mills a full-term parturition, or even a fetiparous one, can be downright dangerous, believe me."

This time it was Art who stopped, a few slow paces later. "Even a what?"

Hall was silent. He seemed to be trying to read Art's face. "Fetiparous," he repeated at last. "Bearing young something in the manner of a marsupial, before they are fully developed."

"What? What kind of parturition, live birth, is there in humans except full term? Are you talking about premature?"

Hall prolonged his intent gaze at the mystified Art for several seconds, and then relaxed. "I think you and I are really on the same side in this case, aren't we, Mr. Rodney?"

"I want my wife at home with me, not getting into trouble. And I don't want the world overcrowded with my progeny—I'm willing to respect the rights of others."

"Fine." Hall was suddenly more relaxed and

friendly. "Then I'd better tell you something you may not know about. Just recently there has come into widespread unauthorized use a method for removing an embryo or even a fetus from the womb, at any time during gestation, in such a way that it can be artificially preserved. The midwifer usually freezes it—"

"Preserved? Alive?"

"If you can call it that. The potential for life is maintained. The frozen fetus can later be thawed and reimplanted, in the same woman's body or in another's, or even put into an artificial womb, and it will grow and develop eventually into a child. None of these methods are really new as applied to early embryos. They've been successful experimental techniques for a long time. But now as I say they can be applied even to late-term fetuses, and their abuse is becoming widespread, to thwart the law and produce unwanted children."

"Oh."

"You begin to see. Now if we at Family Planning seize a frozen embryo or fetus, our legal situation is tricky, because current federal law states that if nine months have passed since conception, the fetus has become a child. Unless we can demonstrate certain categories of deformity, which is unlikely. Calendar age, not developmental age, is the way the law reads. We're trying to get it changed, and we probably will, but right now . . . there have been articles on this recently, and stories on the sollies. I would have thought perhaps you would have heard or read something about it."

"I've been busy," Art said. "Not keeping up with the news."

"You see, with just a frozen fetus in our hands,

we have a purity of a time proving the calendar age. Can't even take a tissue sample that might prove the parentage, since that would constitute damage. If we can't prove it's a superfluous third, and nobody claims it, why then believe it or not it has to be treated as a potential child, in effect an unidentified orphan."

"It does? Why? I don't see . . ."

"Well, it *might* be someone's first or second child, you see. It might be the result of a wanted pregnancy. We can't even put it in permanent cold storage. We have to take it to an orphanage, if we can find one equipped to take it in."

"But it wouldn't seem likely to me that—"

"Oh, some of these religious and so-called humanist institutions will take them right in. They're building artificial wombs at a furious pace, calling them experimental scientific equipment of course. But they just happen to have them on hand when frozen fetuses show up. And they seem to have unlimited money and personpower."

"Ah."

"You may have heard something about the riot just recently in Iowa, where a Christian monastery was destroyed. I understand the ringleaders of the riot are now in jail, where they should be. Can't have people taking the law into their own hands. But those cultists are facing legal action too. Pretending to be scientific experimenters and getting grants . . . they had no interest in deriving scientific knowledge from all those specimens they had They were interested in increasing the population.'

Art, without realizing it, had started walking again, on newly shaky legs. Cultists. He thought of the carven image on the wall above the children's beds. He knew Ann. He thought of the scream coming out of the woods, and he thought of Rita.

He said: "But then . . . suppose, as you say, that the fetus is thawed and put into one of these artificial wombs, and a child results. What then? Could the mother claim it?"

"Sure. She'd probably have to serve a term in prison if she did, after admitting it was hers. Then while she was behind bars her husband would be at home, coping with the three children. That's another matter these people don't seem to think out ahead of time. Anywhere that this woman and her husband live afterwards, the neighbors are going to be able to count: one, two, three children. You couldn't very well pretend one of them is adopted. There aren't enough adoptable children to even satisfy the childless couples who want one, let alone go to people who have two of their own. So it'll be obvious to all that this couple had three kids, and pretty soon that third one is going to know that he or she is superfluous and unwanted by the world. That's a very cruel situation to bring a child into, in my estimation."

"Mine too."

"No, I just don't understand these women who go to midwifers." Hall had reached his car, and now he unlocked the driver's door and pulled it open. "There's just one more thing I wanted to mention to you, Mr. Rodney. Several times a year we in Family Planning get a massive detailed population forecast for the whole world, and for our own areas in particular; we get it right from the UN computer center. Right now the latest forecast is several days overdue. The rumor is that it's been delayed for re-checking. Because it's a real shocker."

"Ah."

"That'll mean tougher legal crackdowns." Hall entered his car, slammed the door, and then peered out the window. "I hope I can rely on you, Mr. Rodney."

"Certainly I *mean* to do all I can to—"

"That's fine." With a tiny wave and a half smile, his mind probably already at work on his next case, Mr. Hall upped his window, faced forward, and drove off, zooming up an ascending ramp toward the street outside.

—but I don't even know where she is.

SIX

After Hall's departure, Art didn't want to talk to Ann right away. Instead he wandered to an escalator and rode it up from the garage, emerging just inside one of the block's pedestrian entrances. He was jogged partially out of his dazed state by Timmy and Paula, who jumped out of some bushes to ambush their father as he was making his way back toward the Parrs' patio. The children were munching a breakfast of fruit-flavored bars with which they smeared his clothes. Overriding Art's pleas for a delay, they pulled at him to get him moving on a tour of the block's central park, with which they were delighted. Art gave up and went along. He reassured himself that his children were well, and then tentatively questioned them about mommy. About all he could find out was that she had said she would come back to get them soon.

The tour got as far as the nude pool before its directors deserted to join the Parr boys, who were already in the water at the roped-off shallow end. Art sank down on a grassy bank nearby and tried to think, now and then waving mechanically at his offspring when they clamored for his attention.

There were other distractions too. No other men were at the pool, but several women had brought kids or had just come to swim. It was obvious that Ann was not the only bluenose radical in this community; no doubt people with similar attitudes tended to get into the same blockhouse corporation. Anyway these women came to the nude pool wearing only long, loose, dimly translucent jackets, and once there they swam and sat around as bare as babies, without so much as a sequin pasted on to emphasize their sex. It was hard to say which was the more antierotic, being almost completely covered or completely bare. Some of the women cast suspicious glances at the male stranger, who in turn waved at his children to show that he had a good reason for hanging around, and then frowned thoughtfully into space. But only Art's face was truly thoughtful. His brain was getting nowhere.

In half an hour or so the kids were ready to do something else, and Art walked home with the four of them, reminding them to gather up their clothes. When he got back to the Parrs' house he found that George had come home, and promptly took him aside.

"George, have you seen her or heard from her this morning?"

"No, Art, I swear."

"I've got to find her. She's my wife and I have a right to talk to her."

George stood there for a while, looking glum and uncertain about the whole situation. Then he said: "I have to agree with that."

Emboldened, Art pushed harder. "I don't want

to get you, or anybody, into trouble. But if I can't find her I'll have to go to the police and report her missing. It's that important to me."

George came to a decision. "All right. After lunch you and I will go out and see about making contact."

"Why after lunch? Why not right now?"

"Just go along with me. I want to do it my way. After lunch."

And so, a couple of hours later, after Art had spent some more time with his children, and Ann had fed everyone more sandwiches, the two men walked out of the blockhouse and got on a slidewalk together. George didn't have a car at the time, what with one expense and another. Art could certainly understand that.

After a couple of kilometers' slidewalk ride, Art saw a vast domed stadium looming up ahead of them. At about the same time, George came up from deep thought to say: "Understand, it may take a little time to find out where she is. There are several people I want to talk to about it."

"Just so I get a chance to see her, before she commits any irrevocable foolishness. Where are we going now?"

"I expect one of the people we want to see will be at the ball game. You just stand by and let me talk to him."

"All right."

Another kilometer's ride and the slidewalk, by now fairly thick with passengers, deposited them before one of the entrances to the stadium. George said: "Let's not forget to pick up tickets. A dollar is a dollar."

They accepted time-stamped tickets from the jaws of a machine as they passed in through a turnstile.

George led Art through cavernous passageways to an outfield grandstand, where they emerged squinting into the sun. A sizeable crowd was filling a good proportion of the seats. The stadium's domed roof had been opened like a set of gigantic jaws and the people were in a good humor under the warm sun.

George chose seats high in the rear. Once seated, he kept looking around him at the crowd, now and then standing for a better view. "I think I see our man," he said after a minute. "You just watch the game, and I'll go talk to him."

The game was just beginning. The Cubs, the home team, took a one-run lead in the first inning, and gambling in the grandstand seats promptly became fierce and steady. It was conducted mostly by arm-waves and cryptic shouts. There were a few ushers and police in sight, but they ignored the betting; Art wasn't sure whether it was legal here or not. There seemed to be no bookies and no formal organization. Art observed no wagers of more than about ten dollars, but small money passed through hundreds of hands with every pitch.

One of the busier gamblers was the man George had engaged in low-voiced talk, who seemed to be able to keep track of his gaming and his conversation at the same time. They were sitting too far away for Art to be able to tell if George was learning anything. Their talk just went on steadily.

So matters continued until the top of the fourth inning, when the Cubs blundered themselves four runs behind. The emotional climate in the stands changed radically, with the score. The majority of the spectators, grown men and late adolescents who wore the gaudy codpieces and indefinable look of the jobless, lost much of their enthusiasm

for betting. Many brooded in sullen silence. Here
and there some gamblers persisted more energeti-
cally than ever, jumping and shouting like fanatics
when they won, but joyless even then.

George finished his conversation abruptly and
stood up, motioning to Art that it was time to
leave. They met on the moving ramp descending
to street level. A number of other men were heading in the same direction, taking to the exits early.
In the lines forming at the exits there was some
jostling for position, and a few police were standing by. A huge, disheveled man standing in the
next queue glared across a railing at Art and George
and murmured something about jobholders. In present company Art felt secure enough to glare right
back, until the man decided he was getting nowhere and turned away.

"Three innings, six dollars," droned the Bureau
of Sports agent inside the booth where Art pre-
sented his ticket. Art picked up the coins that came
clattering toward him from under the bulletproof
glass. He supposed that watching a whole game
would be worth eighteen dollars. He wondered if
they paid overtime for extra innings.

As soon as they were clear of the stadium crowd,
riding a westbound slidewalk into a part of the
city Art had not visited before, he asked eagerly:
"Did you find out where she is?"

"We're on the trail. Really, we are, Art. As I told
you, we'll have to talk to a couple of people."
George, shaking his head, turned to look back at
the slowly receding stadium, its roof-jaws gaping
at the sky. "I was afraid for a while there we were
going to have a little riot. It gets bad in there
sometimes when the home team loses."

Controlling his impatience, Art looked back too.

"They can get paid something now just to sit and watch a game and keep out of trouble. Or there are a thousand things people can do to win prizes. They don't have to be intelligent or educated, they can win by bowling or pitching horseshoes. Everyone can win a prize at something. I don't know what they want."

George faced forward again. "Did I tell you, I may be going on television? Probably not, though. I think I blew the audition."

"No." Art was surprised.

"That's where I was this morning, auditioning. Just a local station. Oh, it's a real triplet of a mess. They have this monstrous clumsy machine, made up like a woman, for a man to fight. Let's change to the high-speed walk here, the next place I want to stop is way out in the slumburbs."

At the interchange, the local slidewalk they had been riding made contact with an express, by means of an acceleration strip. The strip of viscous plastic remained cohesive and hard-surfaced even though it flowed like water, a platform that supported passengers through the change in speed. With no more balancing than it took to mount a stair, they changed. Once they were whizzing westward aboard the fast, long-distance belt, Art and George sat down on the continuous bench that moved with their new conveyance.

"So, what about this television program?" Art asked, curious despite his problems.

"It'll be garbage. They want somebody to jump through the air like an idiot and scream, and beat up this giant woman. Garbage. There *could* be a good karate program. Showing how the human mind and body can work together . . . I'd like to do a good one someday, but I don't suppose they'd ever let me. I guess I'll do a middling bad one if someone wants to hire me for it. I could use the money."

Art had a sudden realization of the obvious: a midwifer was illegal, and therefore must be expensive. Rita hadn't had much money with her when she fled her home. Might she have fallen into the hands of some cut-rate quack?

"George, are you paying for—Rita?"

"I'm contributing something."

"Then why must we run all over the city to find out where she is? It would seem to me you'd know."

George calmly shook his head.

For a time they rode on without talking, through the warm afternoon. The whispering rush of the express walk, shaded from the sun beneath its endless plastic awning, bore them at highway speed through kilometer after kilometer of the great city. They passed modern industrial blockhouses, and older manufacturing parks surrounded by grimy fences. In all of them machines were laboring for human masters, machines that often could repair and sometimes could redesign themselves, machines that more and more rarely needed human care and attention. The slideway bore them over street after street of the two- and three-apartment dwellings in which the bulk of the city's people seemed to live. Here dwelt the great respectable mass. Here the jobholder might work two or three days a week, here the family owned enough in the way of stocks and bonds to bring in some effective income, here they had more or less success in winning prizes. Altogether it added up to respectability.

Vending centers flowed past, and other more expensive stores that were staffed by jobholders. Streets and parking lots. A school. A park, with a young couple naked on the grass, their bodies locked together and working. A Church of Eros, whose twin towers stood like the raised knees of a supine woman, flanking the main entrance. A superhighway interchange for private surface vehicles, a convoluted structure fallen into disrepair, with half of its lanes closed by barricades, grass growing through the cracked concrete. Nearby was a terminal of the long distance Transcon system. Then more two- and three-unit dwellings, row on row on row of them. And, scattered everywhere throughout the clean and sunlit city, the fortified walls of blockhouses were springing up.

Now Art noticed with a part of his mind that the buildings rushing past were becoming noticeably shabbier; they must be approaching the western border of the city. With another part of his mind, thinking aloud, he said: "Suppose she actually does have a child. Produces a living child out of this. What'll we do then? I tell myself that if it comes to that, we'll just ignore what people say. I'll do all I can to keep the third one from feeling unwanted. But I suppose he will. Or she."

"I just don't know how that would work," George admitted humbly.

"And Rita. I don't know if going to jail would bother her as much as being sterilized."

Another little time passed before George answered. "I know the thought of having that done has scared her in the past. Maybe now, though, it wouldn't seem so terrible. She wouldn't have to worry about this happening again."

"Maybe. I hope she'll see it that way." No more babies for Rita, wanted or unwanted. Art felt a surge of pity and grief for the superfluous one already on the way, unneeded and detested by a world already jammed. Embryo, why do you grow, why thrust with such a mad, blind drive to reach the light? Shrink back to nothing. Go away. There's nothing here in the world for you, that you should fight to reach it. But of course it could only grow, or try to grow, like a planted tree or like a cancer.

"George?"

"Yeah?"

"The man from Family Planning was saying that after some women go through this new method of having the embryo or fetus extracted live, and frozen, then they're content to have the resulting child brought up in an orphanage, or put out to strangers for adoption. I wonder if that's what Rita has in mind. To me that would be worse than having a third child with us—to purity with what the neighbors say. Do you know what she intends? She must have discussed some plan with you."

George, staring off into the distance, only shook his head gloomily.

"Either way," said Art, "it would be pretty grim. And I don't want that kid to ever come into this world. You can see how I feel, can't you?"

"I can see how you feel, and how Rita feels, too. Maybe that's my trouble, I see everybody's point of view. Even that of the kid who isn't born yet." His eyes flicked at Art and off again. "If abortion's not killing, what is it?" It was more an apologetic question than a challenge.

Being well rested and in good control of himself now, Art could have brought out the arguments with which to demolish this simplistic point of view. But he had no wish to argue with George, who must already have heard all the arguments anyway. The main goal today was finding Rita.

The city proper had been suddenly left behind.

No official boundary was visible, but within the space of a few blocks the view changed, as what were unmistakably the slumburbs came rising like a dirty wave about the slidewalk. Art was a stranger to this part of the Chicago area, but it did not look much different from some of the poorer sections of Los Angeles. Here were the endless curved rows of small houses cheaply built, falling apart at the age of twenty or thirty, but still occupied. Not only occupied, but cut up and partitioned into multiple dwelling units. No steady jobholders lived here, nor did many who owned shares of stock or won more than an occasional prize. This was Basic Income territory.

The terminus of the high speed slidewalk was here, incongruously. Maybe there were plans to extend it, or to clear the slums. But right now only a small vending district clustered around. The pedestrian walks through the slumburb itself were stat, as rigid and unmoving as the streets.

Among the automated vendors in the small center a couple of establishments operated by jobholders survived. One of these, a small and dingy tavern at the dead end of a block, proved to be George's destination.

The tavern did not look particularly old, but it was already rundown in appearance, sharing the neighborhood's general atmosphere of defeat. Daylight was shut out from the interior, and the artificial lighting inside was dim though garishly colored. As Art's eyes adjusted he could see a couple of obscene words scrawled on the shabby walls, and the crudely drawn images of concealing garments, opaque hip boots and overcoats. All in all, Art supposed, a typical BI barroom; not that he had seen many such, except in sollie stories. Four or five apathetic male customers perched along the bar on stools. Above and behind the bar, the legally required police eye roosted like a robotic vulture, now and then turning its glass eye on its scrawny metal neck.

The bartender raised his head, sizing up his two new customers with eyes blank as the vulture's lens. Then he fixed his gaze on George, as if deciding he was the one who had to be dealt with.

"Couple of short ones," George ordered, resting an elbow on the bar. When two small glasses of beer had been poured, he asked: "Is Alfie around?"

"Maybe shootin' pool," the bartender grated. There was a back room. POOLHALL $2.50 ADM.

George strolled that way. "I'll just see if he's there."

"That'll be two-fifty, see the sign?"

George just glanced back as he strolled. "I won't touch a cue." He went on into the POOLHALL.

The bartender hesitated briefly, then picked up the coins George had left on the bar and slouched away to tend another customer.

Art sipped his beer, which for some reason tasted quite good. He wished he knew how to talk to these people and act with them. George's and Rita's background was as middle-class as his own, but George had picked up the knack somewhere. Maybe in karate, though George had mentioned once that most of the students and practitioners he knew were not the tough-guy type. Couple of short ones. Get tough with me and I can break your ribs—this last was only implied, of course, never verbalized or even stated in so much blunt body-language. George was just this somewhat undersized fellow who was not at all intimidated. What others read into that was what intimidated *them*.

There was a stir in a rear booth, and a pair of B-girls materialized out of the dimness there, to come flowing forward to the bar. Art felt a mild twinge of alarm. The girls' license buttons were prominently displayed on their kimonos, but the garments were probably longer and thicker and more shapeless than the letter of the law allowed. The young women approached the bar and stood there, closer to Art than to anyone else. Not that they were looking at him. Their pale-painted faces were averted slightly, their mouths pinched in professional haughtiness and cool reserve. Art uncomfortably shifted his stance.

George stuck his head out of the back room. "Not today, girls," he called. "Art, get a beer for Alfie, and get us a booth. We'll be out in a minute."

The girls' faces relaxed into more natural scowls and they moved away, resuming some private conversation in bored voices. One pulled her kimono off to scratch beneath her bikni straps. Art bought three more short ones, and carried the filled glasses to an empty booth.

From the booth he had a good view of the tavern's huge sollie stage. For some reason the ball game was not being shown; maybe the game was already over, or he supposed there could be rioting at the stadium. Instead, the barrel-sized image of some announcer's head had just begun reading a news story: "This afternoon in the General Assembly, chief Chinese delegate Lu Ti-p'ing accused a neighboring government, Southern Pan-Asia, of using biological weapons against its own—the Southern Pan-Asian—people.

"Lu quoted statistics from UNIMED which indicate that deaths from uncertain causes may have reduced the SPA population by nearly ten per cent during the last three months. According to the UNIMED report, most of those dying have been the elderly and the chronically ill. According to the Chinese accusation, disproportionately few of the deaths have occurred among members of the Patriots' Party, now the ruling group of Southern Pan-Asia.

"Finally the Chinese delegate expressed regret that, in his words, the SPA government has chosen such an inhumane method of trying to strengthen itself economically. Is this, Lu asked, to be the first step on a road of dangerous economic aggression?"

As if on cue, the announcer's head was abruptly replaced by that of another, equally big, who with a tyrannosaur's smile read hastily through a perhaps ill-timed commercial for a Chicago vending chain. The presentation was so inept that Art assumed this was some small local station, maybe the very one George had auditioned for. Probably there were a hundred of them, though.

Art sipped his beer. The newsmonger was soon back on stage, saying: "Then it was the turn of Cao Din That, chief SPA delegate, to reply."

The enlarged head of Cao Din That now appeared on the sollie stage of the tavern in the Chicago slumburb, where nobody but Art seemed to be paying the least attention, and the Asian's translated words were heard, categorically denying all the charges leveled against the leaders of his suffering country. Possibly some foreign government was really to blame for the surplus deaths, which were, if anything, mostly among the young, the helpless children. If so, let the aggressors beware, they would shortly be found out. In any case, UNIMED should mind its own business; it was overstepping its authority by interfering in SPA internal affairs.

That point made, the tone of Cao Din That's speech became milder. Possibly the deaths were the unforeseen side-effects of a new insecticide, employed by many countries in the region in the desperate struggle to increase food production. Also to be considered were the airborne viruses that had been accidentally freed during the recent UN police action against the Nile Republic; no one knew where those viruses might have landed, nor would anyone even admit to knowing exactly what they were. The UN was to be applauded for its prompt action along the Nile, which had liquidated some planners of biological war, but still some of the consequences had been unfortunate.

"Ah, th' world's gone t' repression," said a colorless little old man who must be Alfie, for he arrived at that moment with George. Art slid over to make room.

Alfie seized a beer, downed most of it in a couple of gulps, and went on talking. "The whole world's crazy. Y'know what happened the other night? Somebody bombed Vic Rizzo's townhouse. It musta been just vandals. They couldn'ta known it was his."

"That so?" George asked indifferently. Art wondered who Vic Rizzo might be. After a few more social noises had been made, and Alfie further supplied with beer, George got to the point.

"Alf, you know the city pretty well."

"I guess I do."

"Then tell me something." George dropped his low voice even lower. "Who might a nice girl go to see, if she got kind of carried away and emotional, and wanted to finish an extra baby. She's got two kids now."

Alfie gave facial demonstrations of thought. "Married?" he asked, just as if being married or single made any difference in the number of children a woman was allowed to bear.

"Yes," said George.

Alfie glanced at Art, wordlessly identified him as the worried husband, and winked at him. Then, obviously pleased to be consulted, Alfie assumed an air of wisdom and began to talk. He seldom really finished a sentence, however, and his speech was thickly interlarded with allusions to people and events that Art had never heard of. Also Alfie used a number of slang words and expressions that were strange to Art, or maybe Art was only mishearing them, because Alf's whisper was almost too low for him to make out. All in all, the dissertation was just about perfectly unintelligible. George, though, kept on listening with apparent satisfaction, now and then encouraging Alfie with more beer.

"Some characters you know," Art reflected aloud, as he and George rode the express slidewalk into the east again. Twenty kilometers or so ahead, near the shore of invisible Lake Michigan, and farther east in the city than Art had been as yet, the unbelievable central towers rose.

George grinned "Alfie has his uses."

"I hope you found out something from him. I didn't. Do you think Rita's with one of those people he mentioned?"

George turned to look back into slumburb country, a desolate jumble of rooftops beneath the hot sun of midafternoon. "I think Alfie may be on the phone to Family Planning right about now, trying to sell them the information that you and I were asking about midwifers. The man I talked to at the ballpark may be doing the same thing. Family Planning knows what Rita's trying to do, but I want 'em to think she doesn't have a midwifer yet. They can't arrest us for asking general questions. All I've been trying to do so far today is put 'em off the trail a little.''

Floundering well off the trail himself, Art could think of nothing to say.

SEVEN

Art maintained a somewhat surly silence through several slidewalk interchanges. He and George were deep in the city again, moving on a fairly crowded walk that angled to the southeast, before he spoke again. "Where are we going now?"

"The dojo. Fred's supposed to be there at three-thirty so I can watch him work out. And then I have a private lesson to give. Come along and watch."

"Look, George, are you going to help me find Rita or aren't you? If you can't or won't, just say so. Don't keep stalling me along."

George was unperturbed. "Just come along to the dojo. I said I'd help you and I will."

Art puffed out his breath. But he went along; somehow George's words carried conviction.

Under an unpretentious sign that read PARR'S KARATE DOJO Fred Lohmann stood waiting for them, holding up the front of a modest building in a small middle-class vending district. Under one arm Fred was carrying a whitish roll of what appeared to be clothing.

"Art, you and Fred remember each other, right? Sure you do." George unlocked the ground-floor door and stepped inside, waving the lights and air conditioning on with a passage of his hand over the switchplate on the wall.

"Sure we do," agreed Fred, clearing his throat nervously. He towered over the two older men. Art's hand was squeezed in greeting. "Art, how's your wife and kids?" Then Fred looked as if he had just remembered something.

"Oh, they're fine. I guess you met Rita yesterday? Over at George's place?"

"Yeah, sure, that's right." It was an abstracted answer; Fred's eyes slid away.

It seemed obvious that Fred wasn't really in on the midwifery conspiracy, but still Art thought it might be possible to get some clue to Rita's whereabouts out of him. But the effort would have to be made later. Right now Fred was out of touch, all nervous anticipation of whatever test he had come here to undergo. And of course George was present now, busy raising his window blinds, checking his terminal for messages, and in general opening up his shop.

The interior of the dojo was mostly one big room, about twenty meters square and two stories high. You could have fitted a very small house inside it. The floor was of polished wood. At the front of the big room, beside the entrance from the street, an area marked off by a low partition contained a desk, with phoneplate and computer terminal, and a few chairs, some of them arranged as for spectators. In the rear of the big room an open doorway led to a bank of lockers, and, Art supposed, a shower. Large flags of the United States, the United Nations, and Japan were formally and correctly displayed together on one wall, the UN flag a little higher and in the center. The general impression was of functional orderliness.

On entering, George and Fred both bowed, seriously but not deeply or very ceremoniously toward the flags. Then they slipped off their sandals and padded back toward the locker room, bare feet seeming to grip the floor familiarly. "Make yourself at home, Art," George called back.

Art put his own sandals into the convenient rack by the front door, then wandered about looking the place over. The floor felt smooth but not slippery underfoot.

Something here reminded him of chess. He wondered if it was the square arena of polished wood, or some faint scent of conflict lingering in the conditioned air. Or perhaps the present quiet. Glancing up, he saw some of the pieces. Four android fighting machines were hanging like executed murderers near the high ceiling, above the center of the open floor. Art looked about and spotted their control console, near the desk. Feeling a technician's curiosity, he walked over and looked at the controls.

While he was occupied with this, George and Fred emerged from the locker room, clad in loose whitish jackets and trousers that were only moderately translucent, and wearing athletes' codpieces of hard protective plastic. "I guess I just *lost* my own belt somewhere," Fred was saying, meanwhile accepting a brown belt, an overlong strip of tough-looking cloth, from George's hand.

George looped a black belt twice around his own waist and knotted it in front. Out in the middle of the open floor the two men began to limber up, swinging their legs like ballet dancers, crouching and twisting and stretching their bodies to unlikely extremes, then shaking wrists and ankles as if their hands and feet had fallen asleep. Art stood watching the process with some interest.

"Ready?" George asked, after a few minutes of this. "Let's go five-time sparring, then."

"Okay." Fred drew a last deep breath, and gave his arms another shake.

George, with nearly the full length of the floor clear behind him, drew himself up facing Fred, and they exchanged bows, similar to the salutes they had given to the flags. Then the two men stood erect, each with arms slightly bent and hanging in front of his body, fists loosely closed. "You first," George directed.

Fred snapped into a much lower stance. He was tense now, poised to attack. His right fist was cocked back near his hip, his left arm curved before him in a blocking position.

"Jo-dan!" The word came out of him in an explosive breath.

George grunted: *"Uhss!"*

Fred sprang, not up but forward. He advanced in long strides, each stride a rapid lunge. With each advancing step, one of his fists drove like a piston straight at George's chin. George flowed backward easily, staying just ahead of the punches, pressing each of them aside at the last moment with an economical open-handed block timed perfectly against Fred's extended arm. The older man's short legs gracefully matched the speed and rhythm of the long ones driving at him. George made it look quite easy. After he had gauged the first punch, his eyes moved downward between punches, appraising the movements of Fred's feet and hips.

With his fifth punch Fred halted and stood motionless, his right arm still extended. Instantly

George came blurring back at him with a counter-punch that was evidently an expected part of the ritualized combat; his fist snapped to a halt a centimeter from Fred's unmoving chin.

Now it was Fred's turn to draw himself up straight, while George crouched for the attack.

"*Jo-dan!*"

"*Uhss!*"

George charged. Somehow he made his short-ness look like an advantage. The sleeves of his white jacket snapped audibly with each straight punch. Fred retreated, his movements looking com-paratively stiff and hurried, even to Art's untrained eye. Fred's arms swung hard, parrying the punches with heavy blocks. When it came time for the counterattack he essayed an arm-grab and kick to the stomach which George did not attempt to avoid. The snapping kick just touched George's jacket, as it was evidently supposed to do, but George still seemed to find it unsatisfactory.

"Try again," he ordered.

Fred went through the grab-and-kick again. George said nothing. Art had a growing impres-sion that Fred was failing his test.

George exchanged bows with his opponent, and turned to Art. "Art, switch the andys on, will you? That little console right by the desk."

Art found the console and the power switch. There was a whispering of light cables up above, and the four androids started to descend, hanged men coming down for vengeance. The wires low-ered them like puppets, slowly, as their faces, still blind and lightless, turned this way and that and their plastic limbs began to stir and quiver. By the time the androids' feet had touched down on

polished wood, their legs had life and balance
enough in them to let them stand.

The cables detached themselves from the figures
and were quickly reeled up out of the way by the
overhead machinery. Four men of about average
height were left standing in the middle of the floor.
Their heads and hands and feet were smooth tan
plastic, the rest of their bodies clothed in white
beltless karate outfits. At the crotch of each android
appeared a small, formalized codpiece-bulge. And
each android had a number—one through four—
marked in red and white in the middle of its
forehead. Otherwise their tan faces were almost
featureless, marked only by small recessed eye
lenses and flattish dummy noses. Like superior
creatures lost in their own proud thoughts, the
four of them stood with loosely hanging arms,
ignoring the three real men who watched them.

George, coming over to the desk where Art was
standing, called back to Fred: "Want to run through
heian number four?"

Fred shrugged. "Okay." He was frowning at the
man-like figures, as if hoping to intimidate them.

The four androids were warmed up and fully
active now, and as George set up their controls
they obediently rearranged themselves. Now they
were facing each other across the center of the
floor like four cardplayers at a large square table.
Each was crouched in the same attacking position
that the men had used in the five-time sparring.

"You don't fight all four at once, do you?" Art
asked. "I've seen karate on television a few times,
but I confess I never paid too much attention."

George dismissed television karate with a mere
lipcurl of contempt. "What speed do you want,
Freddy? How about three or four?"

Fred flushed slightly. He stood with his hands on his hips, swinging his legs again, keeping them loose and ready. "I can handle one-point-five, or two."

After a moment George said: "Try two-point-five, then," and set a dial. "Better get a helmet."

"Okay." Fred trotted to the locker room.

Art was interested. "Then he is going to fight all four at once."

"Not free-style. That would be quite a trick at two-point-five. Just in a kind of formalized way, a pre-arranged exercise. They'll come at him one at a time, and anybody who has some training and has memorized the moves of the particular *heian* can do it. If he keeps his nerve. And if the speed's set low enough. He wants to do it pretty fast." For a moment George's face said openly: *It's his funeral.*

Something about the fighting machines continued to fascinate Art. The way they stood there on the polished wood like outsized chessmen, waiting for an act of human will to impel them into ritual battle.

He asked: "Is it all right if I take a closer look?"

George glanced at the control console. "Go ahead."

Art padded over to the androids, that were still waiting with impassive and impressive poise. They did not react, but he had the feeling that they were aware of him as he approached. Peering into their dull lens-eyes, Art wondered what kind of an image his face made, how that image was experienced by an electronic brain.

With a cautious finger he touched the plastic knuckles of one cocked tan fist. The fingers of the hand were not really separate, only indicated by grooves in the one plastic piece. The knuckles felt perhaps not quite as hard as the proverbial rock, but they were not what Art would call safely padded, either.

"Feels as if it could kill you."

"Not likely." George smiled briefly. "Does sting a little, though."

"You've been hit, then."

"Oh sure. Not seriously. Yes, these things can be dangerous. We sometimes put big padded hands and feet on 'em for novices. But if there's no real element of danger when you train, you can't really train properly." There came the sound of a toilet flushing, and George glanced back toward the locker room. "Fred's no novice. But he's nowhere near as good as he's been telling me he is. I just can't hire him now."

"Then why—?" Art gestured at the androids.

"Oh, I guess I owe him a full fair tryout. And he's got good potential if he'd settle down and practice every day. I've told him he can work out here free, all he wants."

Fred came back, fitting on something like a fencer's mask. "I found a face protector. I like it better'n a whole helmet."

"All right," said George, standing by the console.

Fred moved in among the androids and oriented himself carefully at the center of the space between them, facing android number one. He drew a deep breath and then stood up relaxed. "Ready."

George touched a red control on the console, and instantly bright red warnings glowed into life in the eyes of each of the mechanical figures. Somewhere a small repeater chime began to sound. One, two, three, four, five notes and the android at Fred's left lunged at him with a punch too fast for Art to follow. Fred was ready for it though, and his left arm snapped up to block the attack while his right hand came whipping around edgewise to hit home like a hatchet on the tan plastic neck. The aggressor machine was sent staggering back. Meanwhile another was already charging.

Each android charged in turn, was beaten back, reset itself quickly, and in its next turn came back to the attack again, aiming another blow or kick at Fred, or grabbing at his jacket with clamplike fingerless hands. About half a minute passed, while Fred piled up points.

Fred spun from side to side, defending himself with vicious blocks, counterattacking with fists and feet and elbows. His face was rigid with concentration. Art thought he could see fear and hate as well. Fred reached out and pulled down an android's head, smashing the blank uncaring face against his driving knee. Again he spun around—

Not quite in time. A savage punch glanced off his skull, and down he went.

Art, moving with an electronic technician's instinct, went for the power switch, but George's hand was there already. For an instant the androids hesitated, looking for fair game, a standing human within range. Then their eyes died and their bodies fell clattering to the wooden floor.

Fred was rolling over on the floor, gasping and moaning, clutching at his head. Art and George went to him. He rolled again just as Art bent down, and Art's hand was smeared with a drop of Fred's blood.

"They changed speed!" Fred sat up, dripping blood onto his white jacket. "I just about had 'em, and then something went wrong . . . ah, triplets, that hurts! I swear the chaste things changed speed on me . . ." Fred was practically sobbing with exertion, pain, defeat.

Having played chess against some of the best computer programs, Art thought that perhaps he understood Fred's feelings. But since he had risked no blood against the chess computers, Art said only: "Lie still, I'll get a towel." Fred's scalp was torn, but still the damage didn't look too serious.

George stayed with the victim, gently getting his face-protector off, while Art went to the locker room and found a couple of towels, and also picked up a first aid kit that hung there on the wall. He had just returned to the disaster area when the street door to the dojo opened and a tall man came in.

The new arrival was well dressed, in translucent shorts and business jacket, and had dark skin and Oriental eyes. As he was starting to bow to the flags he noticed what was happening and immediately slipped off his shoes and came across the floor.

"Have an accident?"

"Oh, hello, Doc. Yes," said George, getting to his feet. Fred also started to get up, then sat back on the floor as the man who had just entered the dojo bent to look at his torn scalp.

Accepting the towel from Art, Doc dabbed around the wound. "This looks like it'll need some glue. Ivor, fetch my bag in from the car, will you?"

Another man, youngish and of undistinguished appearance, who had followed the doctor in and then had remained near the door, gave a little salute with his fingers, like a chauffeur or a servant, and then ducked out.

"Doc," said George, "this is Art Rodney, my sister's husband. Art, this is Dr. Hammad."

With a look as of recognition, the doctor nodded, and reached to shake Art's hand.

George said: "Art, when you have a chance, you can ask the doctor that medical question you had. He's your man."

"I happened to see your wife this morning," the doctor was telling Art a few minutes later, back in the locker room. "She's in good health and good spirits." The doctor was hanging up his street clothes, getting ready for his private karate lesson. George was out in the main room of the dojo, discussing some refinement of mayhem with the bodyguard Ivor, both using gestures. From where Art was standing he could see Fred sitting out there too, the picture of defeat. Fred's head was resting in his hands, blood spots were drying brownish on his white jacket. His brown belt had come unknotted.

"Where is she?" Art asked the doctor.

"Understand, I have no direct connection with the place she's staying at. It's been my experience, though, that they do a good job of taking care of paying guests."

"You have no connection? Aren't you the one who's planning to perform the operation on her?"

"Oh, no, no, I'm not handling your wife's case myself. No, the connection between myself and George is too obvious, you see. In such cases a referral to another physician is more prudent."

"All right, who is she, then? Or he? When am I going to get to see Rita? When is the operation supposed to be?"

"I would think it'll be scheduled very soon. She's young and healthy, and I would anticipate an uneventful parturition and cryogenic interval."

Cryogenic interval. What was about to happen to Rita, what she was about to do, was suddenly more real to Art than it had ever been before. He thought he could feel a touch of frost in his own bone marrow. He had no very clear idea of what a three months' fetus looked like, but in his mind he saw a brainless finger of tissue, extracted like an appendix and then frozen into an icicle; Rita's icicle. His too. And a very expensive icicle in many ways.

Art asked: "If a fetus is treated this way, then grown in one of those artificial wombs, what are the chances of its becoming a normal baby?"

"Oh, very good. Excellent. Is that what's worrying you? Don't let it. Freezing an organism that small and then revivifying it is nothing, these days. Much easier than at five or six months, when it's larger. And an artificial womb actually offers several advantages over a full-term pregnancy, for mother and child alike. We can watch the development of the fetus easily, day by day. The flow of nutrients can be perfectly controlled. Physically it's much easier for the mother too of course. I expect the FDA is soon going to release the wombs for unrestricted use with legitimate children; they're probably only delaying because more women would want kids if pregnancy wasn't such a bother." Dr. Hammad pulled on his loose karate trousers; he was smiling reassuringly, as if confident that he had just solved all Art's problems for him.

"That's all very well, doctor. That helps to ease my mind of one kind of worry. But now what about my wife?"

"Oh, this is even safer for her than a normal birth would be. I understand that she's had two of those."

"I'm not talking about that. I mean legally. Suppose she's caught and convicted and sent to jail and sterilized against her will? What effect is all that going to have on her?"

"See here." Hammad's expression was no longer reassuring. He said sharply: "I thought you wanted this child. There are always certain risks involved, for everyone."

"I don't want this frozen so-called child, Rita does. What I want is to talk to her, to reason with her, before it's too late."

The doctor had turned partially away from Art, and was adjusting his karate jacket, slowly and meticulously. "You'll have to see someone else about it, then, Mr. Rodney. I told you I'm not operating."

"You said you've just seen her. You know where she is."

Hammad looked at him but did not answer.

"I insist that I be allowed to see my wife, face to face!" Art was keeping his voice low, but he could feel it becoming shaky with his anger. "You know where she can be found. Don't try to tell me you don't. And I'm quite ready to stir up trouble, if you refuse to help me talk to her!"

Knotting a green belt at his waist, the doctor glared at Art as if he had found the wrong specimen laid out on a dissecting table. Art glared right back.

"All right," the doctor said at last. "I'll find out if some arrangement can be made for her to phone you. Though it's not wise; phones can be tapped. Where are you staying?"

"No. I want to be able to talk with her face to face. In person. Alone."

Hammad was all ready for his lesson now, but he remained in the locker room. "All right, all right. It's against my judgment but since you insist on taking the risk I'll see if there's any way a meeting can be arranged."

"Arrange it soon. Very soon. Before the operation."

"All right. It's your responsibility. Where can you be reached by phone?"

EIGHT

Fred Lohmann was standing inside the Megiddo Bar & Coffee House, on the edge of a mean little urban BI district near State Street, not very far from the Yipsie where he was rooming. He was alone in a crowd. On a low dais some people with medieval musical instruments were twanging out a ballad about pure-hearted love, and as they sang a chill silence was creeping into the huge dim room. The place was befogged with the exhaled smoke of several kinds of leaves and synthetic mixtures. At every table there were glassy, staring eyes, and more of them to be met in the mirror behind the bar.

Fred slouched his tall frame over the coffeebar, nursing what they called a small Turkish, which tasted like it was mostly coffee but certainly had other things mixed into it. He was also nursing a vague dull hope that someone might ask him about the little bandage on the side of his head. After all, there were mighty few men in all the world who could have handled those andys at the speed they were set for today. Mighty few. And he had been handling them, had been about to handle them, except . . . not one in a hundred guys could do it, probably, even if they were given the chance to train and practice.

Black belt George, of course. Third degree black belt, no less. George could probably set them on speed one and knock them down like bowling pins. Fred felt envious of George, but there was no malice in the feeling.

Karate was a purity of a good business to be in. You could make some money directly, like George, and you could also get to meet some important, influential people. People with class, who wanted to learn karate for self-defense, or exercise, or sport. Like that Dr. Hammad who had come in and patched Fred's scalp today. Afterward Fred had watched the doctor go through his private lesson, and George had used Fred to demonstrate a point or two, and had had Fred spar freestyle with the doctor for a few minutes, taking it easy.

Now Fred made a karate blade out of his right hand and chopped delicately, silently, with it at the edge of the bar. It paid to keep at it all you could. Practice. Toughening. Then he stopped. Who cared? What was the use? George probably could tell without even checking that he had been lying about having a brown belt.

Sorry, George had said, no job now. Practice every day and we'll see. George hadn't said every day for how long, but Fred knew it wouldn't be just for a week or two. Months. Maybe even a year, before he could get his stance and his control and everything else up to the standards George wanted in a brown or black belt, in a paid instructor. There was not much fun in grunting and sweating and working like a machine for that length of time. And there was no guarantee that he would ever make it, so what was the sense in putting out that kind of effort?

Up to the bar beside Fred there stepped a young man who looked like he knew his way around. He was of average height, but so broad-shouldered that he appeared squat. Around his shoulders he wore the pelt, doubtless artificial, of what Fred took to be a wolf; anyway it was some kind of shaggy animal, with pointy little stick-up ears, beady glittering dark glass eyes, and sharp-looking sizeable white teeth in a pink open plastic mouth.

Fred hadn't yet made contact with anyone who could tell him where to buy some gladrags.

"Hey," he called quietly, still loudly enough to be heard in the chill spreading silence.

The wolf-man turned, properly casual, and looked Fred over. "Hey," he answered coolly. "You buyin'?"

Fred waited, long enough to show that he wasn't being pushed into anything. "Got my check today, why not?"

Fred and Wolf ("Call me Wolf, man") sat at a table, where they were soon joined by a friend of Wolf's named Lewandowski, who was drinking herb tea spiked with vodka. Fred bought another round for the three of them and decided it was the last he was going to buy. He sounded out Wolf and Lewandowski about gladrags, and they assured him that a man who sold such things would be coming around later.

Wolf said that he came from New York City. He let it be known that he had led a gang there, and the New York police were looking for him so he had come west for his health. Fred could believe this about halfway. Lewandowski, a fat, strong-looking youth with empty eyes, was a native

Chicagoan. Once he started talking it was hard to get him to shut up. He said he was looking for a job with one of the policy wheels, legal or illegal made no difference to him; his old man was a compulsive gambler and he knew there was good money to be made on the business side of the operation.

Neither of them asked Fred about his bandage, but he faked a little more headache than he actually had and managed to reveal casually that he was a karate expert, working hard for his black belt. He saw the others hardening their faces slightly to keep from showing they were impressed. Probably they believed him about halfway, as he did them. Well, he was telling them about half the truth. If only there were someone he could talk to.

Finally Fred gave up waiting and bought yet another round, for neither of the other two seemed to have any money at all. They both said they had been on BI for about a year, since abandoning school. And Wolf said he couldn't even collect his checks these days or the New York police would find out where he was and have him extradited.

Fred began to feel a little drunk and sick, and his wounded head was aching now in earnest. The gladrag man finally arrived and was pointed out to him, and as soon as Fred had the little carton in his pocket he went back to the Yipsie. Marjorie wasn't in, or at least she wouldn't answer his tapping at the door of her room. He let down his side of the bed, but her side was up, and stayed that way. She must be still out, somewhere.

Fred slouched on his spine in a chair with his feet up on his tiny table. He sat there in dizzy silence for a while, staring into the enigmatic eyes of the Yipsies' founder, whose portrait decorated one wall. On another wall was the predictable print of Caravaggio's *Love Conquers All*, the naked urchin wearing wings and pretending to be Eros, climbing out of bed and knocking books and mathematical instruments off a table and trampling a violin. That Caravaggio had certainly known how to paint. That picture would be something to try to carve in wood.

He wanted Marjorie to come back, and to hurry up about it. But actually he had no idea where she was. Maybe she had checked out today, and tonight he would find himself sleeping with some real old-fashioned sex kitten, some real dog who studied her erotic manuals every day. Fred didn't know if he could take that now.

One thing he knew for sure he wasn't going to be able to take for very long tonight was sitting here alone. It was only about eight o'clock, not yet dark outside, and he was neither sober nor yet really high on the spiked coffee.

Fred got up and went out of the hostel, and found himself on the street with nowhere to go. In a little while he was heading back to the Megiddo.

NINE

The phone call got Art up from the Parrs' dinner table. After Art had let the caller see him, a man's voice spoke briefly through a blanked screen, giving directions. "The corner of Belmont and Halsted. Be there in an hour. Come alone."

"How will I know—?" But the connection had already been broken off.

George, who had been listening in the background, now looked worried, which did not do anything at all to help Art's nerves. Ann, smiling though she was worried too, came up to Art. "You're going, then? Give Rita our love if you do get to see her. And listen to what she says. And don't do anything foolish. You won't get lost now, will you?"

"No. No, I won't. Well then, I'm off." And he left the house before they could change their minds completely and begin to argue with him not to go.

He had prepared himself by purchasing a map of the city's slidewalk system from an autovendor. It was no trouble at all to pick out what looked like a good route to Belmont and Halsted Streets. Art even detoured through a busy shopping center, with the idea of shaking off anybody who might be trying to follow him. Chicago was a place where people walked—or at least where they rode standing or sitting on their moving walkways—as often as they rode in vehicles. In most of mid-California, a person trying to move any distance on foot soon became a helpless alien in a world planned and built and paved and spaced almost exclusively for surface vehicles.

Here in Chicago things were closer together and more accessible. More on a human scale, save for the towers that clustered in the center of the city, the place a few Chicagoans still called the Loop. In this city, signs at every corner named the streets, address numbers were logically consistent, and of course the whole city was netted in a huge slidewalk grid.

Now, at sunset, the walks were only thinly occupied. The crowded shopping center, through which Art passed on his antisurveillance maneuver, had evidently been fed most of its customers by street vehicle, for its large parking facility looked nearly full.

The relatively few people Art did encounter on the slidewalks kept looking at each other and away again, mutually wary as they passed. He kept to the main thoroughfares, which Ann had said were fairly well patrolled by the police, and off the little stubs and branching statwalks. The sun was down now, but plenty of artificial light had been provided along the main walks. Well lighted also were the new, blind, blockhouse walls that now made up so much of the city's face in this region. Some of the blind walls would enclose factories, humming with industry but almost devoid of human workers. Art, seeking out his path between the walls, was suddenly reminded of a maze he had once seen in the laboratory of a psychologist who had been experimenting with rats.

Now, with the going of the sun, the city trees that grew in tended spots and strips of grass took on an unreal, misplaced look. Their June leaves were as green as signals in the streetlights' brightness. And the steady vehicular traffic of the streets, dipping or rising as the streets passed under or over the moving walks, was unreal traffic to a slide-walking man; the people in the cars looked like fish in some dim aquarium, obscure sliding shapes bound into their own world.

"See that one there?" the psychologist who ran the rats had said to Art. "Looks fine and healthy, doesn't he? Fat and sleek and bright-eyed compared with most of the others."

"How do you manage to keep some that way, with so many crowded in?"

"They're supposed to be crowded in. I'm studying the effects of overpopulation. And he's really no healthier than the others are. He's like a sleepwalker, passive, non-sexual . . ."

"What about the others?"

"Various reactions. See the shabby one with all the energy? He's what we call a 'prober.' Hyper-sexual and homosexual. Hyperactive altogether. That type often turns cannibal."

Thunder rumbled somewhere. Or was it thunder? Close above the streetlights the night, opaque and prematurely black, pressed down on Art. Above the brilliant streetlights there might be stars or clouds or staring eyes, but nothing could be seen.

Art ran his maze. After leaving the shopping center he changed slidewalk directions twice, navi-

gating with his map. He was sliding east along
Belmont Avenue, calculating the distance to Halsted Street, when a passing police car slowed, keeping pace with him for ten or fifteen seconds. Art
threw one half-scowling glance toward the car and
just kept on walking. Presently it pulled away.

A minute later he wished it back. Glancing down
a comparatively dim side street as he passed
through an intersection, Art saw a group of four or
five male figures walking together two long blocks
away. They were shouting something in rough
voices and waving their arms. Fortunately they
were a little too far off to pay any attention to Art.
He would have bet that they meant trouble for
someone, though.

Thunder rolled again. Hyperactive, and they often turned cannibal. But the psychologist with his
studies on crowding had been too wise to offer any
simple cure-all for human nastiness. There was
still plenty of violence reported from uncrowded
farms.

Art's nerves relaxed a little when the band of
toughs passed out of sight, then tightened again as
he arrived at the intersection named to him on the
phone. It was a busy place, he saw now, the center
of a small vending district. Art alighted on a section of statwalk bathed in the rippling noon of a
barred display window. People moved around him,
shopping or walking aimlessly. No one approached
him, or appeared to be paying him any attention.

Another police car, or perhaps the same one,
came easing round a corner, and Art turned away
from it, pretending to study the contents of the
vendor's window. He heard the car halt just a
little distance off, and wait there, turbines idling
with a muffled whine. Maybe they were just keep-

ing a protective watch over the shoppers. If they were trying to follow Art to Rita, surely they would be more subtle about it than this. But now it seemed to Art that the police and Family Planning probably knew already where she was. He pictured Mr. Hall of the BFP conferring with other cool and crafty agents, reaching an agreement that they would wait until the crime had been irrevocably committed before they sprang their trap. *We're not out to get her*, Hall had said.

Art inventoried the window until he heard the police car pull away. A few seconds later another car drove up to the curb beside him, one of its windows lowered. A man's voice called softly: "Are you Rodney?"'

"Yes." Art stepped quickly across the sidewalk to the curb.

A rear door was opened for him. "Get in."

He got in, pulling the door shut after him, and the car moved out. There were two other men in it, one driving and one beside Art in the rear. As soon as the auto had turned out of the busy intersection, the man in back took Art by the neck and pushed him impersonally down to the floor.

"We don't wancha see where we're going. Get under this." A musty-smelling, opaque blanket of some kind was thrown over his head.

Decent people didn't commonly have opaque blankets like this one in their possession. It was a trivial point in itself, but suddenly all the possibilities of evil began to open. Art could fear that he was not being taken to Rita at all, he was being got rid of as a troublemaker. Meanwhile the car purred on. It stopped and started and turned in traffic. Art no longer had the faintest idea of what direction he might be moving. There was a faint odor of perfume, or perhaps some kind of drug, in the car or clinging to the blanket. His imagination could make new possibilities out of that. He told himself firmly that his new fears were ridiculous, and anyway it was too late now to start having them.

He crouched beneath the blanket awkwardly, breathing uncomfortably and pulling at his beard. Just let him have one chance to talk with Rita, face to face, and she would not be able to stick to her mad plan. If she had been able to face him with this decision, she would not simply have left him a note and fled. Art had to believe that he would be able to make her change her mind.

How could she have done it? And another question: How could he have lived with this woman for four years and not know her any better than he did?

But Rita didn't know him, either, if she thought that he would simply let her wreck her life this way. Yes, that was the important thing. The legal problems and even the number of children were secondary. To save her was what he was really fighting for.

The car turned, slowed, turned once more, crept ahead, and shortly stopped.

"We get out here. Don't look around, just go straight into the building."

The blanket was pulled away. Art could see that they had parked in an alley. Anonymous rough brick walls were close on either hand. As he got out of the car, one of his escorts turned him toward an open doorway, some kind of unmarked service entrance, in what must be the rear of a building, a sizeable structure only dimly lighted.

One of his guides, a graying, tough-looking man,

came along with Art, walking a pace or two ahead
to show him the way. Art followed this man down
a long shabby interior passage between walls of
painted concrete block, and up a narrow flight of
stairs whose carpet had begun to wear. Some run-
down apartment building, or perhaps a cheap hotel.
Now they entered an upper passage, that turned
first one way and then the other past closed and
numbered doors. The building was certainly old,
but it was at least reasonably clean and well
maintained.

At last Art's guide stopped and pointed to a
door. "She's in here. I'll come back in fifteen, twenty
minutes, and we'll take ya back where we picked
ya up." The man turned his back indifferently and
walked away.

Art tapped on the door, then turned the antique
knob and pushed it open. Rita was sitting with her
back to him, in a worn plastic armchair, wearing a
silvery bikni that sparkled in the light of the small
room's single lamp. She had evidently been staring out of the room's one small window at the
night. She looked around, startled, at Art's entrance,
and he saw that above the bikni bottom her belly
was indeed bulging with three months' illegitimate
pregnancy—he was not too late.

Love and fear and defiance came into her face as
she recognized him, and she jumped up from her
chair. A second later she opened her arms.

"Come home with me now," Art murmured. It
was ten minutes later and he was starting to feel
sleepy. Which wasn't going to do at all. His voice
was half muffled by the single pillow on the small
bed. Rita's hair, spread out on the same pillow
artlessly, was somehow both silver and gold in the

light of the cheap lamp. Gleams of something like the same colors came from the plastic armchair, where her discarded bikni lay.

"No, I can't." His wife's voice was small but it did not hesitate. "They'll kill my baby if I do." Then, unable to lie still after speaking those unsettling words, she got up from the cot and went to close the window, against which rain was just beginning to splash.

Art sat up and put his feet on the floor. His escort would soon be coming back for him, and so far Rita and he had talked very little, and that little mainly about their children and how they were getting on at Ann's.

He stood up and reached for his codpiece, which had been tossed onto the armchair too. "You're coming home with me, so don't argue about it." Not the way he usually spoke to her, but this was different. "You haven't committed any real crime as yet."

"I can't, Art."

"Why not? A man from Family Planning came to see me, and from what he said I'm sure they won't file any charges, *if* we just turn in this fetus as we're required to do."

"I can't, I can't. I wish you would try to understand, Art. I wish you would stand by me." Her tender body turned in the lamplight, naked and unprotected. His heart turned over.

"*Why* can't you do it, for sex' sake?" he demanded, more savagely than he had meant.

"B-because it's living. It's my baby, and it's alive already. And it's like . . ."

"Like what?"

"Like a part of you, that I have inside me. It would be like killing you."

He turned away momentarily, muttering. Even the early stages of pregnancy always made women look ridiculous, he thought, and Rita would look more so when she put the bikni on again. Why couldn't anybody make clothes in which pregnancy would look less grotesque? Art had heard theories about why such clothes were not made. Not that Rita would need them. In a few days, in one way or another, this pregnancy was going to end.

He turned back. She had got her bikni from the chair and was putting it on again. Her breasts were fuller than usual; that would be the pregnancy too, of course. She did look ridiculous, he thought, and fragile and vulnerable and beautiful too, and he loved her tremendously.

"I can't go through this again," she told him grimly, suddenly the practical mother working on a strap. "I'm going to have myself sterilized when this is over, even if the government doesn't make me."

"Rita. That's great. Then why not—"

"B-but I can't let them take this baby who's already here."

"Well. But you have two real children—"

"Three."

"—who need their mother with them. Not in jail."

"You say Timmy and Paula play all day in that b-blockhouse park." Rita only stuttered when she was very tired or upset. "I didn't have time to look around there much. Is it safe? Ann's very nice but sometimes she doesn't watch her children closely enough." She was in front of the mirror now, the little mirror over the little dresser, and was trying to tug the bikni bottom into a better fit.

Art too had finished dressing now. "They're very

safe." Then he wondered if he should have raised doubts as to whether they were. No, stick to the truth. "Come on, Rita, you're not killing any part of me by getting rid of a fetus. I'll still be here, just as I am. It's not my body you'd be disposing of."

"It's not mine either."

"Bah. It's an outgrowth of yours. You have the right . . . how do you know I'm even the father?"

She didn't answer, or look away from his eyes in the mirror, but something in her face closed off.

Art said: "If you had a diseased appendix giving you trouble you'd want it cut out and done away with."

"What's growing in me is not diseased."

"How do you know, have you had any tests made for defects?"

"And even if it were, I'd love it."

The urge to grab his wife and shake her was almost overwhelming. "If you really loved it—loved the potential child it might become—you know what I mean—you'd want to save it from a lifetime of being unwanted by the world."

"He's not unwanted. His mother wants him." Now Rita was growing angry too. "We should kill him now because it's possible that someday the world will give him a tough time? Then let's be consistent. We'll go get Timmy and Paula and knock their heads in. Someday they're likely to have a tough time too."

Sublimation! When she got angry she was really impossible. Art knew that he was right. Rita would know it too if she would let herself listen to reason. But no. He could try telling her what the neighbors would one day say, but no, he knew her too well to expect that line to work.

It came down really to their duty, to everyone's

duty to the overcrowded world. Personal wishes, even personal love sometimes, had to be sacrificed for the general welfare of humankind. Everyone's reproductive urges, weak or strong just had to bow aside. But he couldn't belabor his suffering wife with words like that. How to make the truth sound less self-righteous, speechy and highflown?"

There came a knocking at the door. On his way to answer it, Art said over his shoulder: "You're coming back to Ann's with me now, to get the children. And then we're taking them home, and then you're going to Dr. Kuang and get this taken—"

"No, I'm not." Stubborn as a mule, just like her sister-in-law. You might have thought the blood relationship was there.

The knocking came again, already louder and impatient. Art reached the door and flung it open. The man who stood there, the same graying escort, started to say something, looked at Art's face, and hesitated. Then, in a more respectful tone than he had used before, he asked: "You about ready to leave? Don't worry, she'll be outta here in a coupla days."

"My wife is leaving with me. Now."

Her voice from behind him said: "I'm not going, Art. Don't ask me—oh, I wish you hadn't come."

A pair of young women were coming along the hallway, talking and giggling about something. They eyed Art strangely as they passed, and they looked through the open doorway into Rita's room, their curiosity showing through the pale makeup that masked their faces. These two were made up worse than the B-girls in the tavern had been, and dressed worse too. This pair were both wearing loose, shrouding robes, totally obscene draperies of brown and gray that no woman would wear except . . . except . . .

"What kind of a place—?" Art burst out, glaring wildly at the man who faced him from the hall. The graying man took a step backward, startled.

Art turned quickly and confronted Rita. In two steps he was close enough to grab at her. "What kind of a place is this, answer me, what kind of place?" He saw his hands shaking her, shaking Rita, as if she were someone he did not love.

Rita slapped him in the face. Never before. Art backed away from her slowly, away from her fierce glare. He backed up three steps and bumped into the man who had come to take him away and who now took a grip on Art's arm. When Art tried to pull free the man said something and only tightened his hold. Art turned, all rage let loose, and struck out with his fist. The blow was clumsy but by chance he got most of his weight behind it and it took his enemy by surprise. Art felt human tissue yield with a crunch beneath his knuckles, and then he was no longer being held.

Now once more he had Rita in his grip. She was struggling with him, trying to break free. She screamed: "Do you think I like it, being here in a whorehouse? Do you know what I feel about anything? Let go!"

Even in his rising madness he had no intention of hurting Rita. His only thought was to save her, get her out of here. He was considerably bigger than she was, and when he dragged her with him there was not much she could do. He got her, screaming, fighting, out of the little room. But now there were suddenly frightened faces in his way, and doors, and scrambling bodies. All these were obstacles that must be pushed or knocked aside. Strong hands came from somewhere and fastened on him, but he struck out blindly and kept trying to pull Rita free. Her being here was not to be endured.

An expert foot tripped him, and down he went, onto a dirty floor. His arm was clamped and bent until he must let go of Rita's wrist. Massive weights sat on him, crushing out what little of his wind was left.

"Stop it!" a rough male voice demanded. "Stop. You gonna stop?" It had been barking the same words at him for some time, and finally he had to listen.

"Uh."

A large hand seized Art by the jowls and turned his face up from the floor. "In the name o' pure chastity, you gonna behave?"

"Yuh."

"All right, let 'im up. Sublimation, we get 'em all in here, every kind of a nut there is."

The powerful hands that held Art down reversed themselves and hoisted, and without even trying he was on his feet. He was dizzy suddenly, the world was gray with his faintness. In horrible shape, unused to such exertions. Sweat and dirt were in his eyes, all mixed with helpless tears. His chest heaved in wind-broken spasms. There was a pain inside his shoulder, as if something in there had been torn.

Rita's voice was somewhere nearby, demanding: "Where is he? Let me see. Oh, the fool. If you've hurt him, I'm going to—to—"

"Oh lady, please, he's all right, see? Just his wind knocked out. He was out to tear the place apart. Look at my chaste eye, excuse the language, where he slugged me."

Good.

Rita was now visible as a blur before him, and they were speaking to her with respect. Of course she was only a boarder here, only a fugitive, and she had nothing to do with the—no, of course she was not that.

Art could feel her cool hands, moving on his hands and face.

"Don't start him up again, now, lady, please. Let us get him the purity outta here, we'll see he gets home safe."

"Art? Oh Art, forgive me. Are you all right?"

"Come home with me."

"No."

He nodded. Then he was being led away. He no longer tried to resist.

A man's voice muttered: "Where's the Holy Joe, why don't he look after these celibatin' people of his. I'm sick of the whole celibatin' mess." Then the voice lowered itself to ask a whispered question.

"No! Take 'im back where ya picked 'im up, and just leave him there, nice and safe. Is somebody usin' the car now?" There was a fresh uproar in the middle distance, men's voices raised in some angry quarrel. "What the chastity is that?"

"Sounds like the leather gays again. I tell ya, we get every kind of nut there is. Lemme put this guy in here for a minute."

The grip that had remained on Art's arm now guided him into another room, this one in darkness. "Stay put, hear me? We'll be back to get you in a minute." He was released and the door was closed behind him.

There was a window, framing some brick walls at varying distances, all dimly revealed by distant intermittent lightning. Art groped along the wall beside the door and found a switchplate, which in response to a human finger on its surface turned on a lamp. The single light was dim, revealing a room much like Rita's, except that this one was unoccupied except for Art himself.

Seeking air, Art stumbled toward the window, which was partially open to summer night and rain. Just as he reached it, lightning flared twice, very bright. In the repeated violence of light he could make out a street, or part of one, and the front of an angled wing of the same building he was in. DIANA ARMS APARTMENTS, said a cheap new plastic sign just over the main entrance at ground level. Above that, molded right into the old concrete that arched above the entrance, were other words, not conspicuous but picked out now by perfect light and some trick of the speed-reading brain.

CHICAGO MATERNITY HOSPITAL NURSES' QUARTERS

Art stumbled over to the made-up cot and sank down on it. His breath still wheezed. He had to regain his wind, and more importantly his self-control. Trying to solve his problems with violence was stupid. His game was chess, and not karate. His strong point was supposed to be intelligence, and so he had to think.

Forget the infamy, the shame, of Rita's staying in this whorehouse. But remember this, seen in the fortuitous lightning: DIANA ARMS APARTMENTS. Let them use all the blindfolds that they liked, he could now be sure of locating this place again. But to what end? Should he go now and tell all to Family Planning, and lead them here? Or should he go to George, and tell George what sort of place his sister was penned up in? Art couldn't believe that George would have gone along with the mid-wifing scheme if he had known that. The trouble was that George coming here to drag her out would be likely to kill someone, or else they would kill him.

The attempt to think was doomed. The door of the room opened quietly, and a girl stepped in, completely nude, carrying under one arm a bundle of cloth rolled up, as Fred had carried his karate outfit. Art blinked his eyes, focusing clearly now. The girl was young and blond, flat-bellied and full-breasted, and her face was made up into a cold, pale mask.

She closed the door behind her and then froze, motionless, staring haughtily at Art, as if she had fully expected to find him here but was pretending to be surprised. In a cold voice she asked: "Is this the right room? I don't think it can be mine. What are you doing here? I don't want men in my room."

Art shifted his weight on the cot, starting to get up. Then, when his body made its great reluctance known, he let himself stay sitting there. He knew, he understood perfectly well, that he ought to speak up without delay and tell this prostitute that this time, for once, she really had made a mistake. For once she actually *had* walked into the wrong room. Art understood perfectly well what he should do, yet he said nothing. Maybe he had not yet re-gained his breath enough to speak. Or had some-thing now gone wrong with his throat?

Now the girl was moving away from the door, which she had closed softly behind her. She was edging along the wall, opposite from where Art sat on the cot, trying to give the impression of wanting to keep as far away from him as possible. Already she was gradually unrolling the thick, opaque robe that she had brought in under her arm. As she passed the switchplate on the wall she turned the room's light to an even softer, cooler glow. Her painted face was averted almost completely from Art now. What he could see of her face suggested that it was fixed in a mask expressing bitterness and contempt.

By now she had the robe fully unrolled, and now, with a sudden movement graceful as a dancer's, the robe had been made to cover up her flesh. Her body had vanished, every bit of it below her painted face had gone in a wink from chaste perfect exposure to complete concealment.

This girl was good, she knew her trade. "Don't make a move toward me," she said in a low voice, tense with raw repression. "I don't want to be pawed by anyone, especially not by a man. I don't want you even to stare at me."

Twice during his adolescence Art had visited brothels. Both times feelings of guilt had hampered his performance, and the results had been unsatisfactory. He was still very nearly a virgin as far as sublimation was concerned. Since his marriage he had come to think of himself as grown above all that kind of thing. He had never, since marriage, been seriously tempted toward it. If Rita had ever wanted to do anything like this, he hadn't been aware of it. But—did he know how she felt about anything?—those were her words. He would have done it with her, if she had ever asked. What went on between husband and wife was nobody else's business.

The girl had nearly reached the window now. Suddenly she turned. "Maybe you don't *want* to touch me right now, though," she said, fastening her eyes on Art as if with dawning hope. Oh yes, this girl was skilled. "Maybe you're a pure, chaste man. Maybe you're a person who understands what a human being really likes."

She was standing right beside the window now, and now she turned her pale mask of a face to look up and outward through the upper panes, left unshaded for this very purpose. Her body from the neck down was completely hidden in the long robe. And now her simulated fear and tension were being put aside, were being replaced by—something else. Probably the new feeling was simulated too. Yes, it must be, it had to be, though when a man had let himself be drawn into it this far it was all too easy to convince himself otherwise.

"The stars," the girl said. Her voice was now much softer and far more distant than before. Far more distant, and yet at the same time it spoke to Art directly. "The stars are very beautiful tonight."

A man who had been drawn along this far could make himself believe, perhaps, that stars were visible through clouds and rain. Again Art realized dully that he must move and speak. He must explain his presence here and make her stop . . . before it was too late. Before the exaltation gripped him and could not be broken. Already his breathing had slowed to a normal rate, and it was slowing still further as he watched the girl.

Her hair reminded him of Rita's hair, and there were other ways in which they looked alike. This girl was physically quite attractive, as were all the most successful whores. That increased his danger. The more lust there was to sublimate, the more the act could mean. Of course, nothing having to do with sex was ever reducible to such a simple formula as that; but it seemed to Art that with this girl the meaning of the act of sublimation was likely to be very great indeed. The urge was well-nigh overpowering. To drop sex like a burden from his back. And then to stand on top of it. To stand there with this girl, and look with her at her imaginary stars, and take their light into his being. Art now yearned very powerfully to do just that.

He knew that it was a wrong and perverse yearning, and he struggled against it manfully. Not long ago he had been sure that such secret urgings were all safely behind him, that marrying and accepting responsibility had changed all that. But now, in his moment of weakness and defeat, the craving rose up and assaulted him once more. Well, since an act of sublimation promised all the comfort of which he stood in need, why not? Why not, just this once?

No. He was not going to be so spineless, so weak-willed. Art resisted. He closed his eyes and called up images of Eros, of lust-knotted, bikni'd bodies sweating and writhing together, raging to attain and then prolong a pinnacle of urgency, then raging more to find and climb another higher still. Away with thought, away with fantasy. Flesh was real, reality was flesh. Art fastened his mind upon the image of the girl's bare body, as he had seen it when she first entered the room. His imagination dutifully sketched a bikni on her skin. That's it, that's it.

But lust was faltering. And he could not let it fail. All the fleshly stirrings that he could arouse would, he knew, be nothing more than fuel for sublimation if his determination weakened. He must not weaken.

But erotic awareness, the consciousness of sex-as-god, that must never entirely leave an adult's mind, was flickering now and fading dangerously in his.

"The stars are beautiful," the girl's voice said again. She could make the words sound like winter bells. "So beautiful, so far away."

Art opened his eyes. The rain drummed on the window steadily, but had no power to make her words ridiculous. Feebly he tried to cling to his sweating, struggling, mental images. But they were going still and flat and lifeless, becoming as remote and meaningless as old photographs of strangers.

Just as he might have stood up and gone to join the girl at the window, he suddenly recalled the men, his escort. They could and likely would come walking in at any moment to reclaim him. The thought of their laughter, their comments if they found him stargazing, was enough to tip the balance.

"I'm sorry," he said, and stood up with a grunt. His hands and his knees were quivering still from his recent exertions and his wrenched shoulder hurt. He fumbled in his pockets for some money to tip the girl with; probably she would make a fuss if he tried to walk out without tipping her. At least things had been that way in the brothels of his youth. He said: "I'm not a customer."

She had turned back from the window now and was regarding him with great surprise. As he handed her money, he explained: "There's really been a mistake." Mechanically a gentleman, he squeezed the girl's breast through her robe.

"Mistake? I'll say!" The wintry voice had broken suddenly to nasty shrillness. "This is only ten you gimme!"

"It's all you'll get," said Art, now dangerously calm in his exhaustion. "I told you I'm not a customer."

"You owe me forty!"

"Ten's all you get."

With the money in hand the girl rushed out of the room. Art followed, wearily, as far as the hallway, where he stood waiting for whatever happened next. In a moment his guide, wearing a swelling high on his cheekbone but the same indifferent expression as before, came into sight. Another man was with him. "I'm ready," Art told them. "Take me back."

He rode under the blanket again in the rear of the silent car, and managed a grim private smile. DIANA ARMS APARTMENTS. He had that much anyway, if he could determine what to do with it. He was let out of the car at the busy intersection where he had been picked up. After what he had just been through, a late trip home by slidewalk seemed nothing at all to be concerned about, and Art did not even look around when once there came to him the sound of distant screams.

He arrived back at the Parrs' townhouse to a demonstration of anxious relief by Ann and George, who were both waiting up for him. Art had been gone longer than they'd expected. He did not have a great deal to say to them. Yes, he'd seen Rita, and no, he hadn't been able to get her to change her mind. She was still bent on going through with it. At least she appeared to be all right, and she said that everyone was treating her well enough.

"What kind of a place is she staying in?" Ann wanted to know. "And what's wrong with your arm? You keep holding it oddly."

"I, ah, twisted my shoulder somehow, opening the car door."

Ann, evidently assuming from Art's defeated attitude that he was now going to let his wife do as she chastely well pleased, became very comforting and motherly. Art let her rub his shoulder with some kind of medicine that George used for his occupational aches and pains. Art also let her go on thinking what she liked.

"I should have gone," George muttered several times.

No you shouldn't, thought Art. At last Ann released him from treatment and he dragged himself upstairs and fell into the guest room bed.

In the morning, he decided painfully, he would go to Family Planning, and try to catch Mr. Hall and have a talk with him. Tell all, or nearly all, and plead for help. There was really nothing else that he could do.

Sleep was a long time in arriving.

TEN

"Mr. Barnaby of the Gay League is here asking to see you, sir."

Oscar Grill, director of the Chicago office of the Federal Bureau of Family Planning, slumped back in his chair and gazed unhappily at the intercom plate bearing the sollie image of his secretary. "What's he here for? The same as usual, I suppose."

"I asked him that, sir, but he was vague. I suppose the same as usual."

Grill allowed himself a grimace of annoyance. He had barely had time this morning to sit down and assure himself of what a busy day he had ahead, and now here came Barnaby again. About a year ago the president of the Illinois Gay League had begun to pay the local head of Family Planning a series of drop-in visits. There had been one visit about every two months or six weeks since then. Barnaby would come in, and talk in generalities, and depart. Sometimes they had lunch together. Grill had never been able to understand just what his visitor was after. The two men were agreed on just about every aspect of public policy,

131

so it didn't seem to be a campaign to change Grill's thought on that. Nor was it that Barnaby was sexually attracted to him; that surely would have been made plain by now, and didn't seem too likely anyway, given Grill's paunchy, jowly appearance and the fact that he was fast sliding past middle age.

What really made the situation difficult for Grill was that the president of the IGL was much too important to be casually brushed off. No politician wanted to risk alienating a bloc of votes of the League's size, and Oscar Grill was, among other things, very much a politician. The general elections were coming up within a year.

Grill sighed, mentally trying to rearrange his morning schedule. He wondered which appointments he might be able to put off. At last he said to his receptionist: "I suppose you'd better send him in right away. Maybe I can cut it short."

"Yes sir."

Seizing the fragment of peaceful time that was still available before Barnaby walked through the door, Grill closed his eyes and tried to achieve an instant of total relaxation. But it was not to be. Today's thoughts were not to be so quickly quieted. Today there was to be an obligatory luncheon meeting, with the local heads of other bureaus, notably Art, Poverty, and Vandalism. There were, as always, important political decisions to be made—or at least to be foreseen and postponed as much as possible. And sometime today Grill wanted to talk again with his semi-official contacts at the UN's Chicago consulate, to try to find out what might be delaying the latest population forecast. A fog of rumors already surrounded that ominously tardy report; when he did learn what it contained, he would probably wish that he hadn't.

His moment was over, the door was opening, and Grill opened his eyes and stood up and came around from behind his desk, setting himself to be courteous while he went about the job of easing his visitor out as quickly as he could. At least he had an obviously and honestly cluttered desk for Barnaby to notice.

The president of the Gay League entered, moving with his usual slightly feminine walk. Barnaby's basic physique was that of a male of about average size and build. His face was strikingly handsome—or perhaps pretty—and his long hair was a natural-looking bright red. In the IGL as elsewhere, appearance apparently counted for a lot in getting to be president. Also a leader of the Androgyne Society, Barnaby wore a conservatively tiny bikni very little different from a standard female business model, the bottom lacking the exaggerated fullness of the usual male codpiece. Mr. Barnaby's bra was functional, courtesy of modern medical science.

"How do you do, sir?" Grill asked formally, extending his hand. Andro or not, Barnaby was a stickler for preferring the male form of address for himself.

"Not well today, Oscar, not very well." Barnaby's voice was husky rather than deep. He shook Grill's fingers, as always, rather than his hand, and delicately. "I am becoming afraid to travel through the streets. There is an organized harassment that I must endure. Good citizens pay taxes, then find that their government offers them no protection."

Grill said: "Won't you sit down? You mean you're being picketed by that bluenose group again?"

"Again? One might say that it has become almost continuous." Adjusting his shoulder bag with a large smooth hand, Barnaby settled himself in a visitor's chair. "Not only is our headquarters under siege, as it were, but some of these Young Virgins have taken to following my car through the streets. Some of them have followed me here today."

Grill had seated himself behind his desk again; as soon as he was seated, as if unconsciously, he was toying with the corner of a stack of printout—though he had little hope that the hint would be taken. "Well, I can certainly sympathize. I really wish that there was something I could do. But twins, we're sometimes picketed here ourselves."

"Yes, I'm sure you are, and by many of the same people." Barnaby crossed his legs, which were hairless and slightly plump. He drew a breath. "Oscar, it seems to me to be of the utmost importance that those of us who lead in conserving traditional values should support one another, for the cause of Eros and the good of society. Women and men of good will should stand together whenever possible, that's all I mean. I realize that you have no power to punish those wretches who are out there picketing."

"I certainly don't," Grill said sympathetically, and sneaked a quick look at his clock.

"I did go to the police about the picketing, as I believe you suggested once before." Barnaby seemed unable to keep from exciting himself over the pickets. "I tried to point out to the police the difference between our country's traditional freedoms and the anarchy those bluenoses want. They think they have a license to paint their dirty words right on their signs, and wave them about in public places, and the police and courts will do nothing to put a stop to it!"

Grill shrugged. "Freedom of speech and all that, my friend. I suppose that if the police are providing you with physical protection, that's really about all you can expect."

"Oscar," said Barnaby reproachfully. He leaned across the desk and lowered his voice. "Which is the more to be feared, injury to the body or poisoning of the mind? I'm much more concerned for the youth of this country than I am for myself. What will happen to them, growing up in a world where nothing is considered obscene any longer?"

Art woke up slowly. He was aware of morning sunlight coming in a window, but, at first, of very little else. There was something very nasty he had to face, as soon as he was fully awake. He couldn't remember exactly what the bad thing was, but he knew it would be preferable to fall asleep again instead.

Then he moved his arm, and the resulting twinge in his shoulder brought memories of yesterday flooding back. With a groan he sat up in the guest room bed. His watch read half past eight.

Art's situation looked no better to him in the morning light than it had in midnight gloom. There was nothing for it but to be a good citizen and go to Family Planning and tell them what he knew, bargaining with them as well as he could to keep Rita out of trouble. Mr. Hall had said they were not out to *get* anyone, at least not anyone like Rita. Certainly the attitude at the BFP *ought* to be that people like her were only the innocent victims of the midwifers and their gangs. And of their well-meaning relatives as well. Too bad, thought Art, if the relatives got in trouble. It was their own fault. His first responsibility was to his wife, not to the people who never should have got her into this mess in the first place. Even if they were only trying to help.

Art didn't want to think about the Parrs at all right now, but it was hard to avoid thinking about them as long as he was in their house. Rubbing his shoulder, he got out of bed and began to get ready to go downstairs.

While he showered and trimmed his beard and dressed, he pictured raiding police breaking down the doors of that former nurses' quarters, carting off hysterical whores, handcuffing thugs. He supposed there would be some such scene as that. Then along came the quietly efficient police lieutenant, leading Rita safely out. When she saw Art (who had ridden along in the lead car with the lieutenant) Rita burst into tears, and threw repentant arms around his neck . . .

More likely she would hit him in the face again. The whole scenario was fundamentally unconvincing. Art had to give up on it, and try to think of something else while he held fast to his determination.

Aromas of coffee and warm food now reached him in the upstairs hall. Art promised himself suddenly that he would say nothing to the Family Planning authorities about George and Ann. Well, sooner or later he would doubtless have to say *something* about them, for he was going to be asked a lot of questions. But he might be able to make their immunity a condition of his giving information. Something like that. Anyway, he kept telling himself, if Ann and George wound up in trouble it would serve them right, for helping Rita to get herself into such a mess.

His shoulder definitely felt a little better this morning, but it was still sore. He would get Ann to rub it with liniment again tonight. If he was still staying here. If *she* was still staying here, and they were still on speaking terms with each other. Sex, what a mess. It would be so good to enter a big tournament, and think of nothing but chess for the next week.

After taking a quick peek into the children's room and finding it already deserted, Art went downstairs. In the kitchen he found George and Ann facing each other somewhat glumly across the breakfast table, where Art's place was already set. Copious garbage on the table testified that the children must have already breakfasted; doubtless they were already outside, playing.

Even as Art's in-laws bade him good morning, they seemed to him to be exchanging guilty looks between them. They were feeding Art and his children, and giving them lodging, but what did that count for, compared to the harm that they were doing to Rita? The Parrs' intentions had been good, of course, but what of that?

George raised troubled eyes across the table. "Art, what are your plans now?"

"I don't know." As soon as Art was seated, Ann began silently to ply him with toast and protein bars and coffee. Art's fingers fumbled on the jelly jar. He asked unnecessarily: "Are the children out on the playground?"

He was assured they were, and with that an awkward silence fell. He wished he had gone straight out of the house, but that would have demonstrated an anger against his relatives that he could not really feel. Besides, he always needed breakfast.

But now he couldn't stand to sit here in this silence. He took another large bite of protein bar and pushed his chair back and got up quickly. "I'm going out," he said. No one answered him as he fled the house.

It was a bright, warm morning; only puddles here and there gave evidence of last night's rain. Once outside the blockhouse walls Art breathed a little more easily, at least at first. But not for long. He took a slidewalk, aiming vaguely for the city's center.

As soon as he came to a public phone facility, he went in and from the directory computer obtained the address of the Chicago office of the Bureau of Family Planning. With a slight feeling of relief, he saw that he would have to travel a considerable distance to reach the place. That was good, because he needed some time to think over what he was going to say when he got there.

The Bureau wasn't out to get Rita, though; they were really on her side. He felt confident of that.

Once on the proper slidewalk, he drew a deep breath and told himself that he felt better for having come to a decision. He told himself again that the weather was fine today.

But who cared what the weather was like?

Reaching the BFP office seemed to take no time at all, and somehow Art was unable to do any constructive thinking en route. The office evidently occupied the whole of a new, fairly large building, one of the foothills that surrounded the central Loop's high range. From several blocks away Art could see that there was an unusually dense crowd gathered on the statwalk in front of where the main entrance ought to be. And as he drew a little nearer he quickly realized that this was more than an ordinary pedestrian jam. In an out-of-the-way spot against the wall of another building, a stack of placards waited on the pavement, as if ready for distribution. Some kind of demonstration must be shaping up, though whatever it was it hadn't really started yet. Should he go in?

If he didn't make himself face the authorities now, he never would. Ignoring the murmuring, jostling crowd as best he could, he pushed his way through it and into the lobby.

In the middle of the vast ground-floor lobby of glass and marble he approached a receptionist, a voluptuous young woman who smiled at him enticingly from behind her desk. As befitted her place of employment, she was very conservatively dressed, wearing only a few electrostatically clinging sequins and pads.

When Art halted in front of her desk, he had the sensation of a complete loss of momentum. This was it. He was finished. His mind had gone as blank and bare as the smooth expanse of receptionist's skin confronting him. Somehow he had earlier convinced himself that once he got this far everything would be all right, that at this point the right words would flow from him. But that had been panicked self-deception. He had no more idea than ever of what the right words were. All he was certain of was that to ask for Mr. Hall would be like leaping over a cliff.

"I'm from California," he began with a great effort, helped along by the young woman's encouraging eyes. "But I have important business with you here. I'd like to talk to—the director. Or someone." Art was suddenly and completely sure that he never wanted to talk to Mr. Hall again. He would never be able to convince Mr. Hall that George and Ann were innocent, or at least that they deserved a break. Not after the tough time that Ann had given him. And she and George hadn't even asked Art where he was going this morning.

The receptionist's eyes turned grave. "The director is a very busy man," she said. "If you'll tell me the nature of your business, I can probably find someone to help you."

"My business is, uh, important." Of course the director of an establishment the size of this one was not going to see everyone who just walked in. One could even hope that all the important people were too busy to see anyone today. No, one couldn't.

The eyes of the young woman narrowed slightly, searching Art's face. He could not escape the thought that she could see his guilty knowledge, that she might be already pressing an alarm button somewhere underneath her desk. She said: "I can arrange for you to talk to a social worker. Are you in a hurry?"

"I—" Of course the instant their computer learned his name, it would give him to Mr. Hall. And Mr. Hall would seize upon him, not to be denied a single scrap of information. Art would stumble helplessly into a complete betrayal of the Parrs, and Rita would hate him for that, even if he kept her from being thrown in jail and forcibly sterilized. "No, there's no hurry," Art told the young woman.

"May I have your name, please?" The receptionist pulled a computer-input slate toward her on its decorative fiberoptic cable, and took up an electronic stylus.

"I—" Ann was at this moment caring for Art's children. George was risking bloody beatings from

machines, to pay for safe blockhouse playspace
and midwifers, and cinnamon-flavored protein bars
that tended to turn lumpy in the stomach. Art's
thought, now scrambling like a cornered animal
for some way out, seized suddenly upon the possibility that Rita's illegal operation was being per-
formed this very morning. If so, she would certainly
be jailed instead of rescued if Art led Family Planning to her.

In Art's present state he took this as excuse
enough to flee. Without even delaying to pinch the
receptionist goodbye, he took a step backward from
her desk. He blurted out wild words about return-
ing later. He turned and fled.

"Radicals and bluenoses. Repressors of all that
binds humanity to its billion-year heritage of sex!"
Mr. Barnaby's voice had grown shrill. "Are we to
abandon the youth of the world to them?"

Looking down with Barnaby from an open window of his office, Director Grill had a good view of
the wide statwalk in front of the Family Planning
building. Two competing picket lines had just been
organized down there, and both of them were on
the march, weaving and writhing like antagonistic
serpents. The lines had formed with a healthy distance between them, but they were coming closer
to each other, in part because of the pressure of a
mass of onlookers, whose expectation of a riot was
probably going to fulfill itself. It seemed likely to
Grill, who had observed this sort of thing before,
that a critical mass of active humanity would soon
be reached down there. A block away, a column of
helmeted city police was marching in. One could
hope that the effect would be like that of a damp-
ing rod of moderator thrust into an old-style atomic

fission pile as it began to overheat. One could hope.

Sporadic shouting drifted up from the mob scene below, but as yet Grill had seen no actual violence. He was not too high above the scene to be able to tell that one of the picket lines was composed mainly of radical-looking young people, the girls wearing their hair long, sometimes curled, the men short-haired and clean-shaven, both sexes dressed in opaque garments that covered half their bodies or more. These were of course the Young Virgins, the objects of Barnaby's wrath. In the opposing picket line, men and women of ordinary appearance were in the majority, though their group contained a noticeable admixture of men in biknis, and women in codpieced, translucent business suits.

"I see the Gay League has some counter-picketers out today," Grill commented.

"Naturally we do!" Barnaby ran nervous fingers through his bright red hair. "We don't intend to succumb without a struggle."

Grill turned in from the window. He decided that the time had come for bluntness, whatever the result might be. "Frankly, I wish you hadn't decided on counterpicketing. Not in front of my building."

"What? But we must take action. Look, look down there. A sign that says 'sublimate,' in big bold letters, being waved around in a public place!"

Grill looked down and saw. He saw also another sign, in bigger and bolder letters yet: STOP MORAL FREE FALL. He wondered honestly which side that one was intended to be on.

"Let them go to their monasteries and lamaseries and nunneries to have that kind of freedom,"

Barnaby was saying. "Let them go behind walls, away from the innocent, and do what they like."

Grill drew a deep breath. "You know, if I was coldly logical about my job . . ."

"Yes?"

"Well, I might look with official favor upon the bluenoses. After all, the less sexual activity there is, broadly speaking, the fewer pregnancies and the less population pressure."

"Only in the most primitive societies!" snapped Barnaby. But then he fell silent, and seemed to have put on a mask of careful control. Grill got the odd impression that the emotion being concealed was more fear than anger.

Emboldened by this impression, Grill went on, determined to set things straight now that he had started. "I don't know if any society has ever been run on the basis of cold logic. Probably not. I'm sure ours isn't. People's emotional attitudes are the ultimate power, of course. And most of the people are with you, at least in your attitude toward bluenoses. If I were to come out strongly in favor of chastity today I'd doubtless be fired tomorrow."

Barnaby relaxed slightly. "You are joking. Of course there's no excuse for chastity. No comparison between *that* and what my League represents. For a long time our people have shown the way toward the fullest enjoyment of sex without the slightest risk of adding to the population."

"Most people just don't enjoy the kind of sex you do, though," said Grill deliberately. "At least, not as a steady diet. And the monasteries and other religious places you talk about are from my point of view very much like Gay League resorts—they all have a vanishingly low birth rate. So, while I

may not agree with the bluenoses emotionally, I'm
not going to try to put them out of business. I still
won't say so publicly, but I don't mind telling you
in private that I'm rather glad there are more and
more lamaseries and nunneries these days."

There was silence in the room except for the
noises drifting up to it from below. Then Barnaby
cleared his throat. He seemed to be giving some
point a deep reconsideration. "Really," he said at
last, "I didn't come here with the main objective
of getting your help against the bluenoses. I know
I let them upset me too much. I can see how they
help you in your difficult job. But we've helped
you even more, haven't we? For many years? I like
to think that we in the League are your favorite
citizens, so to speak. That there's a large backlog
of goodwill built up between us."

"Of course." Grill sighed, left the window, and
walked back to his desk. He did not want to watch
another riot. That many police were sure to handle it, one way or another.

Privately, he had no more emotional sympathy
for homosexuality than he did for chastity. Professionally, he was glad to accept every bit of help,
from any quarter, that Family Planning and the
world could get. The human world was in danger
of collapsing under the weight of its own numbers,
even though you might not be able to tell that
from what went on in Illinois.

On the walls of Grill's office the computer-drawn
curves of the world demographic charts showed
the danger. There were ever and everywhere more
people, who inevitably ate more food. While around
the world the food suppliers struggled to get ahead,
sometimes they could not even manage to keep up.
There were now laws restricting births in every

country on the planet. It was mathematically and physically inevitable that at some future time, by some combination of peaceful or violent forces, the world's population growth would finally be stopped. Obviously it could not continue until human beings stood jammed shoulder to shoulder on every square meter of solid land.

The approximately eight billion people who inhabited the world today could, in theory, probably be stored within Chicago's borders, standing indoors and out, leaving the rest of the Earth on which to grow their food. But reality was something else. Frighteningly many of the eight billion were hungry and sick today. And many more would be sick and hungry tomorrow, even though science had boosted the world's supply of available energy beyond all foreseeable needs by achieving controlled nuclear fusion, by beginning to harness tides and the heat of the inner Earth itself. The problems of actually producing and distributing adequate food, and providing medical care, had proven less amenable to research and engineering. Most of the leaders of have-not nations spent their careers in power in a state of chronic desperation, weighing and selecting gamblers' moves to keep themselves in power and—sometimes this came first—to help their people.

One time-tested solution to the problem of maintaining oneself in power was to point out to the people a scapegoat or two on which they might vent their hate, their dissatisfaction with their lives. If some real justification could be found for the choice of scapegoat, so much the better.

Another gambler's move was the creation of an external enemy by the utterance of overt or implied threats. Often, now, the threats were serious, even when spoken by some leader of a poor but desperate nation against a wealthy and much more powerful one. Today at least eighty nations were theoretically capable of producing atomic weapons, and perhaps fifteen or twenty of these had the technological capability to hide such outlawed weapons from the UN inspection satellites and surface teams. Nuclear weapons had not actually been used since the last Mideast War in the 1990s, but everyone knew that delivery of such a bomb could be accomplished by stealth as well as by missile or aircraft. Biological weapons were easier to make, conceal, and deliver, and could be just as deadly if not as quick as nuclear blasts. Thus the voices of the have-nots must be heard in all the greatest capitals of the world. Thus if a newborn baby in Chicago consumed, statistically, three times the food of one new-born in India, it was considered only just and decent and prudent to limit the number of new-born Chicagoans, and the same with Londoners, Muscovites, babies of Peking and Tokyo. The starving child in the Indian village or the African bush might never see a bite of the food thus theoretically saved, but who could say it was not just and necessary to offer him at least a theoretical chance? Thus, even among the haves, compulsory sterilization and abortion for women who could not or would not limit their fertility in any other way. Thus the illegitimacy of the third child. We may not feed the world, we may lack the knowledge or the will or the resources for that, but we will not let it watch more and more of us overeat.

Again, as he looked now at the charts, there darted across Grill's mind the question of why the latest population forecast had been delayed. He felt a foreboding chill.

"It seems to me," Barnaby was saying to him now, "that in fact you owe us a real debt. Very few of the League's members have brought any children at all into the world—as yet."

Something in Barnaby's tone brought Grill's thoughts back firmly to his office. "As yet? Why do you put it that way?"

Barnaby did not answer immediately. An alien hardness was shadowing his face. He continued to stand at the window, watching Grill from across the room.

As Grill stood waiting beside his desk his mind started to relate that odd phrase "as yet" to the chain of Barnaby's odd visits, and to certain other, more terrible, hints that Grill had lately received from other sources. The hints concerned recent advances in surgery, in genetic engineering, and in hormonal chemistry; until now, Grill had managed to avoid directly confronting their implications.

Barnaby, as if he could read the director's mind, was nodding now. It was a slow and solemn gesture. "Maybe you've heard something about it? True male to female sex reversal is going to be possible. It's been achieved in animal experiments. Doctors have been working on it in Sweden, and lately in Japan, and both groups seem to have been successful."

"Well. That's fine. I suppose many members of the League will want to avail themselves of the operation, to become practically complete women."

"Not just practically, Oscar."

"What?"

"Truly complete. I want that. Does that surprise you?" Paradoxically, as he spoke of becoming a woman, Barnaby looked straighter than he had before, a male trapped in a masquerade costume that he could not shed, a man grown weary and desperate beyond all words. "Does it make you laugh, to hear that I will want to bear a child? Two children, if I can."

Grill was very far from laughter. He whispered: "This is—beyond belief."

"Not to me." Barnaby's husky voice was quavering. He spoke now as if he were confessing some terrible crime. "All my life, ever since I was a child myself, the thought has been in my mind that somehow—if I could have a son—what do you know about me, anyway?"

Like the first thunder of an expected storm, the sounds of rioting burst up abruptly from the street outside. Director Grill hardly noticed. He moved behind his desk, without taking his eyes off Barnaby, and sank slowly into his chair. "So," Grill said in a faint voice. "Today you have come here on business."

Art, while he was inside the Family Planning building and agonized by his own problems, had forgotten completely about the demonstrations being organized outside. When he emerged from the lobby to the statwalk, practically at a run, he was at once engulfed in chanting swirls of picketers and counter-picketers. He managed to push himself free of the first entanglement, found he had been turned around, and stood for a moment, disoriented, in the middle of the pavement.

A short, fat man bearing an armload of cheaply made, stick-mounted signs appeared at once beside Art, haranguing him. "Get yer sign, get yer placard here. Do yer *part*, sir. Only two dollars." STOP MORAL FREE FALL, said the signs, or some of them at

least. Others, interleaved, bore the proud legend
LOVE CONQUERS ALL.

"I'm not involved in this," Art muttered, trying
to get free of the peddler, not knowing which side
the man thought Art was on, or even who the two
contending parties were. As soon as Art was able
to spot a small gap between the writhing lines he
made for it. The picketers now were chanting louder
and louder, faster and faster, mouthing unintelligible rioter's warcries. The peddler would not give
up, but stayed at Art's side like a stubborn con-
science, trying to sell him a sign. Moving as a couple
they were too big to get through the gap between
lines, and they, or Art at least, collided with people
in one of the lines as it writhed toward him. A
shout of anger went up from those he had bumped,
followed by a cheer from the opposing ranks.

"Filthy censor! Bluenose!"

"Smear the queers! Smear the queers! Smear—"

A tall male figure loomed up in front of Art.
Above the words STUDENTS FOR A CHASTE SOCIETY,
handpainted on a dirty, opaque sweat-shirt, the
young man's face was clean-shaven, angry, florid,
shouting. Someone bawling a song about love
pushed Art from behind, whereupon the young
man in front struck Art on the head with his sign.

Something was wrong, the blow with the flimsy
sign should not have hurt so much, should not
have been a great deadening bash that had dented
a vacuum into his skull, a hole into which a tremendous pain was now about to rush . . .

There was suddenly a policeman in Art's field of
view. And other people, he could not tell who they
were . . . Art was down, on the pavement, but
somebody had him under the arms and was drag-
ging him along . . . now he was dying, or else . . .

ELEVEN

After Art had hurried out of the house, George and Ann remained seated at the breakfast table, alone together now in the silent house, facing each other with glum expressions.

"I wonder what's happened to Fred," said Ann distantly, turning her head to look out her window at the genengineered fast-growing patio vines. "And I wonder if Rita has her baby yet." Then she gave up on making conversation and brought her hands up to cover her face. "Oh, if Art turns us in today it's going to be all my fault."

"He won't turn us in," said George, putting into his voice a lot more certainty than he felt.

"He might." Ann spoke through her muffling hands, around her silver wedding ring.

"No. He doesn't want to get Rita in trouble. Anyway, there's no use blaming yourself if he does."

"You and Rita will be the ones who go to jail for conspiracy, but it'll be all my fault. Why can't I mind my own business? Why'd I have to tell her you had a student who could arrange things? Some criminal doctor."

That irritated George. "Hammad's no criminal, as far as I know, or I wouldn't have him as a student. I don't consider arranging births to be a crime, and you don't either. I don't know of anything else he does that's outside the law."

"He arranges births and breaks the law just for money. I don't like that. Why couldn't I have waited until I heard from the Order of St. Joseph people?"

"You might have waited a long time, with their monastery burned down. Anyway, it might even be one of them who's doing the operation. I think it was a smart move for Hammad to farm it out."

"Someone else is doing it, while he gets paid. Hammad . . . I don't trust Hammad."

"Now's a fine time to tell me that," George grumbled. "Anyway, Rita's no Christian, she won't care who does it or why, as long as it's done competently." Of course, if it wasn't done competently—but there was no reason to speak of that, there was nothing they could do about it now.

Ann was silent behind her hands.

"Art won't turn us in," George repeated, trying to be comforting. To himself he thought that he could hardly blame Art for anything he did today. Art was the one they hadn't allowed for in their plans.

Still silent.

He reached across the table, pried one of Ann's hands down from its job of eye-hiding, and held it softly in his own. "Hey, things aren't that bad," he said. "Hey, lady, do you need some help?"

The first time he had made that offer to Ann they had both been aboard a bus, cruising at thirty kilometers per hour along the thirty-two-lane freeway that ran from Bear Canyon to Pasadena, near

the middle of Los Angeles. Five apish young men
had also boarded the vehicle at Bear Canyon,
though George had not paid them much attention
then. Perhaps they had only got on the bus to
follow Ann, who had had five or six small children
with her that day.

The five young men had taken seats just a little
forward in the bus from Ann and her brood, and
once the bus was isolated from the rest of the
world in the flow of traffic they had begun to talk
loudly among themselves, boasting in obscene language of their skills at stealing, fighting, and
sublimating. Ann was pretty good at ignoring them,
but then one of the apes began to toss little wads
of something or other in her direction. "Hey, lady,
those all yours? Quint-up-lets! Looks like you waited
too long deciding which ones to keep."

By now most of the other passengers had con-
gealed in their seats, seeing and hearing nothing.

"Hey, girly?" called the youth who had been
tossing the spitballs. "Anyone ever tell you you'd
look nice wrapped in a blanket down to your
toenails?" He turned to a friend. "Red, you got
some gladrags with you?"

"Sure."

"Break 'em out. Girly's gonna gaze at the stars
with us."

An old woman sitting beside George muttered
something to the effect that girls who dressed that
way were just asking for trouble—and true enough,
Ann had on an opaque blouse, and an opaque
skirt that came down nearly to her knees. Her
dress was probably one reason why George had
noticed her as early as he did. But that was irrele-
vant now.

"Do you need some help, lady?" he called to Ann

politely, at the same time getting up to stand in the narrow aisle between seats. He just stood there, swaying slightly with the motion of the bus. George was then twenty-one, half trained in karate, proud owner of a purple belt. He stood up with a feeling of necessity, without much fear or much sense of heroism either. Vaguely he wished he could have a chance to limber up before any action started.

"Yes, I believe I do." Ann's voice was as calm as if she had dropped a package in some inaccessible place and some presentable man had offered to retrieve it. George, though he had hardly had time to look at her yet, was in love with her already.

So George cleared his throat like a nervous orator and faced forward. He met the eyes of the five troublemakers, one pair after another, and wondered if there were any words that he might use to stop them. A wise old instructor had once told George that if you were really ready for street trouble the readiness showed somehow, and trouble never came—unless you went out of your way to make it, which wise people in or out of karate never did. What words would have stopped me, George wondered, when I was just a kid and up to something wild? But he had never been as wild and apey as these five looked and acted now, and magic words eluded him. At the same time he was reassuring himself on a comforting point he had already taken into consideration: the narrowness of the aisle. He might be facing five opponents, but they could only come within reach of him one at a time.

If they were going to come at him at all. George could see in their faces that he had frightened them just by getting up to face them, and he hoped that his continued calm and that of the girl might

be enough to keep them paralyzed. Raising his
eyes toward the front of the bus, George met the
driver's eyes in a mirror inside the driver's personal shield of armored glass. All around the bus
the sixteen lanes of traffic proceeding in the same
direction crept on, cutting it off from the rest of
humanity and bearing it along. The driver was
already trying to maneuver the bus into an outer
lane and reach an emergency stopping bay, but
the maneuver might easily take ten minutes or so.
He was probably also trying to radio for police
help, but for that to arrive might need some time
also.

Meanwhile, maintaining a calm silence was not
going to be enough, perhaps because the five had
nowhere to retreat. Now their faces were hardening again; they were more afraid of something
else, something that drove them on, than they were
of George. They looked at one another and got to
their feet and started after him. The old woman
screamed.

The eyes of the first youth to come at George
changed again when the implications of the narrow aisle dawned on him at last. He was a boy of
average size and strength, sixteen or seventeen
years old. His face was too broad to be called
handsome, and his red hair was cut so short that
the top of his head looked bald. His cohort, mum-
bling obscenities, shoved forward behind him, pushing him to the attack, until there was nothing he
could do but lunge at George, swinging his fists in
clumsy desperation.

The bus driver was thinking, as well as watching in the mirror. At that moment he tapped his
brakes firmly, risking a bang from the vehicle

following, but stalling the momentum of the single-file attack.

George saw the first blow of the fight coming at him, and ducked just enough to catch it on the top of his head, where an enemy knuckle was likely to be cracked. Then he leaned forward counterpunching, just as the sudden slowing of the bus rocked his opponents back on their heels. George at the purple-belt stage was already able to crack two centimeters of pine board with the knuckles of either hand. The foe went down like helpless dummies, tangled with one another as they fell. George pressed forward, hammering at the face and body of the hapless youth who had led the attack, getting him down and keeping him down so that the rest were jammed behind him and beneath him.

When the police came aboard the bus, only a couple of minutes after it had reached an emergency bay, they found George still leaning on the pile of inept apes, punching anything that dared to move. The police heard Ann's matter-of-fact story, and the driver's, and those of the few passengers who had really watched what was happening. George was identified and allowed to go his way; the five were removed to a police copter. The red-haired youth had to be carried, and his face was now even broader than it had been before and of a different redness. George knew a moment of sick regret. But no more than a moment.

As soon as the police had departed with their catch, the bus got rolling again and Ann's reaction started to set in. Her hands were trembling and she had to fight back tears. She understood as well as anyone that the five had had more in mind than wrapping her in a plastic sheet. And the children riding with her were getting into a slight state of shock now too, seeing how upset she was. The little kids all sat quietly, staring at her and at George.

George sat down at Ann's side and acknowledged as best he could her choking thanks. He now felt ten feet tall, and at the same time shaky with relief. "Relax, it's over now," he said to Ann. He patted her arm, and slid a hand up under her long skirt, gently squeezing her thigh.

"Please don't," she murmured, shifting herself infinitesimally away from him, pressing her knees firmly together.

His pulse, quieting after the workout, speeded up again immediately. But he couldn't believe that she had meant those words just the way they sounded. Probably it wasn't really the open invitation it sounded like, but just a nervous reaction from the danger she had been in. A lot of people didn't really feel like sex when they were frightened or upset, and under the circumstances her lack of even a polite pretense was quite forgivable socially.

So George restricted himself to holding Ann's hand and lightly stroking her arm, which attentions she accepted and seemed to find comforting.

"I think I know you," he said with sudden mild surprise. "At least I think I know who you are. Your name's Ann something, and you're in my sister's high school class. You were there at school one day with a bunch of girls when I went to pick her up. She's Rita Parr. Oh, excuse me, my name is George."

"Yes, I heard you giving your name to the police. You're right, I know Rita. I'm Ann Lohmann. Oh, why must I start blubbering now, when the trouble's all over?" She was certainly not blubbering, just a little tense and swollen-looking about the eyes. "Thanks to you," she added.

But soon Ann had herself almost completely under control. She looked around, checking on her children, giving them a smile and a few cheerful words, snapping at a boy to get his feet off the seats.

"Where are you taking them?" George asked.

"We're just coming back from Bear Canyon Park. I took them out there because so many never see anything but pavement and little strips of grass." The kids all had a BI look. "They're from my Sunday school class."

"Oh, one of those religious schools?"

"Yes." Ann paused. "I remember seeing you too, now that I think about it. Rita looks a lot like you."

He laughed. "Don't say that about the poor girl. She's all excited about graduation these days. So are you, I suppose."

"Yes, we all are, I guess." But it was evident that Ann was not nearly as excited as Rita was.

George wondered why. "And about going to college. Where are you going your freshman year, if you don't mind my asking?"

"How could I mind *your* asking anything?" Ann smiled beautifully. She was really quite a good-looking girl. "I might go to Mid-Cal my first year. Or maybe Ha-Levy Junior. I'm not sure."

George liked her voice, too, now that he had a chance to listen to it attentively. Women's voices were important, in his estimation. Temper and spirit were important in anyone. There was a suggestion of repression in Ann's clothes and manner, and any normal male would be drawn on by that.

"You're older than Rita, aren't you?" Ann was asking him. "Well, naturally you are. Where did you go to college, or are you still going?"

"I didn't go." Not wanting her to think him lazy or stupid, he quickly added: "Oh, I may go yet. But the year I finished high school there was one problem after another in our family. People getting sick and losing jobs. We were almost back on BI. I didn't have much time or money, and I was a little too dumb to qualify for any good scholarships. Then I got into this karate business. Once you get your black belt, it's really a profession."

Ann looked at him warmly. "I can't imagine that you're lacking in intelligence. Anyway, you've proved that you have courage, and that's more important." She shook her head as if marveling. "When you stood up there in the aisle, I didn't know what you were going to do. But I knew that *you* knew."

Unable to find any words with which to answer that, George changed the subject. "I suppose you're all excited about the Prom? Rita is. She's got her escort all picked out and everything. I don't know if the poor clod knows about it yet, whoever he is."

Once more Ann seemed to withdraw momentarily, as she had when George caressed her leg. "I'm not going to the Prom," she said, and then busied herself suppressing a quarrel developing among the children.

George supposed that maybe she had had a fight with her own most likely escort, and was uncertain who was taking her. He never doubted that a girl like this one would have a choice of invitations to accept. "I'll bet you change your mind about that," he said, thinking back to the windup celebration of his own high school years. "The Prom's half the fun of graduating, or more than half."

She didn't answer. But *surely* a girl like this had been invited to the Prom, so George felt he could safely tease and probe and push a little more without any serious danger of hurting her feelings; besides, he wanted to find out as much about her as he could. "Why," he said, "I'd be tempted to ask you myself, if I was in your class."

"I've been asked." Ann's face was slightly averted from him so he could not make out her expression. And her voice was guarded too. "I'm just not going."

Ouch. He had managed to hit some kind of a sore spot after all. He gave himself mentally a swift roundhouse kick for clumsiness "Anyway," he said, trying to dig himself out of trouble, "your Prom isn't next week, so you have lots of time to think about it. Meanwhile, when am I going to see you again?"

It turned out that he saw her the very next day, at the police station where they had both been summoned for questioning about the trouble on the bus. George came near being charged with aggravated battery, but when the testimony of all the available witnesses had been heard, he was not.

Later, George bought Ann a snack at a nearby restaurant, and then suggested that they find some place a little less noisy and enjoy some kind of sex.

"No, please, I'd rather not." Again, the bluntness of her reply could be taken at face value as an invitation to repression. But at the same time the answer had been so natural and direct, so unembarrassed, that George found he simply could not take it at face value. He told himself that Ann had doubtless been upset all over again by having to give evidence. She was so matter-of-fact about what she said, that she probably didn't realize how it sounded.

At that meeting he asked Ann several times to go out with him on a regular date, but she consistently refused. Still, he contrived to see more of her. His sister Rita told him where Ann could usually be found on Monday nights, playing volleyball, and George went to the gym and managed to get in on the games.

He went after her when she pursued an escaping ball up into the empty spectators' seats.

"Annie, this is fun, but how about you and me going out someplace by ourselves? You like other sports? Bowling, swimming? Or maybe a show."

"George, I . . . you're nice, and I really like you, but I think it wouldn't be wise."

"Why not?" But now people were yelling at them to get back to the net if they ever wanted to play. They never had the time or the place for a serious discussion. Ann seemed to be making sure of that.

During this same period of a month or so George made it a point to enjoy sex with five or six different women and girls. With each of them, at the most abandoned moments, he found himself closing his eyes and imagining it was Ann Lohmann's flesh that moved against his own. The popularizers of psychology on the sollie talk shows and in the newsprints were always warning young people that such behavior could be a danger signal. To focus desire on one individual might be a step toward its repression whenever that individual was not available. Brilliant, thought George. It was just staggering how wise those psychologists had been rendered by all their years in college. Anyway, he wasn't worried. Some of the younger, more radical psychologists held that the occasional practice of sexual repression, or even all-out sublimation, was unlikely to cause permanent harm. That seemed sensible to George, though he hadn't much in the way of personal experience to judge by. He was young and full of health and usually wanted to do nothing with his sex drive but satisfy it every day or so and enjoy thinking about it between times.

But now this thing with Ann—this thing with Ann was something else.

Early on the evening of the Prom—living in the same house as Rita, he could not possibly have been wrong about the date—George obeyed an irrational-seeming impulse and phoned Ann's home. Ann's mother, tight-lipped and looking somehow hurried and harried, answered. When George asked for Ann, she reminded him in a nervous voice that this was Prom night.

After he had blanked off, George sat thinking. Ms. Lohmann had not actually said in so many words that Ann had left already for the Prom or that she was too busy getting ready for it to come to the phone. George went into Rita's room, where his sister was still being fitted into her Prom dress, meters and meters of fuzzy pink transparency. While their mother was out of the room looking for implements or materials of some kind, he took the opportunity to question his sister.

"I really don't think she's going tonight, George. How does this look in the back?"

"Fine."

"She's an honest girl and a good friend of mine

and I love her dearly. If she said someone has asked her, then someone has. I'm sure anyway that someone has." The excitement of the night seemed to be rendering Rita somewhat incoherent. "Also, if Ann said she's not going, then that's the way it will be. I love her dearly, as I said, but I wouldn't be at all surprised if she doesn't go. Oh George, what do you mean it looks fine? I can tell in the mirror it's simply terrible."

But he wasn't looking into the mirror, or at the dress.

Ineluctably motherly even on her Prom night, Rita came over to him, frowning with concern. "Oh, George, is it really getting serious between you two?"

"It is for me. Is she always—like that? You know?"

Rita was worried now, for the moment completely distracted from her preparations. "I might as well tell you bluntly, Ann has a bad rep with the boys in the class. I mean *I'm* not the most prudish and old-fashioned girl around, but *she* is really way out." Rita glanced at the bedroom door, trying to determine whether their mother was still safely out of earshot. "You know she's been excused from Erotic Orientation classes all along, on religious grounds. Don't get me wrong, she's been my loyal friend ever since sophomore year."

"No, I didn't know that about her having no EO. But it's not really surprising."

"I bet you've never got any sex from her."

"Yeah, that's true, but . . ."

"If you ask me, no one ever has. There, I've said it." Rita nodded significantly. "I mean it. She's my friend, but you're my brother. I've seen a lot of the boys displaying a certain *interest* in her, if you know what I mean. And more than one of the men teachers, too. Well, if she hardly ever lets them see anything between her shoulders and her knees, I suppose the men are bound to get the message and come sniffing around. I guess you know what you're doing."

Rita was still looking at him worriedly when their mother returned. George withdrew from his sister's room. A deep excitement was now taking control of him. It wasn't something new: it had begun on that first day on the bus and had been developing ever since. He went back to his own room and spent half an hour alternately lying on the bed, pacing, and practicing his side snap kick before the mirror. Meanwhile he fought through a confused inner struggle, understanding that the whole course of his life might be altered here and now. Again and again he told himself to put dark ideas out of his mind and phone some other girl with whom he could simply and pleasantly spend the night in bed. Then he gave up and started to punch out Ann's phone number again. Then he gave that up too and headed for her house.

The house was all in darkness, and George almost stumbled over a small figure sitting on a step in front of the front door before he realized that anyone was there. Taking a second look, George saw that it was a boy, maybe nine or ten years old, who held in his hands a carved wooden figure about half as tall as he was.

"You live here?" George asked, his hand hesitating over the callplate on the door. His previous visits here had been few and brief, and he and Ann had avoided talking much about her family.

"Yeah," said the boy. "Nobody's home but my sister," he added gloomily.

George's heart gave a little premonitory throb. "It's her I want to see." He touched the plate, and immediately a light came on overhead, giving the glass eye up there a good look at him.

In the new light George could see that the carved wooden figure in the boy's hands was—or had been—a female nude, executed with some skill. The kid was slowly mutilating it now, moodily gouging and hacking away with a small knife. The step was littered with little chips and shavings.

"Hey, what're you doing that for?"

"I carved it, I can do what I want."

"Well. What's your name?"

"Fred."

"I'm George. You can carve pretty good, Fred, if you did that. Why don't you save it?" Though it really seemed too late for that. Now one of the house's barred windows came alight; someone was on the way to answer the door.

"Oh, you're karate-George from the bus." Small Fred looked up with interest for a moment, but then lowered his brown head again and dug in with the knife. "Why should I save it? Nobody wants to look at it."

Ann opened the door, and stood there rubbing her dark hair with a towel. She was wearing a translucent pinkish sarong kind of thing, not radically concealing, with apparently nothing under it. "Hello, George." She didn't sound surprised. "Freddy, I thought you were at the Scout meeting. What are you doing, *destroying* that?"

"Nobody cares about it."

"I care. I told you I like to see anything you do."

"You don't know nothin' about it. And nobody

else cares." Freddy flung the scarred chunk of wood and was gone running into the night, across the little front yard and then in an instant swallowed by the shadows along a narrow statwalk, with bushes and a river of vehicular lights beyond.

Ann called after her brother in annoyance, but evidently without any real expectation that he would turn around and come back.

And then she and George were looking at each other. "Come in," she said, and again it was almost as if she had been expecting him tonight.

"Thanks. Is your brother going to be all right?"

"Oh, I suppose so. I think he'll stay in the neighborhood. Anyway, I don't know what I can do."

George, as he stepped into the house, daringly omitted giving his hostess even the slightest pinch or caress of greeting, even on the hand or arm. Ann did not blush or giggle at the omission, as most of the girls he knew would certainly have done. Nor did she take offense, as the really nice conservative ones might have. A bad girl, then, as Rita had warned him, as all the signs so plainly showed.

But still . . . somehow he couldn't really believe she was.

"Let's go out beside the pool," she said. "It's nice outside tonight."

"All right." He followed Ann through her house. "I called earlier, and your mother sort of implied you were going out tonight, but I just had a hunch and came over anyway."

"I'm glad you did." Just as they were leaving the indoors for a palm-fringed patio Ann stopped and turned to him. Her gladness, if such it really was, was quiet and melancholy. "My parents have gone to the Prom, they agreed to be chaperones. They were very upset when they found they couldn't talk me into going, even going with them at the last minute instead of with a boy. My mother is Church of Eros, you know, quite devout, and she's been going there for guidance day after day, and trying to get me to go with her. But her church and mine just don't agree. My father went to his playclub and talked to the philosopher. Finally my parents had to give up on me, but they're still chaperoning. I guess that's partly why Freddy is upset. He thought Dad might go with him tonight to some Scout meeting."

That was about the longest speech that George had ever heard from her, and she was perhaps a little less melancholy when she had finished it.

"I'm glad your parents decided to go ahead and do their social duty," said George. "Now I have you all to myself."

"I'm glad you do. I had to talk a little bit to someone." Ann stopped rubbing her hair and let the towel hang down in front of her. She seemed innocently unconscious of the concealing effect. Now, for the first time since George had come in, she smiled. "Would you like a swim, George? I just climbed out."

"Sounds like a good idea." He followed her around the bend of the L-shaped patio to the pool, which was irregular in shape and fairly small, bordered along most of its perimeter by genengineered grass and flowers. His mind pictured Ann climbing from the pool, slipping on her sarong, going to answer the door. Suddenly George was sure that she had been swimming in the nude. His inward excitement—if excitement was really a good word for the chill need that had brought him here—

took a deeper hold on him than ever. Of course there was no sensible reason why a girl alone should not slip off her bikni and swim nude if she wanted to. Only the most satyrish reactionaries would insist that a solitary person wear clothing to emphasis his or her sex. But still the mental picture of Ann floating alone, all chaste and bare as a lily pad, smooth as a snake, divorced from sex, was overwhelming.

"Still, the air is getting a little cool now," said George, suddenly afraid and stalling. Standing beside Ann on the edge of the pool, he felt very unsure of himself. If he mentioned his lack of a swimming codpiece would she laugh at him for an old-fashioned clod? On the other hand, if he just stripped bare and dove in, would she, after all, be shocked? He couldn't really believe, in spite of the evidence of her own words and actions, that she was the bad kind of girl. But hadn't he come here tonight hoping that she was? Trying to prove it, yearning to get from her what only bad girls gave?

"You're right," Ann said calmly. "I wasn't in the pool for very long."

They sat down side by side on the pool's curved grassy edge, and George pulled off his sandals and dipped his feet into the water. In his knitted translucent shorts and jacket he was quite warm enough, but he saw Ann shiver just slightly in her sarong with the damp towel around her shoulders. In a minute, he told himself, he would suggest that they go back inside where it was warmer. Meanwhile he wanted to watch her as she stirred the water gently with one toe, scattering a thousand California stars.

Only once, as an adolescent in the grip of a way-out mood, had George visited a brothel. There a pretty young woman had draped herself as he watched, and had talked to him about stars and purity and poetry and other high, mysterious things, until she had him sexless as a mushroom. Then he and the woman had lain chastely side by side on her narrow bed and talked. Between other topics of conversation George had tried to explain to her the mental processes of karate, how the mind could concentrate the body's force sufficiently to drive the hand uninjured through a slab of wood.

Probably his dissertation, delivered largely out of adolescent ignorance, hadn't made too much sense. But the girl was a skilled listener. George supposed most whores were that, and sexually desirable too. He had heard Japanese in the dojo speculating, arguing, over what the old-time geisha must have been like, and he supposed that they were something similar. In the brothel, George had never forgotten how desirable the woman beside him was, and at the same time his mind had deliberately, daringly, pushed the desire for her farther and farther away. A door had opened for him, to a bittersweet world of controlled power. A different metaphor had occurred, later: free-style sparring, and Eros's feet of fleshy clay were swept out from under him, and down he came with a great ignominious gonad-jarring crash, to be made to bend his neck before a single rebellious human slave. The power . . .

Still, when it was all over in the brothel, when George's half hour was up and he was being expertly shown the door, he found himself somewhat disappointed. Was this all that sublimation amounted to? It hardly seemed worth all the fuss that people made about it.

Now, sitting beside Ann on the grass rim of her

swimming pool, he watched a movement of her hips under the sarong as she shifted her weight slightly, and felt a sudden physical urge to have her. He suddenly remembered—or thought he remembered—that he had seen and responded to just such a movement of the prostitute's body as she began to cover herself in front of him.

He had to talk, to say something. He cleared his throat. "So. I guess you're still working with that Sunday school religious class, huh?"

"Oh yes. When I have time."

"Have you been in that Christian group for very long? I mean, I gather that the rest of your family aren't members."

"It's a Christian school, but ..." Ann spoke slowly and carefully now. "I'm not actually baptized into the Church yet myself. I just help out there. I've been hanging around the school and church there since I was about thirteen. You're right, my parents are much against it and of course they try to argue me out of ever being baptized. I guess my adolescence has been difficult for them, with me always hanging around Sunday school instead of going to the young peoples' orgies in their church. The philosopher at Daddy's playclub says I'm looking for a crutch to help me get through life. And really it is such a tremendous step—being baptized, I mean. In a sense I'm still free now to do anything I want, but after baptism I won't be."

"Huh."

"For example I'll be practically restricted to marrying someone who's also a Christian. If I get married at all."

"Really?"

"Well, I just mean it takes an awful lot of work to make a marriage a success even when the two partners agree on the important things such as religion. And my marriage will have to succeed because Christians don't have divorce, or at least not very often."

"Aren't they still divided into a bunch of splinter sects? I was reading about it the other day." George, who had rarely given the subject of religion much thought, had been reading up recently on Christianity, knowing of Ann's involvement. He didn't think it was for him. He couldn't determine if violence was ever allowed or not.

Ann said: "Christians used to be divided. Now they're pretty much reunited again, what's left of them."

"Well, I never even go to Church of Eros any more. I think religion's not for me. They say that some of those churches, once you join them, they never let you alone again afterwards."

After a little silence Ann said: "There are a number of things that never let you alone."

"Yes," agreed George, wondering just what things she had in mind.

"George?" Her voice was different.

"What?"

"Would you like to have sex with me? Here and now?"

"Why, yes." In his surprise the answer came out mechanically. "That would be nice."

For long seconds Ann did not reply. She sat there so motionless that her toes in the water no longer troubled the reflected stars. George tried to read her face in the near-darkness. Then abruptly she turned her face away. "The way you say that!" Ann said, and made a frightened, twisted sound that had some resemblance to a laugh.

"It's just that you took me by surprise." George

slid closer to her along the side of the pool. "Oh, Ann. Annie? You've never wanted me to give you an erotic touch before."

"Oh," she said. "I've wanted." She leaned away from him, supple and graceful in her sarong, her toes leaving the water with a tinkle of tiny drops. She stretched out on her back along the grassy rim of the pool, covering her eyes with one slender wrist.

George could no longer control himself. He crept very close to Ann and bent over her, daring not to touch her at all. "Don't be afraid," he said.

"I'm not afraid. I'm not ashamed." Her voice was surprisingly firm and proud, and she was watching him from under her arm. "You don't know me very well, George. But maybe you've heard some of the stories."

"Yes, I have. I don't care if the stories are true."

"What do they say about me? Those stories that you don't care about?"

"They say—" His voice suddenly went shaky on him and he had to pause. "What they amount to is that you're still a virgin. And that you ..." He couldn't really say it.

She moved her arm away, and now he could see her face in the starlight. It was becoming calmer now, with an inner change, the blooming of some beauty that George could not have named. "Yes. And I sublimate." She said it without a trace of shame. "That's why I'm not at the Prom tonight. Nothing but one long orgy. George, just now I offered you my virginity. Can you understand what that means to me?"

Watching her, listening to her, he thought perhaps he could. Now, as if his body and mind were both following some biological imperative, his desire for her was pushed away, while at the same time there rose up in him—something else. Something else that made his throat ache with the joy of it. He straightened up, so that he was no longer bending over Ann, but sitting at her side.

Looking at George steadily, she asked again: "Now, do you want to have sex with me?"

"Yes. Sometime. Right now I want—something more."

Ann nodded agreement and lowered her eyes. Her breathing, that had quickened momentarily, now once more grew slow. In a gentle voice she asked: "Shall I take this sarong thing off? Or put on something thicker?"

For a few moments George could not find his voice to answer. What had happened to him in the brothel had afforded him an enjoyable, way-out kick, a fancy kind of a reverse tickle. That tremendous gulfs of experience lay beyond what had actually happened to him on that occasion had been suggested, but no more. In itself the visit to the whore had been not quite worth the effort to repeat it.

This event impending now, beginning now, was going far beyond that one. A winged thing had been born inside his chest and it was lifting at the roots of his being, lifting and pulling and expanding what was in there until it seemed to George that sex itself might be dissolved out of the flesh and carried outward to the stars.

"Oh, I don't care what you wear," George groaned in a failing voice. "Oh, I love you, love you, love you. Oh, sublimation's such a dirty word, there has to be a better."

"I know," Ann whispered to him. "I know. Don't

talk now." She had done this before. He was the virgin here.

Their hands came together, clasped together. They were just human hands now, more than they were male and female, and they were male and female more than they had ever been before. Ann raised her eyes to his, and then on past his eyes, and he knew that she was looking at the stars. No turning back now. Never. They rose on the great lifting wings.

TWELVE

Waking up, rejoining the inhospitable world, was a slow and intermittent struggle, conducted on instinct rather than on any conscious wish to be revived. Art understood from the beginning of the struggle that he was not just asleep. He was hurt, or sick, and in a way this knowledge was pleasing to him. If he was sick or hurt less would be expected of him. They would have to take care of him instead.

. . . they? Yes, someone was trying.

When his eyes at last were firmly open, he saw that he was lying in what had to be a bedroom in someone's home. Able to focus and to think at last, he made out that he was in one of two beds crowded into the small, cheaply furnished chamber. He had the vague impression, not really a memory, of having seen someone in the other bed. But now when he looked carefully no one was there, though certainly the covers were rumpled. Perhaps, too, someone had once shared this little bed with him. He rather hoped not. But maybe they had. He should have been polite and pawed at the anonymous partner's genitals at least but he doubted that he had. Right now Art felt tired of genitalia, male or female, his own or others'. And thank Eros he was sick or hurt and nothing much could reasonably have been expected of him along that line.

Art drifted.

. . . should have grabbed and pawed as those little plastic figures were doing to each other, those cheap Church of Eros icons that someone had shoved to the rear of the top of that high plastic wardrobe over there and then forgotten.

It was a BI bedroom, from the look of it. Or could it be after all a room in some cheap hotel? Some rented room where tenant after tenant rushed through, forgetting or abandoning things, with the result that none of the haphazard assembly of objects in the room fit with anything else. There on the wall was the founder of Christianity nailed up, as in Ann's house, but on this wall two pieces of plastic were doing the job instead of handcarved wood. And there on the other wall, a reproduction of a painting that looked like a Caravaggio, but a Caravaggio that Art had never seen before. Nothing like Eros trampling the violin, or Bacchus lounging amid bowls of fruit. Here instead we had men in ancient, opaque dress around a table doing something, counting money, and on the right of the picture two more men entering. One of these was important, a mysterious figure of light and shadow and power. He was extending a hand toward one of the men on the left, a hand that said here, *you*, enough of playing with those trifles on the table, more important things are waiting. The summons had come, and everyone in the painting knew about it except the man for whom it was intended.

. . . and Art himself was still drifting. Sick, no, he was hurt, for now he remembered something about how frightened he had been out there in the street in the middle of some crazy riot, and now there was this sexawful pain in his head that only intermittently would go away.

And now truly there was a girl, a young woman, with long dark hair, resting, indecently covered, tucked into the small room's other bed. And now, *whup*, a trick of the illusionist's art and she was gone again.

Meanwhile it might have been that Art had slept.

Standing before him was a man, a tall, narrow-shouldered man with a sandy beard and impressive eyes. His eyes were green or gray or blue, it was hard to tell which because the color seemed to change as they kept looking at Art intently. And this man was a somewhat familiar figure, because now Art could recall that he had been standing in the same place a few hours ago (a day ago?) and asking questions.

"What's your name?" the man asked now, his eyes boring into Art. He had a mild, slow voice that contradicted something in those eyes, a look of being fierce and concentrated and ready to pounce.

"Arthur Rodney." Somehow it came out almost a question.

The man smiled and nodded at Art, as if this were very good news indeed. He had shut the door of the room behind him when he came in, but outside somewhere in the background printout was clacking noisily from some kind of computer or teletype in need of mechanical adjustment.

"Art, what year is this?" Art's second answer

was just as satisfying as the first. "How do you feel, Art?"

"Not good. I've got a real triplet of a headache." All of a sudden the lobby of Family Planning came back to him, and then a clear memory of the frantically waving signs outside, the jam of bodies, the fat man trying to sell him a placard from his armload of them. What should come after that? Art didn't know. He had reached a real blank.

The man with the impressive eyes stepped closer to Art's little bed. "Let's have a look at that." With what were unmistakably a doctor's hands, professionally sure and gentle, he probed through or around some kind of a dressing on Art's scalp.

"Ouch."

"Sorry. Well, that's not looking too bad. And I'm glad you've woken up fully now." The man stepped back, pulling at his curl of sandy beard. "But I still want to make an NMR scan or two of your head. Haven't been able to as yet."

"How long have I been here? And where am I, anyway?"

"You've been here several hours. Let's say you're with some people who wanted to give you shelter, when it appeared to them that otherwise you'd go to jail." The doctor raised a hand, forestalling questions. "May I ask—what is the last thing that you remember clearly?"

Art closed his eyes. His head throbbed. Nothing new appeared. He said: "Coming out into the street in front of the Family Planning building. There was some kind of demonstration, or a riot . . . why should I have gone to jail?"

The doctor shrugged and gave a tiny smile. "I don't know that you would have. Some of the Young Virgins on the scene evidently took you for

one of their own casualties and brought you here.
Some of them think that if a person gets clobbered
in the street she or he must be a good guy, and
anyone who's a good guy is automatically in danger of being thrown in jail."

He approached Art again, and with the aid of a
tiny light looked closely into his eyes.

"How am I doing, doctor?"

"Not bad, not bad. I want you to rest. It's important that you take it easy for a while. Don't worry
about a thing. I'll be back in a bit."

When the door had closed behind the doctor Art
lay still for a while, alternately opening and closing his eyes, living in silence with the pain in his
head. Somewhere in the middle distance, the faulty
printer mechanism clacked again.

The room had one small window, with bright
daylight coming in around the edges of the old-
fashioned shade. Some Young Virgins' refuge. But
he had not wound up back in the Diana Arms. At
least he didn't think so. Rita's room had looked
very little like this one.

The door opened without warning and a young
woman came in, wearing a long, opaque sweater.
She smiled at Art, bringing him a cup of something to drink. He was abruptly conscious of being
entirely naked underneath the bedsheet.

He thanked her for the cup and tasted it; something warm and chocolatey. "Medicine?" he asked,
while routinely starting to put his free hand up
under the bottom of her sweater.

"No." She gave him a cool smile and turned
away, perhaps to do something to his bed, tucking
in covers. But the effect was that his hand slid
free. She said: "Just a drink. Thought you might
like some."

He could have asked more questions, but already the young woman was gone again. The stuff in the cup tasted good. Soon, Art thought, he might try getting up. His clothes, his watch, his money should be here somewhere. Maybe in that plastic wardrobe. The doctor had said to take it easy, but not that he couldn't move.

But about the time that Art finished the drink, sipping it slowly, the doctor was back. He looked into Art's eyes again with his little light and murmured with satisfaction. Then he pulled up a chair and sat beside Art's bed.

"Art, I took the liberty of going through your wallet while you were unconscious. Just to see if there was a record of anything, epilepsy, allergies, or so on, that might have a bearing on your medical condition."

"That's all right. And so you found out my name. I didn't catch yours." There was a pause, with no name offered. "No doubt I owe you thanks for taking care of me."

"That's quite all right."

"But now I suppose I'd better get up and put on my clothes and leave."

"I don't want to scare you, Art, but before you do that I must insist on a couple of NMR scans. I hope to be able to make them downstairs here in just a few minutes. If the scans show no skull damage we can drive you home right away, take you anywhere in the city you want to go. If they do indicate serious damage we are going to have to *somehow* arrange to move you on a stretcher to a hospital."

"I—see. Or maybe I don't."

"Well. The point is that your presence here puts us in something of an awkward position. If you do have a fracture, we can't simply call an ambulance to come and get you. And for your own good I wouldn't want you riding folded down and blindfolded in the back of a car."

"I know how that works," Art muttered, feeling a little sick.

"Beg your pardon?"

"Nothing. Evidently I'm in some kind of a— secret hideout."

The doctor looked relieved. "I'm glad you understand. It's quite important to a number of us here that the location of this house be kept a secret. And we've realized by now that you're no sympathizer of ours. Nevertheless we wish you well. We don't want to—to make you feel you're being held a prisoner. As soon as some materials I need for the scans arrive, which I hope will be any minute now, we'll take a couple of pictures and then you'll be on your way. One way or another."

Art relaxed wearily in the bed. "All right. All right. I guess you know what you're doing."

"I'm *really* glad you're being understanding about this, Art. I feel a personal responsibility in the matter. For your being in the Family Planning office to begin with, I mean, and then caught in the riot."

Art looked at him, trying to puzzle it out.

"You see, I'm Rita's midwifer."

Shortly a couple of sturdy male Young Virgins came along, pushing a regular hospital cart. They got Art's clothes out of the wardrobe, and helped him pull on his codpiece-belt. Then they loaded him onto the cart, beneath an opaque sheet. They piled the rest of his clothes on at the foot. Meanwhile he was of course demanding again and again to be told if his wife was here, and if she had done anything illegal yet.

"She's not here, not in this building," the doctor kept answering him calmly. "She's well. The parturition will take place quite soon. And she's worried about you—more precisely, as I interpret what she says, she's worried about whether you'll want her back when she has her third child."

It took Art a moment to understand. "You mean she thinks I might divorce her? But that's foolish. It wouldn't help her or the children, and it certainly wouldn't help me." Now he lay on his back with his head on a low pillow as the two husky Virgins propelled the cart out of the room and along a rambling hallway, through what appeared to be an ancient house of mansion size, or else perhaps a rundown dormitory belonging to some private school. Not at all like the Diana Arms. "Sure, I hope she doesn't have a third baby with her when she comes back. But even if she does, I most certainly want her. So, you're the one who's doing it. How can you interfere in people's lives like this? How much are you being paid?"

The doctor was walking beside the cart, now and then going ahead of it or falling behind when the way became too narrow. "I'm not getting a dollar from Rita, or anyone in her family. If she's paid out money it must be going to the doctor who referred her to me, or to someone else along the line. In a clandestine business like this you're always going to have some people going into it for the money."

"And you? What are you in it for?"

"For the fetuses whose lives I save. For the good of my immortal soul. That's how I see it, that I have an inescapable moral duty to do what I am doing here."

The cart rolled into a small, old-looking elevator. The two orderlies remained outside as the door closed and the elevator started down, with Art still lying on the cart and the doctor still standing beside it.

"You don't inspire a great deal of confidence, doctor. If you are a doctor, really. If you're not you'd better keep your hands off my wife."

"I assure you that I am an obstetrician. And you'll be glad to hear that I haven't lost a mother in years of practice. Nor have I lost anyone to a head injury." The slow descent of the elevator stopped and the doors slid open. "But then, yours is about the first head injury I've treated since I was an intern." And with that the cart was rolling again.

Now almost at once the opaque sheet came over Art's face, folded over to be two layers thick. The voice of his captor said: "I'm covering your eyes up here, so that later you won't be able to locate or identify this house."

Art only grunted. He felt the cart jolt lightly over a threshold, and there came a whiff of outside air, summer-warm and fragrant with flowers he could not identify. But he stoically refused to look or listen or sniff for clues. Once before he had been granted knowledge that secretive guides were trying to withhold from him, and that knowledge had done him no good at all. This game was hopelessly lost, and Art was about ready to give it up. Not that he accepted that his opponents were in the right. It was just that they had him beaten. The law, and the bulk of society, were or ought to be on his side, but there was no way for him to call

them in. When you went into the endgame in a
lost position, a piece down and your clock running
out, maybe you had better resign and save some
energy for the next game. There would be a lot of
tough games to play against the world when Rita
came home again, with a third child on her lap
and on her record, whether she had to go to jail
first or not. Sex, but he hoped she didn't have to
go to jail.

Now the cart was on a descending ramp. Art
found it impossible to judge whether it was going
down one meter or three. Then the floor leveled
out, and a door closed, and the cart stopped, and
the doctor carefully pulled the sheet down from
Art's face. The two of them were alone now, in a
kind of laboratory or treatment room that was
crowded with a jumble of shelves and boxes and
equipment, and lighted by some old-fashioned overhead fluorescents. The walls of the windowless
room were lined nearly from floor to ceiling with
shelving, and the shelves loaded with boxes and
bottles labeled in what Art took for the jargon of
medicine and technology. There was a door nearby,
no doubt the one through which they had just
entered. It was closed. It was hard to guess the
size of the room, or area, because sections of it to
both right and left were blocked off by portable
white screens.

"Now where is that damned stuff? They said it
was here." The doctor had turned to a large desk-
like metal table nearby, and was ruffling through
the stacks of paper, journals, printouts, and other
forgotten-looking material that it held. "They told
me that they left it here." Somehow the archaic
swearword, the like of which Art had not heard

since the sollie play went dead on the Transcon train, sounded natural the way this man said it.

After fruitlessly searching a few moments longer, the doctor muttered an excuse and went out impatiently, closing the room's door firmly behind him. His feet stomped away outside it. Art could hear the opening and closing of another door, some distance off.

Apart from his continuing headache, he now felt tolerably well. Healthy enough to know a sense of awkwardness and vague shame at lying here on a cart like an invalid. He raised himself on one elbow and looked about. There on the foot of the cart were the rest of his clothes. He could see part of his watchband, protruding from a pocket, and he didn't really doubt that his wallet was still there too. That was not the kind of thing these people were going to steal from him. Should he dress and stagger out into the street, calling for the police? That certainly wouldn't win Rita over to his point of view. No. No more. He had tipped his king and resigned the game.

An unobtrusive background hum of electric power and electronics permeated the room. Near at hand Art could recognize a portable NMR machine, a familiar sight from occasional visits to other physicians' offices. And now Art became aware of another faint sound, an antique watch or clock ticking, tick-tick-ticking, except that this was a little faster and perhaps less regular than even an old watch would be. Still alone, Art swung his feet over the side of the cart, moving cautiously, and sat up. His head ached, but he felt able to stand and walk. Now, if that was truly a bathroom over there, as a tiled interior glimpsed over the top of a white screen seemed to promise, then his body might soon be made quite livable again.

He slid off the cart and walked around the screen, leaning at intervals on the wall. He went past glassy tanks and a maze of plastic piping and a computer terminal, all set up on a dimly lighted workbench, and found the hoped-for toilet.

He was on his way back to sit on his cart like a good patient when, just around the shadowed workbench, he came to a full stop. "Ah," he said aloud.

The fetus was in the central glassy tank atop the bench . . .

The light in the area of the workbench was quite dim, and Art didn't want to test any of the wall switches. So he could get a clear view of the thing only from certain angles.

Art stepped closer, staring, then abruptly relaxed. There was no umbilical cord, only a blind knot of tissue at the navel. For a moment he had thought that the complex of equipment beside him formed an artificial womb—beside the tanks and piping, there were innumerable valves, at least three oscilloscopes, counters, and other complicated gear that Art could not at once identify. He had thought that the fetus before him was one that had been frozen and then in some sense rendered viable again. But now he realized that it must be only an abortus, being used in some experiment. Thin tubes or wires (peering into the dim tank he could not be sure which) were attached to it inside the tank, but since it lacked an umbilical cord, he supposed, it could not be receiving oxygen and nourishment. And Art could see no placenta, nor analog of one.

There it sat, or rather floated in an upright sitting posture: the thing that so much fuss was made about. It was very small, only about the length of Art's middle finger from the top of the bulbous, hairless head to the ends of the inconsequential legs. Its proportions were much different from those of a normal full-term infant, and of course even further from those of an adult. But the thing was unmistakably *Homo sapiens* all the same. What other earthly species would develop such a bulging brow, or hold up two such human hands? When Art bent closer, the fingers were fully distinguishable, as were the toes at the ends of the insignificant legs and feet. What with the shadows and the angle of his view, the sex was not quite visible.

Art started back from the tank, with a quick intake of breath. Only then was he aware of the doctor, standing watching him at the corner of the white screen only a couple of steps away.

"Feel all right?" the doctor asked him. "You shouldn't be on your feet unnecessarily."

Art raised his hand, to gently touch the side of his head, at a good safe distance from the wound. He turned his gaze back to the tank. "It moved."

"Oh yes, they move. I've located the NMR materials at last. Get back on the cart, if you will, and we'll finally be able to make sure about that head of yours. Yes, the little girl in there happens to be about the same developmental age as Rita's fetus is right now. About three months as near as I can tell. At that age they've usually been moving spontaneously for several weeks, though the chances are the mother can't feel the movements yet."

Art walked away, pausing at the corner of the screen to look back once more. "I didn't know it was . . . there was no cord."

The doctor held out a hand to give support if needed. "Oh. But usually we take that off at parturition. Tapping into the circulatory system elsewhere serves the purpose, and has some technical advantages. Yes, she's very much alive and growing. That's her heartbeat you can hear in the background, sounds like an old-fashioned watch ticking. And with those scopes back there we're continually monitoring brain activity; that won't settle into the regular rhythms for a few more weeks."

Art lay back carefully on the cart, settling his head down gently on the pillow. "Is that a living human being?" he asked the old fluorescent lights above. The vision of the grotesque, almost fish-like head was still with him. And of the tiny hands that seemed about to be raised secretively, protectively, before the face. "Is it?"

"You tell me," the doctor grunted, moving the cart. Art recognized an NMR scanner when they stopped beside it. The doctor continued: "Frankly, I've had my doubts. Sometimes I feel I don't know where to start in thinking about it any more." His tone was mild and preoccupied; his hands had begun a delicate positioning of Art's head.

Art, still looking at the ceiling, said: "Maybe it doesn't matter if a fetus is a human being or not. Maybe such a question is meaningless."

"Take a deep breath—hold it—don't move." There came the usual audible hum from the machine. "All right, you can move. What do you mean, it doesn't matter? Human beings matter. You know, if these embryos and fetuses turn out not to be human individuals after all, then some of my friends and I have gone to a hell of a lot of trouble and broken a hell of a lot of laws for nothing."

Art twisted on his cart. "You just said that you yourself have doubts."

"*Doubts*, yes!" The man was vexed. He tore free printout that had been spat from the machine and waved it forcefully. "I might have very strong doubts that there's a child hiding under that overturned box that I see in the middle of the road, but that doesn't justify my running it over with a truck. Not without some life-or-death reason to run it over." He looked at the paper in his hand. "Let's take one more to make sure. Turn on your right side this time, if you will."

"How about the welfare of society as a whole? How about overpopulation, people starving? Aren't those life-or-death reasons?"

"To pull the plug on that little girl in there? In a word, no. Take a deep breath again, hold it." Again a powerful, focused magnetic field twanged imperceptibly at Art, set atoms in his body vibrating. The machine sucked back those reactions. "That's fine."

Allowed to move again, Art got up on one elbow. "I suspect neither of us is going to be able to change the other's mind on this by arguing."

The doctor grunted, grabbing and looking at another printout.

Art said: "All right, I know that thing in the tank has the potential for some day being a full human being, with all the rights thereof. But not yet, surely not yet. It may generate a brain wave or two but it can't think. It may twitch but it can't act. It couldn't survive for three minutes without artificial help."

"Neither could you if you had a really massive coronary. And she could have survived quite well in her natural environment, had we been able to leave her there." The gray-green eyes gave the paper printout a final stare and then turned to Art with evident relief. "You're all right. This second picture makes it unanimous. No fracture, no intracranial bleeding. You ought to take things easy for a while, but you can go."

"Good . . . great. Tell me, why does that have to be a baby?"

"I'm not sure I . . ."

"Why must you break the laws, as you admit doing, to make that point?"

The doctor sighed, and let himself down in a chair beside a small, paper-burdened table, as Art sat up on the cart and reached for his shirt. "Art, I can't make it a baby or not a baby. No one can. We can only try to determine to which category it already belongs, and act accordingly." He wearily rubbed his eyes. "Damn it, it *looks* like a baby now, right? In a few weeks it may begin to suck its thumb. A cute little human touch, right? Not necessarily convincing."

"Wait a minute. How about gill slits? Doesn't it have those still? Are they cute little proofs of humanity too?"

"An early embryo has pharyngeal pouches. If it's growing up to be a fish, they turn into gills. In mammals they turn into glands. What do you think that proves, if anything?"

"I . . . how am I supposed to know? You're the scientist, or at least the expert, though most of the scientists and experts don't seem to agree with you on this. What has you so convinced?"

"Art, I know of no solid scientific definition of humanity. As an expert in biology, what can I communicate to you? Only facts, and people, experts and otherwise, interpret them in different ways. Both parents of that organism in the tank were of course human. But its cells are different from either of its parents' cells. It's a genetically unique individual. With human parents.

"It . . . no, I have to say *she*. What you see as a living organism in a tank I see as a little girl. But if you try to pin me down on when she began to be a little girl, I'll have to admit that I just don't know. Teilhard says that the beginnings of all things tend to be out of sight. Was a unique human soul infused when the sperm first pierced the egg? When the nuclei of the two parent cells were first completely united? With implantation of the blastocyst in the uterine wall? Or maybe a few days after that, when the time of possible twinning had passed. I don't know. I don't know if a soul can twin like an aggregation of cells."

"If you're bringing souls into it, you're leaving me out." Art was off the cart now, getting dressed. In the background the steady tick-tick went on, soft and rapid and determined. "Just let me get out of here."

"Of course." As if caught derelict in his duty, the doctor jumped up and went to push a button near the door. "But I can't help bringing souls into it, though I tried. I'm a Christian priest as well as a doctor, you see. I suppose when one's humanity is questioned one must try to prove it by appealing either to God or to some review board composed of one's fellow human beings. I know which I prefer to do."

"No one's questioning your humanity."

"No. Not now. But governments in the past have decided that certain people were of inferior races. Or property that could be bought and sold. And suppose I suffered a stroke tonight, and still hadn't come to by next week. A panel of my fellow physicians would soon be questioning whether I was human still." The doctor paced, hands clenching. The naturally fierce look in his eyes grew more intense. "Maybe it would be the kindest thing in such a case to let me die. But I would still be a *human being dying*, not—not a specimen reacting!"

"All right," said Art, in slight alarm, speeding up the fastening of his shirt. "All right, take it easy."

"Yes. I'm sorry." The tall man stopped pacing and let himself slump back into his chair. "In my opinion there are a few rare medical situations where an abortion may be justified, at least where there's no artificial womb available. But it's still a *human being dying*, and there's not many reasons that justify that. Surely not some non-specific good intended for the world in general."

Art, dressed now and putting on his watch, shook his head. "Do you think a single human being dying matters that much to the universe? Appeal to your God if you want to, the rest of us haven't heard anything from him lately. We have to look out for ourselves as best we can."

The priest-doctor pulled himself to his feet once more. "Let me go and find someone to drive you home. We'll feed you something first if you prefer."

"No. Just wait. I'm not through talking yet." Art moved to stand between the other and the door. "You are about to inflict a third child on me and my wife, because your God wants you to. The least you can do is listen to me for a minute longer."

Abruptly the priest turned fierce again. "I am sincerely sorry for the danger and expense and inconvenience that the third child is going to cause you. But it is still better than inflicting death on your third child. If you find his presence unendurable, why there are people in the world who will take him in."

"People in the world! Yes, I'll say there are." The two men were now standing almost toe to toe, Art with his arms folded like an umpire. "About eight or nine billion of them at last count. And how many of them are starving now?"

"Quite a few are starving, Art, quite a few. Maybe you've seen more starving people than I have. Maybe you've fed more of them. Maybe you promote contraception even more enthusiastically than I do."

But Art seemed to have stopped listening. He was standing staring, with an altered expression, into a far corner of the room. The priest looked there and saw only a red picnic cooler with a white handle.

"Art, here, sit down again. I'm sorry, forgive me, we shouldn't have been arguing."

"No, I'm all right," said Art. But then he did sit down, in the chair that the other pulled up for him. "That cooler over there. I believe I may have carried that across the Mississippi River a few days ago. It was very heavy and very cold. Now I'm just realizing what must have been inside it. That was while your monastery out there was burning down."

"You were there?" The priest sat down facing Art, and leaned anxiously toward him. "Can you tell me anything of what happened? I've seen and read the news stories, but . . ."

THIRTEEN

Art told the priest-doctor what he could about the incident, leaving out the name of the young woman for whom he had carried the container. He concluded: "And the man with her asked me to look out for her, and then just ran off. Back into the woods. Now I think maybe he was trying to help someone. Then I thought he just had diarrhea. He yelled something back just as he left, but I didn't catch it."

"He was sort of flabby-looking, you say. Tall? Short?"

Art tried to remember. "Oh, middling. Nondescript. As I recall, he was sunburned."

The priest-doctor nodded. He had his hands clamped on his knees, and was squinting as if he were in physical pain. "I think he may have been a friend of mine. His name was never mentioned in the official accounts. Maybe the police never knew that he was there."

"I suspect he probably got away all right." Art, remembering the yell coming out of the woods, was being optimistic.

"Do you? Well, I hope so. I pray so."

"I'm really sorry," Art said impulsively. "At the time there didn't seem to be anything that I could do for him."

"Of course not, Art. It's not your fault. Listen, I'd better get you on your way home before I'm charged with kidnapping. But you must be hungry; let us feed you something first."

"I could use something cold to drink. And maybe just a protein bar. I never got around to thanking you for this patch-up job, did I? Thank you." Art brushed a hand gingerly over his scalp bandage. It wasn't nearly as big as he had expected, and very little of his hair had been removed.

In a few minutes one of the stalwart Young Virgins brought him a glass of milk, and a couple of food bars on a plate. As Art munched and drank, the priest-doctor asked him: "Would you object very strongly to a blindfold when you leave? I'd accept your word if you gave it, but some of the other people here might not."

"Blindfold? Oh, I don't care." Art wasn't thinking about that. Foodbar in hand, he got up suddenly and went to push one of the white screens aside.

Like an idol in a temple, he thought suddenly. Surrounded by screens and paraphernalia like an idol, or like a statue on an altar. Suddenly the minuscule statue frowned at him, averted its blind face, then stretched an arm.

Not an idol, then. Far more than that. Inscrutable as a flower or a nebula, it could be contemplated, never fully understood. Tick-tick-tick. And again the firing neurons in the developing brain smeared green traces across the three oscilloscopes.

*   *   *

Shaking hands with the doctor on his way out, Art said: "Thanks again for the treatment. You know if I could find a way I'd still stop Rita from going through with this. Because of the kind of world we have to live in. But I wish it wasn't so; I wish the world would let your way be possible. Anyway, you tell her that I want her back, whatever happens. I want that most."

"I'll tell her, Art. I'll be very glad to pass that word along."

At one o'clock in the afternoon Art, once more shrouded in an opaque cover—this one smelling more medicinal than musty—was led out of the building that housed the laboratory. Outdoors, he was guided blind over an area of long weedy grass and some uneven paving stones that he thought must be very old. Then he was put into the back seat of a car, where without being told he hunkered down so as to be invisible from outside.

The car, when at last it started, jolted slowly for about a minute over rough terrain before reaching some kind of a regular street or road. Very shortly thereafter Art began to hear the noises of other traffic around him.

"You can come up," said one of his Young Virgin escorts, in apologetic tones, only about five minutes after the start of the trip and well before Art had expected any such permission. He pulled the blanket gingerly from his sore head, and eased himself up into a normal position in the rear seat. The car was traveling through some middle-class jobholders' residential neighborhood that Art could not recognize. One Young Virgin sat beside him in the rear while another drove.

"Sorry, we're not going to be able to take you all the way to the Parrs' house," the driver said, still apologetic. "It's possible their place is being watched—you know how it is."

"I don't know whether I do or not. Not any more."

"Pardon?"

"It's all right. Let me out, give me some directions. I can take a slidewalk."

"Oh oh," said the escort seated beside Art, swiveling his head to peer back through the rear window. A moment later the police car with its blue lights flashing came alongside and with its foamy plastic bumpers nudged their vehicle neatly to the curb.

Art didn't have to walk far at all.

From the questions asked by the police before the van arrived to cart the three suspects off to the station, Art gathered that his escorts' car had been somehow identified as one used by participants in the morning's infamous Family Planning riot. All present occupants of the vehicle were therefore immediately under grave suspicion, the sullen one with the lump on his head being no exception. When the van unloaded at the lockup Art was at once taken underground, to a large cell with padded walls. He recognized it from sollie crime-dramas as what they called a DDT, or drunk-drug tank. In this instance of real life he found it crowded not with hallucinating drunks or druggards, but with loudly vocal Young Virgin types, several of whom complained loudly to the walls (where perhaps there were microphones to listen) of their real or supposed injuries suffered at the hands of the police.

The complaints did not appear to be doing any good. "Shuddup in there," advised a ceiling loudspeaker, from time to time. In reply to this the Young Virgins would more often than not break out in some new verse of largely unintelligible song. Approaching Art through this milieu, smiling as if at some old friend, came a suddenly familiar face: that of the sign-peddler of the morning's riot.

"It's just a mistake I was picked up," Art could hear the sign-peddler telling him, just as the latest outburst of song trailed off. "My signs were useful, weren't they, to let the world know what was going on? A man tries to be an influence for peace and communication in the world, to mediate the intelligent expression of differences in the community, and this is the thanks he gets. Hey, bud, which side *were* you on?"

"Shut up," communicated Art Rodney.

Now another fifteen or twenty prisoners were being brought in in a group, adding to the crowding and confusion. These looked like Young Virgins too. Art supposed that any Gay League members arrested were being held elsewhere, in the interest of relative peace. He had got the impression that the corridors under this police station were lined with these large, tank-like cells. Through the air drifted a steady animal murmuring, as of innumerable inmates, along with more dust than was comfortable. A muffled roar could be heard, as of heavy machinery at work nearby. Probably, thought Art, more cell space was being excavated.

He stood around—the places to sit were all taken—and waited. At length three police came to the door of the cell and set up a kind of shop there, a table behind which they sat and began processing the prisoners.

"One at a time, people. Form a single line. Come

up here and present your identification and we'll take your prints and picture. After that you can make one phone call. Form a single line."

A Young Virgin girl, a beautiful girl with dark devilish eyes, pushed herself forward to the table at once, and demanded: "How about separate facilities for men and women?"

The policeman who had already spoken eyed her warily. His lined face was on guard against any of these young punks attempting to get smart. "Separate what?"

"Latrines!" The girl waved at the open urinals and water closet along the rear wall of the huge cell. "We want separate latrines for each sex, with walls closing them off."

The cop's hardened face showed his disgust. "Oh, and no doubt you'd like to open a whorehouse in here too. You'll take what the city gives you, and you'll do your carrying on outside of jail."

Just as if that were the very answer she had hoped for, the young woman stepped back smiling. With a gesture and yell she started up another loud song, all the Young Virgins in earshot quickly joining in. But their rebelliousness now appeared strictly verbal; they were not slow to line up before the table for processing. Jail probably turned into a big bore in an hour or so, and now it was time to call one's parents to get one out. Art wanted to reach that table too; he used his weight and his elbows, refusing to be pushed to the rear.

Someone shouted at him: "Do you know the song?" It was a comradely shout, coming from just behind him in the newly formed queue. The shouter was a tall young man, wearing a sweatshirt, none too clean, with STUDENTS FOR A CHASTE SOCIETY handpainted on the front. Something about him looked vaguely familiar to Art.

"No, why should I know your song?" Art answered, as soon as the noise of it had abated enough for words to be heard. "I was just caught up in all this by mistake."

"That's the way it was with me," said the sign-peddler's voice, from up near the head of the line.

"Are you with us, though?" asked the devil-eyed girl of Art. She was just ahead of him in line, having squeezed her cloth-shrouded body in place there as the line formed, her eyes daring him to protest.

"I'm not with you or against you. I just happened to get caught up in this."

The young woman's eyes, those of a determined persecutor, attacked Art's beard and the conservative near-transparency of his clothing. She was silent, perhaps making plans.

The tall young man demanded: "Sir, if you're not really with us, *why* not?" His tone was meant to be not threatening but inspiring. "Now I judge you're a man who in the past has supported the Establishment, who has upheld all its outworn dogmas and twentieth-century beliefs. And now the Establishment has thrown you into jail anyway. What good has worshipping the sex gods and goddesses ever done you? Think about it."

"Oh, shut up." Art was done with arguing. He shuffled forward with the line, which at least was moving fairly briskly, the people at the front end being taken right off to meet their several fates, whatever those might be. If it came to posting bond, he didn't have a great deal of money.

So, he never knew what Rita, his wife, was feeling. Those had been her words to him, words

that he could not put out of his mind. Why couldn't
he have started, sooner, to try to understand her
feelings? Until he did that it probably made little
sense to argue with her. Of course she ought to
have shown him similar consideration, talked to
him more, found out what *he* really felt. Maybe
they really weren't so utterly, terribly far apart as
it had seemed when she ran away. Of course he
didn't want her to have another baby ... but if
she was going to do it anyway, if it was something
she really had to do, then he wanted to be with her
while it was going on. Now he had sublimated
everything up, it was too late even for that. No
matter what, he wouldn't be able to reach her
until the thing was done.

"Everybody be careful!" cried the devil-eyed
young woman brightly. She had been whispering
with a couple of her girl friends who were just
ahead of her, and now she was ready to have some
more fun with Art. "Everybody be on their proper
behavior while Mr. Whiskers is here. Maybe we
should all undress a little. Tear holes in our
clothing."

"Eunice ..." chided the tall young man. She
wasn't helping his recruiting drive at all.

At least Art was now soon going to have a chance
at a phoneplate. Did he have the nerve to call
George and Ann? To tell them that he had been
caught in a riot in front of the Family Planning
building, and then ask them for help? Not if he
could help it. Better if he never saw them again
until this thing was somehow over, concluded one
way or another. But of course his children were
there with them. He really had no choice but to
call the Parrs.

"I do hope they let us out soon," said Eunice. "I

want to pack as much sin into my life as I possibly can!" She stepped defiantly up to face the three sour police at the cell door.

Art followed in his turn.

After he had been fingerprinted and made to fill out a short identity form, Art got his chance at the phoneplate. Behind him other prisoners were waiting. Reluctantly he punched out the Parrs' number, and felt more relief than anything else when he was answered only by George's recorded face and voice, telling him that he might leave a message if he wished. Art left no message and after a moment's thought his relief turned sour. Maybe the Parrs had been arrested too, and his children were now being cared for in some public home.

He was allowed one completed call. Who else in the city did he know, where else might he turn for help? There was the dojo, but he couldn't remember either its name or address. There was Doctor Hammad. Ugh. After thinking a moment longer, Art dug a piece of folded paper from his wallet and, without much hope, punched numbers on the phoneplate once again.

"Jamison residence," said a male voice, answering through a blanked plate on the other end.

Art cleared his throat. "I'd like to speak to Rosamond Jamison, please."

"Who should I say is calling?" The voice had some thick and awkward tones in it, those of a man who would rather be doing something more physical than taking messages.

"Tell her it's Art Rodney. Tell her the man from the tube train from California. She'll remember."

"The tube train. From California. All right, just wait a moment."

Art waited, gazing around him. The prisoners in line behind him to use the phone looked in their frozen impatience as if they expected him to forget about his call and get out of their way at once. And now the nearby police had all come to something of a halt too. They were all watching Art, with peculiarly blank, controlled faces. He hadn't noticed them doing this when other prisoners were phoning. If it was just a game they were playing to make him nervous they were succeeding.

"Hello?" It was Rosamond's voice. Then on the phoneplate appeared the image of her pretty face, the cat's-eye lenses gleaming darkly. "It *is* you, my handsome protector! I'm so glad! I've been hoping you would call, and Daddy has too, he's wanted to thank you."

From the corner of his eye Art noted, without understanding, that the nearby police had suddenly lost all interest in him, were turning away and getting back to their jobs.

"I'm glad I could reach you," he said. "I'm afraid I need help, and I don't know where else to turn. The police have made a mistake, and they have me in jail here—"

"Wha-at?"

"I innocently accepted a ride with some strangers." Which was quite true. "And it turned out that the police were looking for their car. So now I'm being detained for questioning, as they put it. Or else I'm held for investigation on a charge of conspiracy to riot, something like that. I'm not sure I have it straight. I was hoping you might be willing to call a lawyer for me. Or something. I'm afraid I don't have much money with me, and—"

"Oh my, oh my. Poor Art. How do you spell your

last name? And what station are they holding you at?"

He spelled out his name for her. "And the sign here says Tenth District Detention."

"Just wait there, wait!" Rose counseled him excitedly. Then she blanked off.

Art took a step away from the phone and a policewoman was there to touch him on the arm and beckon him away. This officer for a change had a friendly-seeming smile. She led Art down a corridor to where a bulky, middle-aged man in civilian clothes was sitting behind a desk. On the desk were computer printouts, on which appeared small photographs of Art, both full-face and profile. The bandage on his head with the small bald spot around it showed on the photos, and he wondered when and how they had been made.

The bulky man looked up. "You're Mr. Arthur Rodney? I see here that you're from out of state. Did you know when you accepted a ride in that car that the police were looking for it?"

"No, I—no."

"Well, we find that there's no evidence to the contrary. We're very sorry about the inconvenience, but you can understand that we can't take any chances."

"I suppose not."

The man behind the desk nodded in a friendly way, and the interview seemed to be over. Another smiling uniformed officer, this one with an unusually large number of stripes on his sleeve, was holding open a door at one side of the desk as if he expected Art to pass through it. Beyond the door was an ascending escalator.

After he had started to ride up, and realized that

what appeared to be a public lobby was at the top, Art asked: "This means that I'm free to go?"

"That's right, sir." The smiling sergeant had come with Art onto the rising stair. "By the way," the sergeant added, his voice lowering, "if you're talking to—anybody, you can let 'em know that the people on the Force are a hundred per cent behind the campaign to get tough with the apes and get 'em off the streets."

"Huh?"

They had reached the marbled, busy public lobby on the station's ground floor. With a gesture the smiling sergeant directed Art's attention to where the air-curtained main doorway stood open to the world.

"I'd better wait here for a while," said Art. "I think someone's coming to see about getting me out."

"That so?" The sergeant winked. "Tell 'em they needn't have bothered. Still, you're welcome to wait for 'em here if you like. Have a seat. Excuse me, I'd better get back to work."

"Certainly."

As soon as the man had gone, Art went to a public phone booth in the lobby and tried the Parrs' number again. To his surprise, Ann answered almost at once.

"Art, what's up?"

He stood with his head held high; maybe at that angle the bandage on his scalp wouldn't be noticeable to the plate's pickups, not with his hair sort of piled in front of it the way it was. He asked: "How are the kids?"

"Why, they're fine, fine. Timmy scraped his knee, but it's all right. How are things with you?"

"Ah, fine. I tried to get you a few minutes ago, but no one answered."

"I was just out in the park with the children. George is working. Where are you now, Art?"

"I—I'll be talking to you again soon, Ann." And with that he blanked off.

He went to sit in the public lobby of the police station, in a place from which he could watch the public flow in and out at a brisk rate through the open doors. All of these people were in some way involved with legal trouble, even if they had only come here to report it, so Art supposed it was natural that they should look frightened or dazed, indignant or stony-faced as if in pain. What bothered Art was that when he looked out through the front window at the throng who were just passing the police station, the faces he saw there looked much the same.

He had been sitting in the lobby for less than ten minutes when Rose came in through the air-curtained front door. She spotted Art at once, smiled, and came marching clack-clack toward him across the marble on new hard-heeled sandals. It struck Art now for the first time that her walk was somewhat too childlike and bouncy for a normally mature young woman. She was wearing a red bikni, daringly opaque and almost padless. Art stood up and greeted her with an embrace.

"My good friend Art! How have they treated you?"

"Fine, ever since they heard me talking to you on the phone. Before that they practically had me sentenced, and now they tell me I'm free to go."

Rose laughed prettily, and linked her arm through his. "Then let's be going. We have a lot to talk about on the way."

He walked out of the station with her, asking: "Did you call a lawyer?"

"I thought you couldn't be in any very serious trouble," Rose said obliquely. "Here, get in." She was unlocking the door of a very expensive car parked right in the NO STANDING zone in front of the police station. The Illinois license plate was number four. *Four.* Great sex, had his luck changed at last?

Art got in obediently. "Where are we going?"

"I want to take you home with me, Artie. I told you, Daddy's been anxious to meet you."

Once in on the driver's side, Rose scanned the readiness indicators on the dash, as a cautious driver should, and then punched keys quickly. Then she sat back and turned to Art, giving him a long, unfathomable look while the programmed car started its engine and radared its way out into traffic.

"Artie?"

"What is it—Rosie? Do you like being called Rosie, by the way?"

"Yes, I do. Or Rose. Either one, it doesn't matter." She tilted her head, making the lenses shimmer beautifully. Probably she practiced with them before a mirror. "Artie, my father's a very nice man. A kind man. He's not one to fly into rages or anything like that."

"Well. That's fine." Art supposed she wanted him to ask some favor of her father. "Just who is your father, by the way?"

"He's the bishop, silly. Church of Eros Archbishop of Chicago. Everybody in Chicago knows him. Artie, we really are good friends, aren't we?" Taking Art's hand, Rose swung his arm back and forth over the seat between them. It was a child-

like action, and when a basically sexy girl like
Rose did it, a man could be seriously tempted
toward repression. Especially a weary man, drained
of his energy to fight. The vision of Rose crouching
on the bank of the Mississippi, veiled by the shadows of sunset and his own dirty shirt, rose up in
Art's mind's eye. But he managed to thrust it down.

"Of course we're good friends, Rose. Anytime I
can do you a favor I hope you'll let me know."

"Today I just want you to meet Daddy." She
giggled nervously.

"I'm looking forward to that. Especially . . . Rose,
I won't lie to you. Especially now that I know your
father is someone with influence." An hour ago Art
had been ready to resign the game, but now things
might just be a little different. "Because you see I
have a problem, one that I really need help with. I
hope your father may be able to at least give me
some advice on it."

The cat's-eyes seemed to offer him sympathy. "It
isn't a really big and nasty problem, is it? Oh, I
hope not."

Art laughed feebly. "Big and nasty enough. Oh, I
haven't murdered anyone, at least not so far."

Rose snatched her hand away, letting his fall.
"Don't say things like that! Don't even make jokes
about them."

"I'm sorry." He hadn't realized how sensitive
she was to even the suggestion of violence—or was
it something else in what he'd said that had upset
her? He looked around at the passing city. The car
moved fast on its radar guidance. "Do you live
nearby?"

"Not far." The neighborhood through which they
were now passing looked much like that around
the Parrs' home, except that here the blockhouses

were set back farther from the streets, occupied larger plots of land, and their walls looked even higher. Just ahead was one whose granite walls were extra high.

"We're almost home, my big handsome protector."

The car measured the traffic and the traffic-spaces round it, chose an opening and shifted precisely into the street's curb lane, from which it dove a moment later onto a ramp that swept it down beneath the granite walls. A man in a guard's booth, behind a portcullis, gave Rose a casual wave, which she returned while in the act of switching the slowing vehicle back to manual control.

Here, as in the Parrs' blockhouse, the underground garage was divided into an area for visitor parking and one for owners' stalls. Rose turned into what appeared to be the largest stall. There were two cars parked in it already, both new and luxurious, and there was room for several more.

She switched off her vehicle's turbines and turned to Art again. "Artie, if your problem is—nothing like the horrible thing you joked about—then you can tell me what it is. In fact I think you'd better tell me, before you go in and meet Daddy."

"Rose, it has nothing to do with violence. It's somewhat similar to—your problem. To the problem you were faced with when you and I first met."

She had pretty teeth, and moist, full lips. "However did you figure out what that was?" She sounded a little wary, but at the same time intrigued by his cleverness.

"Oh, just putting two and two together. I know now what you must have had in that picnic cooler."

Now Rose's lips were pouting. Was she going to

cry? It seemed to Art that without eyes her weeping would be tearless and therefore especially repulsive. He added: "Not that I care what you were doing, Rose. Not that I'm in any position to talk. It's just that my wife is now having difficulties along the same line that you were. I don't know that your father would be able to help me with that kind of a problem, or that he'd want to get involved in it."

Rosie dabbed with a tissue at her nose, and yes, at her lidless lenses too. "I'm glad you understand, Art. What happened to my fetus is another thing Daddy mustn't know the truth about." (*Another* thing?) "Of course he thinks that I simply had it aborted. But I can't even think about such violence, let alone permit it inside my own body. Ugh."

A final dab of the tissue, a deep breath, and Rose was back more or less to normal. She smiled. She said softly: "Now you'd better listen to me for a minute, Artie. Because I haven't told *you* everything yet."

Art leaned back in the car's luxurious seat, closing his eyes for just a moment's rest. Then he opened his eyes and checked his watch. It was a little past three. He turned his head and looked into Rose's lenses. "What is it you haven't told me?"

Once more she took Art by the arm. She became clinging. "Oh, Artie, I was just desperate. You see, there's a man I . . . like. I like him very much indeed. You know what I mean?"

He was afraid he did. "I—"

"In fact I've come to—to revere him."

"Revere?"

"Art, I put my fate into your hands. I know you won't betray me. Just recently my father has found out that I'm having an affair, or at least he's become very suspicious. But he doesn't know who the man is, and I didn't dare confess the truth, because ... anyway, I just didn't dare. So today when you called I told him that it was you."

"Oh." Art closed his eyes again. He supposed he could push Rose out of the car, seize the controls, and go roaring up out of the garage, perhaps crashing through the barrier at the outer door. Transporting an illegally frozen fetal specimen. Rioting. Midwifery. Auto theft, gatecrashing ... was there a crime called gatecrashing? There would be. No previous convictions, or even arrests. That Rodney must have been a cunning one. But sooner or later the cleverest criminals trip themselves up. They say he seduced a bishop's daughter, that's what really wrote *finis* to his career. They say just the other day he was in the Family Planning office, bold as you please, talking about an appointment with the director himself. They say ...

"Artie, dear?" Rose's voice dripped honeyed anxiety. Probably she didn't even like to be called Rosie. "Artie? I was just desperate, or I would never have done it. I had no one else to turn to, and I just had to keep Daddy from finding out who my true cavalier really is ... Art? Oh, I promise it won't be so bad. Daddy really did want to get you out of jail, even after I told him you were the one."

Art nodded slowly, meanwhile keeping his eyelids firmly closed. If he could somehow get out of the bishop's dungeon here and reach the Parrs' castle, maybe Ann could hide him under a bed and no one would ever find him. Drape him in an opaque sheet. But that might constitute another crime. Oh chastity, what a mess. Maybe he was dreaming.

"I was just in despair, Art, when suddenly you called. Then it seemed so logical for you to be the man that I told Daddy you were. Don't you see? Art, are you all right? *Poor* Art!"

Poor Art opened his eyes. Now then, what did he have to do to attain success and happiness? Meet the bishop and prove himself innocent of Rose's seduction. Then, with or without ecclesiastical aid, find Rita and get her safely aborted, while keeping George and Ann, and Rita and himself of course, clear of the law. That about covered it.

He opened the car door and slid out. The situation was clearly beyond worrying about, and from that fact he derived a kind of second wind. Bring on the bishop.

"Shall we go in, Artie?"

"Oh, why not?"

Rose led him directly from the parking stall through a double door that might have served to seal a bank vault, and up a private escalator. The door at the top was opened by a huge man, rough-looking though well dressed, who eyed Art with suspicion. Art in turn suffered a momentary fear that this was the bishop himself.

Rose said: "Jove, this is a friend of mine, Mr. Rodney. Daddy wanted me to bring him home so they could get acquainted."

Jove grunted. "Have 'im wait here and I'll see." It sounded like the voice that had answered Art's phone call. He looked Art over some more. "Or would you rather go in, Miss Jamison?"

"No, you go. I'll wait here with Art." She took Art's arm and they stood in the elegantly carpeted hall like, he thought, a couple waiting to be married.

"The bishop's chief bodyguard?" he asked, when the giant was gone.

"Yes. Don't mind Jove's rough manners, he's really quite sweet." Rosie squeezed Art's arm meaningfully. "So is Daddy. Now I put all my trust in you, darling."

Jove was already coming back through the plush hallway. "The boss says you should bring him on in. Hey, Miss Jamison, you're looking real hot. I'm off duty in a little while, could we maybe get together for some sex?"

"All right, Jove. I'll see you in the chapel. Art, dear, let me introduce you to Daddy first."

At the end of the hallway Rose tapped on an old-fashioned wood-paneled door, then pushed it open without waiting for a reply. The room revealed was a large study, the walls lined with bookshelves and taperacks. A massive, brown-skinned old man rose from an armchair and favored Art with a reassuring mild smile of greeting. The bishop was wearing the exaggerated white codpiece of his office, under a vaguely transparent robe.

"Daddy, this is Art. I've been telling him how nice you are, and that he really has nothing to be afraid of, meeting you. Now I want you to *be* nice to him."

"Why, I'm generally at least sociable, dear." The old man accepted his daughter's kiss on his worn, sagging cheek. "Dear, why don't you buzz away now for a little bit? Mr. Rodney and I are going to have a chat."

"Sure, Daddy. I'll be in the chapel with Jove if you want me." Turning toward Art with an expression that was doubtless meant to be encouraging, Rose stepped past him and out of the study. Art, who had reached out his arm mechanically, caught himself at the last moment and let her go without so much as a goodbye pinch. They were supposed to be having an affair; let her at least believe that he was going along with that pretense.

Bishop Jamison continued to smile as the door closed behind his daughter. "Mr. Rodney, that sofa there is very comfortable. And how about a drink? I have vodka and bourbon and beer and even a little sherry on hand."

"Uh, thank you, sir. Your Potency. Bourbon on the rocks would be fine." Art sank with resignation into the sofa, while his host turned away to a cabinet holding bottles and glasses. Poison in the whisky? All right, he'd drink it anyway.

The room might have been the study of any successful man of conservative tastes, though, not surprisingly, there was something of an emphasis on religious art. Rodin's *The Kiss* in nearly lifesize reproduction. *Leda and the Swan*, there on the wall, a sollie by one of the newer photographic masters. Painting had been dead for a century now, along with poetry and story-telling, or so most of the critics said. And there, of course, above the mantel, *Love Conquers All*, Caravaggio's Cupid trampling triumphantly the symbols of the callings by which a man sometimes allowed himself to be lured away temporarily from his true master, Lust.

The old man was back, standing in front of Art and holding out a glass. Art got halfway to his feet to take it from him. "Thank you, sir."

"Quite welcome." With a wheeze, the bishop settled his bulk in his own leather chair; he was holding his own drink in a tankard, around the outside of which some kind of an oriental orgy marched in bas relief. "Mr. Rodney. Rose tells me that you and she have become quite good friends."

"Uh, yessir, we have." Art's intended sip of bourbon somehow transformed itself into a gulp.

Jamison emerged from his tankard, traces of beer foam on dark lips. "She's a lovely girl in her way ... her mother was a lovely piece, and I oughta know, though I was an old dog even then. How was it that you two happened to meet? On the tube train coming in from Iowa, wasn't it?"

"That's right, sir." Art drew in a deep breath. "Bishop, I don't mean you or Rose any harm. Far from it. So I'm just going to tell you the truth. I don't know what Rose may have told you, but the fact of the matter is that I've met her exactly once in my life before today. For a few hours on that train. If she has any, ah, involvement with any man, it's certainly not with me." So far the news was being received with apparent calm. "I'm sorry about her problems, Your Potency, and about yours, but I have problems of my own that are at least as bad. I'm sorry."

Jamison leaned forward a little in his great leather chair. "Would you like a refill on that drink?"

"I'll get it myself, sir, thanks. Another beer? I'm telling you the truth, Bishop, I never was any good at lying."

The bishop indicated with a headshake that his tankard as yet had no need of refilling. He swiveled his chair to keep facing Art, who was now at the bar. He said: "Some people never realize they're not very good liars, and it gets 'em into endless trouble. Most of the time honesty at least simplifies things, if it doesn't always pay. You really did help Rose, out there in Iowa, didn't you? Her own story is a little muddled. She was coming back from visiting some girl friend in Dubuque, I guess, when that riot broke out."

"Oh yes sir, I had the chance to be of help to her

in a small way." Back at the sofa, Art sank down into the cushions with relief and took a sip, this time truly no more than a tiny sip, of the excellent bourbon. "But believe me, there's been nothing wrong, nothing improper between us. We made it all the way, right there in the park, while we were waiting to get on the train to Chicago."

Jamison was nodding slowly. "Arthur, I find myself believing you. I know my own daughter, and she just gave me your name too suddenly and too willingly. I don't suppose you know the name of the man she is involved with?" Then before Art could try to answer, the bishop scowled and put up a white-palmed, wrinkled hand. "No, I withdraw the question. Don't want to put an honest man like yourself on the spot."

"I really haven't the faintest idea, anyway, who it could be." Numbly relaxing, Art sipped at his icy whisky. His head ached, but not as bad as before. It seemed that he had managed to avert any new and disastrous trouble; he could sit in comfort, and enjoy the beautiful liquid in his glass; and what more could a man hope for in the world than that?

The bishop set his tankard down carefully on a small table, and used a hand to wipe his lips reflectively. "Not that I care an awful lot what kind of fun she has with men." His steady black eyes peered out at Art from their time-ravaged setting. "Probably that shocks you, coming from a churchman like me. But if she wants to sit with some young fella and gaze at the stars and forget all about sex for ten minutes, I can't see how society is harmed."

"Yes sir, I am surprised to hear you talk like that." It would have shocked Art more intensely if he hadn't been somewhat numb with alcohol at the moment, and emotionally exhausted by still more shocking things. "If what your statement implies is true, that society isn't harmed by repression, that it doesn't matter if people abuse their sex that way, why do we have the Church of Eros? I mean . . ."

The bishop heaved himself erect, his erotically decorated tankard in hand, and walked over to the dark fireplace. It looked a lot like the one in George's house, except that this one was bigger. When the bishop switched it on, a very realistic imitation of burning logs, probably a sollie hologram, appeared in the dark cave. The logs crackled, flared, and seemed to send smoke up the flue.

"This thing is a fake," Jamison mused, patting the mantel with one hand. "Lots of fire and noise, but no smell. Ever smell real piñon burning? And no real heat." He set his tankard on the mantlepiece and turned to Art. "You know why it is good for man to worship sex? Why it really is good? Simply because the poor fool has nothing better before which to prostrate himself. Eros as a god is far from perfect. He's just the best of a bunch of failures."

Taking a little time to think over what the bishop had just said, and looking at the old man closely, Art was not so very surprised after all. The reader and watcher of modern fiction encountered such cynical bishops and ministers fairly often. And Jamison wasn't just old; he must be decades over the century mark. He must have spent his youth in the period of moral vacuum before his Church became established. Art had once or twice heard other very old people express similar views, startlingly modern and radical.

Standing massive and ancient beside the fireplace, Jamison told him: "The war god and the wealth god and the heaven-and-love god all have failed. Heaven-and-love came the closest. Best example is the man they nailed up on the cross. He spoke to a lot of people, that one did. He was about the best, except for sex. And then Allah and Buddha and Jehovah and Mithra and all the rest.

"And then there's the man-god. You know what I mean by that? I mean god made by man in man's own image. The apotheosis of humanity: *We will all be god someday, and our great leader, whoever he is, is probably god right now.* He, the man-god, he's the worst, he's the most dangerous, and we're not through with him yet. Damnation, are we ever through with anything?" Jamison's voice, which had begun to take on the tones that it might use on Saturday night in the pulpit above the orgy, fell back on the last words to mere conversational pitch. One other man in Art's recent memory had used such an archaic expletive. "Mr. Rodney, man—and woman too—was made to worship something, and no god they find is worthy of them. That's what the ancients would have called a tragedy. Sex does the least harm, I would judge, of all the gods; and sex is fun. Oh, man, yeah, it sure is fun."

The bishop, smiling wryly at Art as he turned away, made his way back to the bar to get a refill on his beer. Then he went back to his leather chair to let down his weight, he and the chair wheezing together. "The only thing is, if she does like some young man in what to her is such an extra-special way, then I'd like to know his name and what he's like. Rose has had enough pain in her young life already. She tell you about that ape-assault in which she lost her eyes? I don't suppose she did."

"No sir. I didn't know that was what had happened. It must have been terrible."

"That it was," Jamison said shortly. "My much-publicized crusade against the street apes and the dope peddlers, which you will hear a lot about if you stay long in Chicago, stems in large part from that assault on my daughter."

"I believe I heard something about it from the police. Your crusade, I mean. They were in favor."

"I myself am not a nonviolent man," the bishop said. "Not always. Eros does not counsel turning the other cheek except for a caress."

Turning the other cheek? Art didn't understand the reference. He wasn't going to ask.

Jamison sipped at his newly foamy beer. "When I was a boy, a lot of people thought it was having African brown skin, what was then called being black, that made young men go out and act like apes. And there was a grain of truth in what they said, a grain of truth, because brown skin could be a real burden then. It could make a man feel desperate and just lash out."

Art grunted something. He was growing sleepy and would have to be careful that he didn't doze off, what with the drink and the hypnotic fire.

"Arthur, if you ever quote me as saying what I said about stargazing being not so bad after all, I shall of course deny it. Likewise with some of my speculations on comparative religion. On the other hand, if you should want to mention to me now your own problems that you said were so bad, I can at least guarantee secrecy. Maybe I could even offer help."

Abruptly Art was wide awake again. "Well, my

problem involves my wife. And the Bureau of Family Planning. It's a rather serious difficulty . . ."

But Jamison was already shaking his head, and putting up a white-palmed hand to stop him. "No. Not Family Planning trouble. I'm staying clear of that. Sorry, no, it wouldn't do for a man in my position to get involved. Too bad, my boy, but I can only wish you luck."

"That's all right, sir." It hadn't had time to grow into a real hope again. "I understand. And I wish *you* luck. And Rose too. Understand, bishop, I'm not having an affair with her, but she's a very attractive young lady and I can see how a man might wish to do so. I mean that as a compliment."

"Hmf," laughed Jamison. It was a single laugh, and not loud. He was staring into the glow of his artificial fire, and Art could tell that looking into the long scroll of his memories he found Art's words somehow amusing. Then the bishop was silent for a while, and Art was almost dozing again before Jamison asked him suddenly: "You're not angry about what Rose did to you today?"

"Telling you I was the man? I admit I almost fell through the floor. She didn't spring it on me until we were here and I couldn't run out. But I'm not angry now, she didn't do it out of meanness."

"You're right about that." Jamison nodded. "There's no meanness in her. But ever since that assault she's been not quite right in her mind. Too much frightened of any least hint of violence. I think she's scared that I'll have violence done upon the real man, should I discover his identity. Now who could he be, that she should harbor that idea?"

"I really wish I could help," said Art. "But I guess there's nothing I can do."

"She saw psychiatrists right after she was injured,

and now she's talking about going to another one, but I don't put any faith in 'em. Doctors, computers, modern science, and we still live in caves with the doors blockaded. Not that I want to damn modern science, not me with my penile implant, my artificial heart and arteries." Then with a visible effort Jamison roused himself from his musings, and once more got to his feet. "Go with Eros, my son. You have my blessing. Is there anything else I might be able to do for you?"

Art put down his empty glass on a small table and stood up. "I guess not, sir. Thanks again for getting me out of jail. I really was innocent."

When he emerged a moment later from the study, Rose, who had changed her red bikni for a transparent dress, jumped up from a sofa in the hall and came to him eagerly. "What happened?" she stage-whispered. "Did Daddy believe you?"

"I think he believed everything I told him."

She was so delighted that she jiggled up and down like a child. "And he didn't explode?"

"No. Actually he seemed very friendly."

Rose squealed. "My faithful protector! You took such a risk for me." She threw her arms around Art's neck and kissed him on the cheek, with a kind of innocent chastity. "Poor Daddy, sometimes at his age his mind wanders. I hate to deceive him. But I knew you'd manage somehow. Oh, how can I thank you?"

"It's all right."

"It isn't all right. You've done so much for me, that now I *must* do something in return." Her voice suddenly turned cool, and she retreated from him half a step. "If I wasn't pledged to be chaste with only one . . ."

"Please, Rose!"

"You're right, what must you think of me?" She tugged Art down the hallway. Looking toward the door at the top of the escalator, he could see that a different bodyguard was now on duty. As the man glanced their way, Rose snuggled one breast against Art lustily. "I'm not promiscuous, you know," she whispered. "Not like some of those bluenose girls, those terrible ones they throw in jail."

"I can tell you're nothing like that."

As they were going down the escalator, she said to him: "I bet they didn't feed you properly in that awful jail. And, knowing my father, he gave you nothing but drink. Let's go out and get something to eat, and we'll talk."

"All right." He had nowhere else to go anyway. It was about four hours since they had fed him at the midwifers' hideout. That hadn't been a real meal, and he thought he could feel the whisky biting at his empty stomach. "Where shall we go?"

"I know a place. I'm buying."

That seemed no more than fair, and Art went along. They were just getting into the car again, when Rose squealed, suddenly enough to make him jump. "Artie, I forgot all about your problem, trying to help your poor wife save her baby! Did you get a chance to mention it to Daddy? What did he say?"

She had the problem backwards, but Art saw no point in enlightening her. "I did mention it to your father. He can't do anything."

"Tell *me* more about it."

She sympathized and persisted until he had to elaborate on his story a little. Obviously she had the idea that he was trying to help Rita avoid an abortion, and he let her go on thinking that. Why upset the poor girl for nothing? Art would share a meal with her, and maybe some sex again, and go his way and never see her more.

"But where is she now?" Rose questioned anxiously. By now she had driven the car into a drive-in automat of the better class and they had placed their orders.

"She's here in Chicago . . . really, Rose, it's painful for me even to think about it. And there's nothing you can do." He reached to take a tray of food from the robotic servitor at the window. When he looked back at Rose she was shaking her head slowly, and smiling a mischievous smile.

"Artie, as soon as you've eaten you're coming with me to get some help. I know people Daddy doesn't know!"

FOURTEEN

Rose urged Art to hurry through the meal, which he consumed without really noticing what it was. Shortly they were driving again, the luxurious car turning itself automatically from street to street, making good time. "But where are we going?" Art kept asking. "Who is it you want me to see?" Hope was hard to kill completely, the game not easy to resign.

When he began to grow annoyed with her, Rose at last stopped being coy. "All right. We're going to visit my psychiatrist, in his office."

"Rose, what good is that? That's not the kind of help I need. I'm not trying to adjust to my situation, I want out of it."

Rose dismissed such quibbles with a shake of her head. Now, in the midst of traffic, she suddenly took over manual control of the car. She drove slowly and cautiously, with fierce concentration on the job. They were headed, as far as Art could tell, straight for the center of the city. Gigantic towers loomed ahead.

"Now the autopilot won't have any record of

223

where we went. It's a good thing Daddy hasn't
started having me followed yet."

"Are you sure it's a good idea for you to keep
secrets from your father?"

No answer.

"Rose, I'm sure you mean well, but I don't see
how this is going to help me in the least."

"I know you don't. But wait and see."

Art slumped back in his seat. He could demand
to be taken somewhere else, but where? Probably
by this time Rita was waiting for him at the Parrs',
her belly flat and perfect once again, a red picnic
cooler frosting over at her side. Working, perhaps,
on applications to get their child into the best
deepfreeze vault available. Where all the best families sent theirs. All right, Rita and Ann and George
had won. So let them do the wondering and worrying and searching for a few hours. Meanwhile, Art
would let Rosie lead him where she would. Per-
versely, hope still would not die.

Rose parked her car in a highrise public garage,
on the edge of the city's central zone in which
private vehicles, even those of the powerful and
wealthy, were forbidden. Nor were vehicles necessary from here on, Art supposed. From the highrise
garage an indoor slidewalk led them into a forest
of towers, more walks at many levels looping the
towers together like treetrunks bound with jungle
vines.

At about forty stories above ground level, Rose
and Art entered an office building, and boarded an
elevator that bore them higher still. From the
elevator, they walked an elegant, skylighted hallway, to stop at last before a door.

RAOUL RIZZO, M.D.

D. PSYCH.

Rizzo. Art had recently heard that name somewhere. He followed Rose into a doctor's waiting room, small and luxurious but empty. Not even a receptionist, human or robotic. An alarmingly remote look had come over Rose's face now, and she put sexless fingers on Art's arm. "Hush. Wait."

He waited. After a moment an inner door slid open. The well-dressed young man who emerged into the waiting room was of no more than middle height, but so emaciated that he looked taller. His eyes did not turn for even a moment to Art, or in any other direction away from Rose.

"My lady fair," he said. His tense voice was hardly louder than a whisper.

"My true knight," Rose breathed in answer. Her expression was becoming, moment by moment, even more remote. "Oh, my champion."

They stepped closer to each other They raised their right hands, and each caressed the air a few centimeters from the other's face. Not once did they make actual physical contact. Staring woodenly over each other's shoulders, they reminded Art of opposing pawns set down slightly off center on their respective squares.

Art just stood there. If they didn't mind his watching, why should he?

At last Rose turned, breaking off the non-embrace. "Raoul, Raoul my cold one, this is Art, the man who helped me on the tube train You remember my telling you about him."

"Rose . . . I thought that today I would have you all to myself," said the psychiatrist in the same dry, near-whispering voice. At last he tore his eyes away from Rose and put out a hand to Art. In Art's grasp the thin fingers felt as weak as they looked.

Raoul's gaze was penetrating at first glance but then kept sliding self-consciously away.

His lover nagged him gently. "Raoul, dearest? Today Art was kind enough to help me *again*, and now he has a problem of his own. We've just got to do something about it for him."

Raoul, nodding slowly, thought this over for ten or fifteen seconds. He dug a tobacco pipe out of a pocket in his translucent shorts. He looked from Rose to Art and back again. "Come in, then, all of you," he invited in the same voice. He held open for them the door through which he had come into the waiting room.

In his inner chamber, anticlimactically ordinary, Raoul pushed a pair of reclining chairs together side by side, and gestured for Art and Rose to seat themselves. Looking out the window as he sat down, Art saw the June sun working its way lower in the northwest sky, beyond a palisade of towers, and a groundcover of more distant rooftops.

Raoul perched himself cross-legged on his desk and lit his pipe, not bothering to ask first if anyone objected. Judging by the first fumes to come Art's way, the tobacco certainly contained an admixture of something stronger.

"Mr. Rodney." Raoul paused and puffed. "You witnessed the greeting that passed just now between Rose and myself. Have you ever beheld even a brother and sister going to greater extremes of antieroticism? My purpose in posing the question is not to shock you."

Art, watching the lowering sun and wondering if Rita could see it too, had not been paying very close attention. "Are you brother and sister? But I thought . . ."

"No, no we are not. Perhaps I failed to make my

meaning plain. Would you have described our behavior as obscene?"

Somewhat obscene, Art answered silently. *Mostly
just exhibitionistic*. He doubted that the greeting
would have been quite so extravagantly repressive
had there been no audience. But, wanting to be a
good fellow, and uncertain whether Raoul wanted
to be thought obscene or not, Art answered aloud:
"I suppose most people would call it that."

Now it was Raoul's turn not to listen. "I just
wonder," the thin man murmured, as if to himself,
"why did I employ that sibling analogy? Brother
and sister may repress a mutual sexual attraction
and that repression is tolerated by society."

"Of course." Art glanced over at Rose, wondering if she still nursed hopes that he was going to
benefit from this visit. Her inscrutable lenses were
aimed steadily at Raoul.

Raoul rocked back and forth in his sitting position on his desk, and puffed his pipe. He said:
"Taking a larger view, are not all women and men
in some sense siblings? What then is more natural
than our occasional urges to escape from sex? We
are all of us subject to the deep powers of the
subconscious. Modern science tells us that dreams,
produced in the subconscious, are attempts of the
ego to flee the restrictions of the body. In every
human adult there lies the buried wish to return
to a sexless infancy. In all honesty, isn't letting
these urges out into the open the only healthy
course to take?"

"I suppose," said Art, after appearing to give the
query a little thought. If he really spoke in all
honesty he would have to say that his own healthi-
est course would be getting up and walking out of
here as soon as he could think of someplace to go.

Rose meant well, and he didn't want to hurt her feelings, but this was ridiculous.

With an unfolding of bony legs Raoul got down, or rather stood up, from his low desk. "Personally, I have never conducted an analysis in which I did not uncover a strong, buried celibacy-wish in the subject. Our differences from other animals are inescapably part of our natures; and we ignore them at our peril."

"You may be right." Now his wife was going to have the chaste baby anyway and he was not going to be with her when she needed him the most. That was all that his campaign to rescue her had accomplished. But what else could he have done?

"Face these things in yourself," Raoul was telling him, in a newly brooding voice. Behind the psychiatrist on his walls were abstract photographs, and also a couple of Vandalist splash-paintings, up-to-date and arrogant in expensive frames. Yes, the art had been dead for a century, all right. "Face them squarely, and they will begin to lose their power over you."

Art cleared his throat.

Raoul's eyes fastened on his, this time not to be easily driven away. "Face the truth about what has happened between you and Rosamond!"

"What do you mean?"

"When you first saw her, she was alone, she was frightened, she was in danger."

"She wasn't exactly alone."

Raoul wasn't listening. "Immediately you went to her aid. Your relationship thus began on a basis lacking erotic values; but society tolerates that in an emergency, and you yourselves did not realize, perhaps, that subconsciously you wanted it that way.

"When the immediate danger was past, perhaps you turned to sex? Yes. *Then*, when desire was temporarily satiated, dangerously weakened, there came the moment of temptation. The forces of the subconscious were no longer to be denied. The fragile remnants of your lust were to be sacrificed upon the altar of repression. You wanted to flee with Rose from the world of flesh, to climb a crystal stair to an ethereal palace, to enter the world of sublimation. Yes. Perhaps you draped her body—"

"Enough of this." Art pushed from him suddenly vigorous memories of that sunset spent with Rose. He tried to stand up with a forceful motion but the reclining chair betrayed him, and he staggered and had to make an effort to keep from falling. "Look here, I haven't asked you to analyze me."

Raoul fell silent, gazing at Art with what seemed to be a mixture of pity and antagonism.

"Dearest?" Rose spoke up timidly. "Raoul? The reason I thought you might be able to help Art is because his wife is looking for a midwifer. Art wants to help her save her baby, but there are obstacles."

Raoul, professionally unshockable, took the news in stride. "I can help him live with the situation, provided he wants to be helped."

Rose shook her head. "No, my chill one, that isn't what I meant."

Raoul blinked. "What, then?"

"Oh, for you to see your father about it, of course!" Rose was lovingly irritated by her lover's obtuseness.

At the mention of his father, Raoul's face twitched, and he laughed bitterly. He sat on his desk again and tried to relight his pipe.

"Please, dearest. You mustn't be jealous. Art and I are *not* having an affair. He and I are strongly erotic together, really we are."

Puff from the pipe, and pause. Raoul stared at Rose. "Why do you say that?"

"Who is his father?" Art asked, standing now with his arms folded.

Rose flowed easily to her feet; probably she had some experience with these chairs. "I say it because *you* are my knight. Do you think I could ever want to sit coldly beside any other man?"

Raoul closed his eyes and let his pipe go out.

Rose hovered near him, avoiding contact, pleading. "My champion! Won't you do this little thing for me? Take Art to see your father."

"Who is his father?"

Raoul's eyes opened. His whisper had a broken sound. "For you, my lady, my chaste one, I will do it. Sometime tomorrow."

"That might be too late for Art's poor wife. Can't you do it right now?"

"I thought that you and I were going to have this evening alone together."

"Please. Take Art to see your father now. I set you this task, to prove that you revere me."

"Then I have no choice but to obey." Raoul came to life, more or less, and slid off his desk. "Will you wait here for me, my lady?"

Rose squirmed, as if with repressed desire, and took a step backward, avoiding any possible physical contact with her knight. "I'll wait here all night for you, if need be. When you come back, maybe . . . we'll play chess."

"My lady, not that childish game, I beg of you. Anything else."

"Who is your father?" Art asked the ceiling. "And

what good is seeing him supposed to do me?" Like as not the senior Rizzo would turn out to be the head of the Chicago branch of the BFP. Soon everyone in the city was going to know about Rita's warped reproductive cravings, her illegal plans. No one would do anything to rescue her, but everyone would know, even unspeakable idiots who thought chess a childish game.

After staring incredulously at Art for a moment, Raoul asked: "You don't know who my father is?" And the young psychiatrist laughed again, bitterly and long.

Still not knowing, Art muttered some goodbye to Rose, and went along with Raoul, first along slidewalks to a garage, and then in Raoul's car. In spite of all, a nagging hope would not be vanquished.

Whatever his occupation might be, Rizzo Sr. had evidently made a success of it. The blockhouse in which he lived was every bit as high-walled and luxurious as the Jamisons'. The Rizzo garage space was if anything larger than the archbishop's, and protected by heavier gates. As Raoul eased his fine car to a stop in one of the stalls and turned its turbines off, Art was once more nagged by the sense of having recently heard the name of Rizzo in some other connection. Was it something about this very structure? *Rizzo's townhouse* . . .

In a short passage that connected the garage with an underground level of the Rizzo home, a pair of non-uniformed guards were stationed. They looked meaner than the Jamisons' Jove, though neither of them was quite as large.

"Who's your pal, Doc?" one of them asked heartily.

"A man I know." Young Rizzo smiled wryly at

the guards. "A man with a problem. I expect my father will be able to help him, if he wants to help."

"Maybe you shoulda just phoned," the other guard suggested. "The Magnifico's sorta been lying low for the past few days."

The what? thought Art.

"You know how my father likes to do business face to face."

The pair of gate-blockers looked doubtfully at Art. He could place them now. They were the ones who had sat on him in the brothel. Not the same men, but the type. Rizzo, Rizzo, he almost had it.

"Well, let's see if you're carryin' anything, mister. Doc, the boss is in his study now, if you wanna go up."

"I'll be back in a minute, Rodney," said Raoul, and went on ahead. The two guards began to pat Art's bulges and probe his pockets, searching him. Rizzo. Little old Alfie in the slumburb tavern, saying Vic Rizzo's townhouse had been bombed. Oh, great stargazing quadruplets.

Raoul was soon back from his filial visit. His face was flushed, though seemingly not with joy. "He says I can bring him up."

"Awright."

Art rose up with Raoul in a large and fancifully paneled elevator, which disgorged them into a room that might have been the entry hall of a small art museum, except who would hire curators with this kind of taste? Marble columns supported a high, vaulted ceiling. Across one end of the room there splashed and burbled a complex of waterfalls and fountains and pools, complete, Art noted, with genengineered goldfish. For all its size, the hall was almost crowded with paintings and statuary.

On the wall opposite the elevator, in a place of dominance over the other *objets d'art*, was an ancient life-sized crucifix of wood, done in a realistically gory Spanish style. Its paint, once red and brown, had aged into a grayish dullness that with the cracks and holes gave the figure a look of frighteningly patient endurance.

Raoul led Art across the museum hall and opened a massive wooden door for him. "In here," he ordered tersely.

The room behind the door was as large as the entry, with a beamed ceiling and woodpaneled walls. Art caught one breath-tripping glimpse of a girl or young woman, heavily garmented in what looked like silk, even her face veiled, before she moved quickly out of sight behind some opaque woven draperies. And there was a huge genuine fireplace that in defiance of every pollution ordinance Art had ever heard of appeared to be consuming genuine logs.

At least four chess sets, of stone or wood or metal, all larqe and ornately carved or molded, were visible on tables or in display cases. At Art's right hand there stood a suit of armor. What appeared to be medieval torches, standing in brackets on the wall, bore realistic electric flames. Despite these and the fireplace, circulating air was keeping the room comfortably cool. On one paneled wall there hung a crossed pair of long, pointed archaic weapons, pikes or lances of some kind; on the opposite wall, a brace of antique submachine guns had been mounted in the same way. Walls and furniture were burdened with framed two-dimensional photographs, mostly in black and white and evidently reproduced from 20th-century newspapers or films, showing men in the obscenely

heavy garb of that time. The men smiled un-
pleasantly, and some of them were carrying firearms. From the upper walls there looked down at
least a dozen paintings from an era yet more
distant, most of them of men in antique costume
who wore swords and were accompanied by crouching dogs or obscure people, servants or hangers-on.
The Magnifico, the guard had said.

Now the Magnifico came forward amid his
treasures. His small torso was plump beneath his
shimmering, partially translucent dressing gown,
but his face still showed some of the leanness of
his son's.

His flat voice came at Art from around a cigar.
"So, you're the man with the troubles. I was curious to see you, I wondered what kinda man my
son would bring here to get his troubles fixed."

Art made himself look directly into the Magnifico's direct and seldom-blinking eyes. The reality of power before him was as apparent as the
hardness of the suit of armor on his right. Art
could feel the world and all its probabilities shifting again, moving crazily and unpredictably beneath his feet. And all hope was not yet dead.

Art cleared his throat. "My problem is a fairly
simple one."

"So. I guess my son can only fix the high-priced
troubles in his office. The simple ones he still has
to bring to me. What's yours?"

"My wife is in a birth-mill, here in Chicago."
Facing the reality of power in Rizzo's eyes, Art had
a moment of weakness, of indecision. But now his
choice was clear-cut, inescapable. "I want to stop
her from going through with it."

"So, who says I know anything about birth-
mills?"

The fireplace roared, and now it seemed to make the room too hot. Somewhere behind Art, Raoul fidgeted. Art said the next thing that came into his head: "I see that you're a chessplayer." Every time he glanced around the room he spotted another set somewhere.

Rizzo removed the cigar from his mouth and raised his eyebrows. "You play?"

Art smiled faintly. "I'm a master."

"No! You are?" The cigar went flipping into the fireplace. Rizzo almost bowed. "Come in here—whazza name? Mr. Rodney? You come in here, there's somethin' I want you t' look at."

He was holding open for Art the drapes behind which the veiled girl had vanished. At the same time he raised his eyes to stare coldly over Art's shoulder. "Hey, Raoul, go fix yourself a drink or something. Or get out. Hey, if you see Penny around maybe she'll wanna screw. She's been sublimatin' her urges quite a bit lately."

The only answer was the sound of the heavy wooden door softly closing; probably, thought Art, it could not be slammed. He went on through the drapes and Rizzo followed, into a smaller adjunct of the study. The young woman Art had glimpsed earlier was not in sight.

"You say you're a rated master, Mr. Rodney?"

"Yes. I play mostly in California."

"I'd appreciate it if you take a look at this position I got set up here. Tell me what you think about it."

On a board on an antique table were ebony and ivory (*real* ivory?) men, arranged in an intricate position, early middle game or late opening. At first glance Art took it for one of the computer-discovered variations of the neo-Shapiro defense.

But one of White's knights was oddly placed, changing the whole complexion of the game. And White's king's rook's pawn had been advanced to the fourth rank . . .

"Interesting," said Art. It really was. "One of your games?"

"Nah, not a real game. Oh, Mr. Rodney, meet Penny."

The veiled girl, moving on soft silent feet, had returned from somewhere amid the velvet hangings. Under the smiling but watchful eye of the Magnifico, Art kissed Penny hello with a fervent show of lust, and pushed a fondling hand inside the innermost of her voluminous garments.

Rizzo chuckled benevolently. "Now run along, little lady."

Penny paused to blow another openmouthed kiss to Art before she let the drapes fall into place behind her.

Rizzo, staring at the place where she had vanished, released a small sigh. "That son of mine just don't know how to keep a woman." Then he brightened. "That reminds me. You hear the one about this traveling salesgirl, she stops at a lamasery to sell blankets?"

"I'm not sure."

Evidently he was not going to hear it now. Rizzo was still gazing after the girl. "That Penny, though. She's been livin' here with me almost a year now, and I've never touched her. Imagine." He sighed again. "I hardly seen a centimeter of her skin in all that time. I did see her ankle once, when she was walkin' upstairs, and I nearly went dizzy. I tell you, when I finally get rid of that girl she'll prob'ly take a lot of loot along, but she's been worth it.

Everything a man could want. Whaddya think about this opening setup, now? Black to move."

"Interesting." With some relief Art turned back to the board.

"Y'see, I'm foolin' around with a little analysis here. I like to take the book theory, you know, and try to find improvements in it. The fellas who write them chess books sometimes don't know much about the practical side of the game. Chastity, I'd like t' get out and play in some tournaments, but I got too much business to think about." Rizzo glanced up from the board. "I'm a investment counselor."

"I see. I was hoping to play in a big tournament myself, but then this trouble came up involving my wife. That makes it very hard to concentrate on chess."

"Oh yeah. She's in some birth-mill, you said. Tell me about that."

Art recited his story. By now he had it down pat, like the standard stump speech of a politician, that even as it was being delivered could be edited a little here and there to suit the audience of the day. "Possibly it's too late and the operation's already over. But if at all possible I want to stop her from going through with it. For her own good."

"And you say you talked to this doctor who's gonna do it, but you don't know his name?"

"Right. He's one of these Christian priests, I know that much. Order of St. Joseph. Tall fellow, kind of narrow-shouldered, with a sandy beard. As to where it's being done . . ."

But Rizzo wasn't worried about where. Already he had nodded and started to pace the room. For the time being chess was forgotten. He lit a fresh

cigar and squinted through the smoke of it, studying Art's face.

"Whatever people she's paid, or promised to pay,
can have their money," said Art, as free with the
Parrs' substance as with his own. "But my idea is
this: the pregnancy can just be terminated legally,
and as far as my wife will ever know, something
just went wrong. The fetus turned out not to be
viable, or whatever the medical term is. That's
simple, and there's no trouble in it for anyone."

Rizzo smiled faintly. "I kinda taken a liking to
you, Mr. Rodney. Course you understand I don't
know nothin' about any midwifers—but what did
you say your wife's name is, and what does she
look like?"

Art told him. He ran through much of the standard speech again, going into greater detail. His
tongue stumbled reluctantly at times. He felt afraid
to start hoping again.

Rizzo heard him out, listening intently, then nodded decisively. "Yeah, I see. Too bad. Any day now
she's gonna have the operation, right?"

"I got the impression it might be at any hour."

"Uh-huh. Some of these priests don't stick to
religion, they're real cultists and mix into things
where they don't belong. Excuse me a minute, I
got a phone call to make. Look over this position
here meanwhile, hey? Tell me how do you like
White's chances."

Left alone, Art heaved a tremendous silent sigh.
He sat down at the chess table, and leaned his
head forward in his hands, letting his eyes close,
pressing the heels of his hands into his eyes. A
great exhaustion was coming down upon him. It
came with a disturbing sense of permanence, as if

he might never be able to rest long enough to recover from it. But his feelings didn't matter, if Rita could be saved. Someday he would he able to tell her what he had done for her, and someday she would understand and thank him for it.

Art opened his eyes and found the chessmen waiting. Rizzo would expect a masterly evaluation of the position, and that was little enough for him to ask.

Black to move.

Four or five minutes of Art's flawed attention sufficed to convince him that the Rizzo Variation was a bust. Rizzo evidently thought that White's advanced knight could not be readily dislodged from its fine post. But Rizzo had overlooked a thing or two, and White was in fact going to have to retreat and waste a tempo, and then would stand poorly in the middle game. These were the facts but they had better be conveyed diplomatically.

In a few minutes the Magnifico was back. His mood had brightened into something like joviality. "Like I said, I know nothin' about any birth-mills. Still, I got a hunch that things are gonna work out okay from your point of view. Just a feeling. Well, should we have a little game? How about a drink, something to eat?"

"Certainly." Art got off another sigh, like a man dropping a weight. But he discovered that the weight was still clinging to his shoulders.

He began to rearrange the chessmen to begin a game. Someday she would understand.

FIFTEEN

Lying chastely beside Marjorie in the dark bed that connected their two darkened hotel rooms, Fred was pouring out his heart.

"Ah, who'm I kidding. I'm not ready for even a brown belt yet. I could be, if I settled down and worked at it. I dunno, though, if its really worth the effort. All the lumps and bruises, and you never get rich. Karate just gets you flunkie jobs, like this part-time bodyguard thing I got going now with this Dr. Hammad. Ivor, he's the regular bodyguard, says the pay never amounts to much.

"George does all right, though, running his own dojo. He must do all right, you should see his house. I don't know what he charges for private lessons. If only I could get myself a setup like he's got. And his brother-in-law does all right too. Ann, that's my sister, says Art holds down an electronics job *and* wins prizes. He must have bread comin' out of his ears. He wins prizes playing chess, pretty good at it I guess.

"You know something I was good at, though, besides karate, was woodcarving. I won some prizes when I was a kid. I even sold a couple things. Little things. My folks never paid that much attention. Finally I didn't carve any more. Maybe if I'd kept up with that I could set myself up handcarving chess sets. Art would probably give me some clues on what sizes and shapes the players like and how to sell them. You know, once I carved a nice religious cross for Ann, when she got baptized. I did it from pictures in books. That was after she left home and married George. She still has it on the wall in her kids' room. George don't go for that religious stuff himself, but he don't care what Ann does."

Fred raised himself on one elbow in the bed, making his plastic gladrag cloak crackle all around him. Marjorie's form, similarly draped, lay still and straight beside him. The room was too dark for Fred to read her face, but he could still perceive the tenseness of her body. A tiny, tinny sound, so faint that he could hear it only intermittently, leaked out into the room from the earplugs of her radio. Fred could not make out any of the words, but he thought it was Orlando, one of the season's top recording stars, chanting his own verse. Marge had said that she liked to have Orlando on for background music whenever she got started outward to the stars.

"Anyway," Fred went on, "the carving business is not bad in some ways if you can get a reputation as an artist, but there are certain drawbacks. You have to have the right wood, if you're using the real stuff. And when you go to sell your work it's hard to prove that it's really handcarved unless they've actually seen you do it. I mean there are woodworking machines that can be set to take off little irregular chips and shavings and leave little marks just like a hand knife, and the machines do the job a hundred times faster. It's like humanity in the modern world has to contend against machines at every turn, you know what I mean?"

Marjorie was nodding, nodding gently. She could understand, she could understand it all, and suddenly it all weighed only half as much as before. She could help him through the puzzling and the difficulty of it all. Above Orlando's tinny moans Fred could now hear another little moan, but in his bedpartner's warm, breathing voice. Could it be that she was weeping for him, had his story of failure affected her that much? Fred reached to chastely touch her hand, and tried to think of words to tell her how much it meant to him to have her here with him tonight.

As he touched Margie, her little moan swelled up into an exasperated snarl. She sat up in her crackling cloak, pulled away her hand that he had touched, and used it to pull her earplugs out. "You twin!" she stage-whispered angrily at Fred. "What's the matter with you? I've run into some horny stallions in my time, but ... what do you think I am, your shrink? If you can't talk it chill any better than you're doing, just fall back in your plastic and let me listen to someone who can."

She flopped her head back on the pillow and turned up the volume of the radio slightly. Into the silence, Orlando's peculiar, almost metallic voice recited:

> ... *up on gladrag hill*
> *You left me so chill* ...

Fred almost hit her. Why didn't he? Only because he was afraid she wouldn't be hurt by his blows at all, wouldn't cry out or fold up or bleed, but would just ignore his efforts the way his dream-opponents usually did.

His hands were shaking with the urge to hit. He got up slowly, on his own side of the bed, and pulled the stiff opaque poncho off over his head and threw it down. He turned away from the bed and pulled his clothes on and went on out of the room without once looking back.

Outside the sky was darkening and the street-lights coming on. Without making any conscious plans Fred headed for the Megiddo. When he got there he spotted Lewandowski and the Wolf sitting at a table together, teetering restlessly in their chairs. Making sure that his face was properly hard again, Fred walked to their table amid the baby-crying music that at least was not Orlando's. Looking at them through the smoke, he saw Lewandowski become aware of his approach, the fat youth's face challenging and welcoming him.

"Let's go cruise, men," Fred challenged in turn, standing beside their table. Wolf's pelt turned to look at him, with the movement of Wolf's own head and shoulders turning, and two more sets of teeth showed Fred their grins.

"Quads and quints, I'm with ya," said Lewandowski, stretching to his feet. "I been sitting here five hours now, let's go find some live fun."

They cruised out of the Megiddo and right away Wolf began talking about how to organize a street gang and establish a territory of streets and blocks. Fred heard it without listening, without caring. As they passed some parking meters Fred tried to smash one with a kick, but the device was too strongly built, and he only hurt his foot. He thought he managed to keep the pain in his foot from showing in his face, as he was keeping a lot of other things from showing, but it was all coming to a head.

They cruised the narrower, dimmer slidewalks. "Hey," Lewandowski whispered, stopping the other two. "Look at this. Here comes fun."

It was a young couple walking alone. They slowed timidly as they drew near, but that only made their fate a certainty. Fred and Wolf and Lewandowski crowded them right off the walk onto the short, thick, genengineered grass.

"You're a jobholder, ain't you, pal?" asked Fred, slapping the young man. The youth began to wrestle ineffectively, and Fred slammed a fist into his ribs full power. The young man collapsed, croaking. Fred bent down and seized one of his manicured fingers and wrenched it back savagely until he thought it must be broken. "Now try and work," he said.

The young man sat on the ground yelping and stuttering with his broken finger and his cracked ribs. Fred had had enough, so instead of shutting him up he walked away, taking a quick glance around to make sure no one was coming to interfere. Then he looked to see what Wolf and Lewandowski were doing with the young woman.

"Don't hurt me!" she was squealing. "Take my money, wrap me, but don't hurt me!"

"Who'd want to wrap you, sister?" Lewandowski laughed. He had her purse tucked under his arm, and he was tearing off her electrostatically clinging costume, while Wolf held her by the arms from behind. Lewandowski peeled the last glitter of silvery film from her plump body, and then Wolf tripped and shoved her so she fell, sadly naked and unattractive. She sat there quivering flabbily, staring at the three of them in abject terror, while Wolf and Lewandowski together rifled her purse.

Now some people down at the end of the block were looking their way and pointing. "Come on, let's go," urged Fred, starting in the other direction.

Wolf delayed a moment, bending over the girl. She screamed loudly and he jumped back and came hurrying after Fred and Lewandowski. For some reason the three of them started running. They ran for a block, switching slidewalks athletically, and then ran again, now and then looking back over their shoulders. There was no pursuit, and they slowed to a casual walk. Fat Lewandowski was puffing hard, Wolf was doing all right, and Fred wasn't even warmed up yet.

Wolf was holding up the head of his pelt, waiting for the other two to notice something new about it. Fred saw that the sharp-pointed plastic teeth were reddened. "I left m'brand on her, where it counts," Wolf snickered. Fred wondered, without really caring, where the place that counted was. He couldn't really think of one.

Lewandowski still had a handful of silvery film, and was tearing it into little bits which he scattered like confetti. Good-humoredly he demanded: "How much dough did that guy have on him, Lohmann? Hey Fred, you get the bread?"

Lewandowski laughed at his own rhyme, and they all laughed, feeling good. Fred's sense of power and self-assertion, brought to a peak by the terror with which the girl had looked at him, was not spoiled by the realization that he had forgotten to take the young man's money.

"Naw, I didn't get it," he admitted cheerfully. "But what th' purity."

"Didn't get it?" Lewandowski too was more amused than upset. "Why?"

" 'Cause I didn't give a quint about it. What the purity!" But now the omission did begin to bother Fred a little, mainly because the young jobholder would be comforted by having retained his money and his papers. All right, next time Fred would make up for the oversight. Fred had never done anything quite like this before. As a kid he had been in fights, but never launched such an unprovoked attack. But already he knew that there would be a next time, and when it came he wouldn't stop with just breaking a finger and maybe cracking a rib or two. Next time? Quintuplets, yes, there would be one.

The Magnifico, when he finally returned to the chessboard, furrowed his brow and took half an hour to make twelve moves. Then Art managed to let him win a pawn. Rizzo was an intense and serious player, with a drivingly aggressive style that would probably win him most of the amateur games he played. Though he vaguely mentioned having taken part in tournaments, he seemed to have little competitive experience since he accepted a pawn from a master without apparent suspicion. Maybe he had played in prison somewhere. Art, headache-ridden, wished he had given away a knight or bishop and so provided himself with an excuse to resign. But no, that might be putting it on too thick. The best thing would be to arrange a draw. If only Rizzo would not take so long to move!

A man, not one of the pair of guards, opened the study door and put his head in. "Chief?"

Rizzo grunted in exasperation, got up, and went out. Art shifted in his chair, took a bite from the tasteless sandwich that had been provided for him, a sip from the accompanying drink, and looked at his watch. Nine o'clock, almost. It would be getting dark outside. His headache was waxing fat. He could ask for aspirin but it wouldn't mix well with the drink.

He meant to spend a lot of time and effort, from now on, making it up to Rita for what she was losing, or what she thought that she was losing. Right now, for some reason, all of Rita's weak points—mostly insignificant things, of course, like her occasional stutter—kept popping up in Art's thoughts. But all in all she was a good wife. What was he thinking? She was a purity of a good wife, the best of wives, and someday she would understand. When that day came, it would be a great relief to be able to tell her how he had managed things, and to have her understand, and thank him for it.

It wasn't as if he had had a real child of hers done away with. It wasn't anything at all like that. Even if they could make movements at three months. Even if there was some activity in the brain. Rita and he would smile over all this then, someday, when he finally told her. Over all their foolish ideas and fears.

Someday they would laugh at it all. It was still only nine o'clock; yes, his watch was still running. Twins, how this night seemed to last and last.

The Magnifico at last came back through the draperies, smiling and rubbing his hands together, looking eagerly at the board. "Where'd you move? Like I said, I don't know about these places where they have your wife. But if I was to give you advice like a father, I'd say don't worry, these things have a way of working themselves out."

"I moved my queen here. And I want to thank you."

"For advice?" Rizzo's laugh was deep and rich, and still managed to be nasty. "Advice is cheap."

The door opened again. "Chief?"

"Oh, Gramma's chastity. Look, Mr. Rodney, you don't mind, hey? I guess we can't continue our game tonight."

"Of course." Art stood up, trying to hide his relief. "Some other time, maybe. We'll call this one a draw."

"Sure, sure, maybe another day. Look, I'm gonna have one of my friends see you safely on your way."

One of the men nearly as big as Jove came out of the house with Art, to guide him on the slidewalks and ride with him; maybe Rizzo's cars were all out on business. The guardian rode silently and protectively at Art's side until they were only a few blocks from the Parrs'. Art didn't want him coming to the door, and said: "It's all right, you can go back now. This is a safe neighborhood."

The man gave a small salute and turned away. Alone, Art rode on under the black sky and the daylight streetlights that somehow were not at all like the genuine light of day. What was he going to tell George and Ann when he got back to them? Nothing. Why should he have to tell them anything?

Never mind, some words would come.

Art looked back sharply, first over the right shoulder, then the left. He had thought he had heard something. But his escort was out of sight already, and at the moment there was no one else in view. He glided past a clock in a vendor's window, and checked it automatically against his watch. Only a little after nine, and why was he bothering so much about the time? What did the exact time matter to him now?

If only this headache would let up.

At an intersection he heard loud voices in the dark, not very distant, coming from along the walk that came to cross his at right angles by diving underneath it. The streetlights must be out down that way, it looked so dark. Still Art thought he saw an arm wave at him from the gloom, an extended imperious hand. A voice called to him: "Hey. Hey you, hold up." At least he thought those were the words.

Art ran. Each pounding footstep jarred pain through his skull, a shockwave springing from the back of his neck to exit at his pate. The voice or voices behind him were raised now in a babble of threats. He thought he heard pursuing feet come pounding in his wake.

He didn't look back, but fled, as in a nightmare. He tried at last to yell for help, but only the tortured wheezing sounds of an exhausted runner left his mouth. A wall of gray faintness rose up soon to mask the world.

Art stumbled, and had the sensation of losing consciousness completely for just a moment as he fell. Were they kicking, hitting him already? No, it was only the pain in his head, and the jarring as he hit the walk with knees and elbows. Where were they? They weren't here.

With a grateful shudder he realized that there was no one at all nearby. They had left him for more sporting game. Or had he really managed to outrun them?

Rizzo sent them. Rizzo sent them, said the irrational panic inside his buzzing head. But that made no sense at all. Rizzo had sent someone to protect him. Rizzo liked him. And, anyway, Rizzo's agents would not have been so easily eluded. But still Art could not get rid of Rizzo's name, and image. They kept coming up, like something that had to be vomited.

The slidewalk was still carrying him as he lay on it. Art glimpsed street signs that gave reassurance he was still headed in the right direction. He tried to get back up on his feet again, but he couldn't, not right away. He rode on all fours, in terror of meeting someone.

The guard at the pedestrian entrance of the Parrs' blockhouse took no chances on being tricked out of his bulletproof booth. First he shut the steel grillwork gate behind Art's crawling figure, then got on the house phone, and only then came out of his booth to try to help.

A few moments later George came running up, his face a taut mask. Once he and the watchman had helped Art to his feet, he was able to stand. The faintness returned for a moment but then abated swiftly, though the headache pain went on and on.

They asked him where he had been hurt, and which way his attackers went. When he came in crawling, looking beaten, it was naturally assumed that some other human being was responsible.

"I—I got away from them somehow. I'm just winded. From running."

George looked at him doubtfully, and said to the guard: "I wouldn't call the cops yet, hey Casey?"

"All right, no law says I have to in a case like this. Wouldn't do any good anyway."

"I'm all right," Art muttered, finding he could

do without support as he and George passed on into the interior of the block. "How are the kids?"

"They're okay. Come on in and rest, Art. You look like you've been through the mill."

At the Parrs' patio door, Ann came to greet them. Her husband said to her: "Put that thing down, we're not invaded."

"Ohh," she breathed, sagging briefly against a wall. Art saw now that in her right hand she carried a carving knife with gaily decorated handle, holding it as if ready to thrust. For a moment he could see in Ann's face all the strain of the last few days, as she turned away to take the knife back to the kitchen.

George pulled forward a chair, and Art sank into it gratefully. Then George said: "We've just now had word from Rita's doctor. I mean the one who really operated. She's all right."

"Operated?" Art started to his feet again. "Then—?"

"Sit down. She's all right. I got the code-word message on when and where to pick up her and the baby."

Suddenly, unexpectedly, this was all, in a sense, old stuff. The essentials had happened to him twice before. Timmy and Paula. His next question seemed perfectly natural as it came out. "How's the baby?"

"Oh, the parturition went okay. Codeword for a healthy boy." George bent down, squinting at Art. "You all right?" His face blurred in Art's vision.

"I'm all right," said Art. "All right now." He was crying.

SIXTEEN

Dr. Matthew Hammad was working late office hours tonight, and in the midst of an abortion when the phone call came in.

"Says to tell you it's life or death," his evening receptionist informed him. "Really vehement about it." Behind the receptionist's image on the intercom screen he could see the wall of his outer office, with just some grapes and Bacchus' elbow showing as a detail of a painting hanging there.

"What name?" Hammad asked the screen, looking across the supine figure of his abortion patient. He was irritated at the interruption, and yet professionally unwilling to ignore the possibility that the life-or-death claim was true.

"A man calling with a blanked screen. He says he's calling for a Ms. Chester. I don't find that name in your file of patients."

"Oh." Hammad glanced down. The girl on the treatment table, draped in translucent sheeting, was sixteen years old. She had the music earphones on, and the look in her eyes was far away. "All right, I'll take it in here. One moment." He touched the girl on the arm, and when she had loosened one earphone and looked up questioningly, he said: "We'll just let this work for a minute. Are you comfortable?" Resting on the table between the girl's raised knees, the Autobort looked something like a small vacuum cleaner, or perhaps some robotic alien in sexual congress with her, its slender sterile organ of plastic and flexible glass extended into her body.

She said: "I'm starting to get a cramp inside." But she gave no sign of experiencing real pain.

Hammad said: "Well, next time come in sooner, and we can do a simple menstrual regulation. Those are easier, you know. Next time don't wait until you're this far along."

The girl, pouting at the mild lecture, put her earphone on snugly again, and Hammad walked around the table, so he was standing with his back to her, close to the intercom plate. He fingered the control to take the incoming call. Ms. Chester was a code word, and one he could not very well choose to ignore.

The caller kept his own phoneplate blanked, as Hammad had expected he would. But the doctor recognized the voice from a few previous calls. What the voice had to say this time was guarded and indirect, and the message was being relayed from someone else. Still the message came through plainly.

"Yes, yes, I understand." Now Hammad was frowning. "Well, it wasn't my intention to cause trouble when I made the referral. Ms. ah, Chester's whereabouts are not known to me now with any certainty." Now Hammad understood why this call was being made; every time the overlords of illegal business had the chance, they tried to embarrass the operations of their rivals in midwifery, the religious cultists who ran their birth-mills without paying tribute for the privilege.

"I can only guess whether I'll be able to reach her and ah, provide the therapy." Even while he was engaged in this difficult call, Hammad kept a conscientious physician's eye on the progress that the Autobort was making. The girl was now quite relaxed, soothed by light sedation and the mild sexual stimulation of the machine. While there was a pause in the phone conversation, the speaker at the other end of it probably conferring with someone else, Hammad chided the watching girl again: "Next time come in sooner."

"I had a lot of other things to do."

"It'll be easier if you come in sooner. You weren't thinking of carrying this one to term, were you?"

"No. Why would I do that?"

"Everyone's given a free choice in these things. Two free choices."

"What?"

"I said everyone in our society is free to make choices."

Through the tubing into the receptacle of clear glass on the vacuum cleaner's back there now flowed the debris from the dismemberment within the womb. Now a few ribs, fishbone clear and soft but recognizable to the trained eye. Now a knee joint, which Hammad could also readily identify. Now parts of the skull and brain.

"What? Everyone what?"

"Yes. I said . . . never mind." Between the earphones and the sedation it was not easy to communicate. The doctor smiled at his patient reassuringly.

The phoneplate voice came back. Hammad's

frown deepened as he stood listening to it. The burden of the discussion was that certain powerful people, those who made it possible for him to continue in the illegal sideline of his profession, were displeased that he still made referrals to the cultists. It wasn't exactly clear just how great this displeasure was.

Hammad said: "Yes, I'm sorry."

Try to help out a friend whose sister was having problems and see where it got you. Now, who would he rather have angry at him, George Parr or Vic Rizzo? There was always South America, Hammad thought wryly to himself. But a less drastic solution than that seemed available. George Parr need never know everything that went on, while Vic Rizzo evidently already did.

The phone voice went on for a while, making sure he understood what was expected of him now. Hammad said: "All right, then, I'll do everything I can. At once. You can depend on me to take care of it."

His caller blanked off. Feeling grimmer than ever, Hammad stayed at the phoneplate and punched a number rapidly. Waiting, he continued to keep a dutiful watch on his patient. She was still coming along nicely.

There was an answer. "Hello, this is Dr. Hammad. Let me speak to Ivor, please . . . yes, Dr. Hammad . . . well, the moment he comes back, will you tell him to call me back at once. It's rather urgent. Thank you."

Hammad blanked off, thought quickly, and at once began to punch again.

When Fred got back to the Yipsie and found a message waiting for him, he wasted no time in hurrying to Hammad's office; Fred wanted to hang on to his job, part-time and poor-paying or not.

It was after midnight when Fred arrived at the office, but Hammad was still there. The doctor ushered Fred directly into an inner consultation room and shut the door, though there was no one else around. "Lohmann, something very important has just come up, and I haven't been able to get hold of Ivor. It can't wait. You haven't been working for me for very long, but I think I can rely on you—right?"

Fred nodded at once, and felt the butterflies start up in his stomach. His big chance—could this be it?

"Fred, the situation is this. There's a fetal specimen that has to be reclaimed. There's a woman— not one of my patients, I'm doing this for a colleague—who has carried off a specimen that according to law should have been destroyed. You follow?"

"Gotcha."

"This woman is likely to get several innocent people in trouble by what she's doing. We have to reclaim the specimen from her. You have to do it."

Fred nodded.

"There'll be a nice bonus for you if you can carry this off. Plus a permanent raise in what I'm paying you. Now we'd prefer that the police not be involved in this at all, if you understand me."

"Yeah. I got the idea."

"Good. Now, from past experience with the people who have been encouraging this woman to do the wrong thing, I can tell you just where she's likely to be waiting to be picked up by some of her relatives or friends, and the approximate time when she'll be there. It's down on South Shore beach.

Do you have a reliable friend or two to take along, to help you look, and to stand by in case of trouble? There could be someone with her. I'll see that your friends are taken care of too. Provided that you get results."

"Yeah, sure, I got friends." With any luck at all he would be able to find Wolf, or Lewandowski, or both of them, back at the Megiddo. Lewandowski, being a native Chicagoan, would certainly be able to lead him to South Shore beach, and either of them would be a good back-up man if Fred should need one. "I can handle it for you, chief. If she's there and she's got it with her, we'll get it. You have to have it back here, or—?"

"Yes, I want to see it. To make sure. But don't bring it here unless you're sure no one is following you."

"Gotcha. Don't worry about a thing."

Art and George had time for only a few hours of sleep before they started out again on the slidewalks, at about an hour before dawn. When Ann came into his room to wake him for the adventure, Art sat up with a start. He felt rested. The pain from the wound in the top of his head was still there, but it was not bad enough to keep him from concentrating on other matters.

George had dug out a couple of old fishing poles and some other anglers' gear for them to carry, to provide a plausible reason for their being out if they should fall under the eye of the police. He told Art that a lot of fisherfolk went to the lake shore in the early morning, this time of year.

On their southwest passage through the city's nearly deserted predawn streets, they twice underwent brief surveillance from police cars, but were not stopped. There were no other problems; Art doubted that street-apes ever got up this early.

In the grayness before sunrise, the last slidewalk brought them to a terminus at the edge of a green strip of parkland.

"Lake's over that way, east," George said. It was obvious that there were no tall buildings in that direction.

Streets and buildings were all behind them now. George led the way into the broad lakefront strip of parkland. They crossed a wide, grassy athletic field, now otherwise deserted. Now Art could smell what must be the lake, fresh dampness without the tang of ocean salt, and billows of morning fog drifted into their faces as they trudged toward the east. The fog turned stands of trees into ominous vague green mounds, and limited visibility in all directions.

George kept looking over his shoulder, and Art looked back too whenever he saw George doing it. Art saw no reason to suspect that they were being followed. Now the ghosts of fog had completely surrounded them, cutting them off from the city behind. Looking to the east again, toward the lake, Art could see nothing but fog. Now, from that direction, he could hear a couple of radios or recorders blaring out pop music.

"We should see some people soon," George told him in a low voice. "There are always a bunch of people out here fishing around this time. She won't be just sitting out here utterly isolated."

"I was wondering." Art was wondering about other things, too, for example whether Rita would really have a picnic cooler or the equivalent with her, to be delivered somewhere else for proper care. According to George, the code message had indicated that she would. Rose had also carried her own fetus away from the midwifer, but that had been under emergency conditions. Maybe illegal parturition was always an emergency condition. Maybe normal birth was, too, not to mention life.

Out of the thick fog there loomed up abruptly a chest-high wall, running directly athwart their path. The wall was a single tier of massive stones, looking at first sight like part of some ancient fortification. Art realized in a moment that just beyond and below this rampart was the lake. Standing at the seawall and looking over it, he could see four or five more tiers of the gigantic blocks, making a rough stair down to the water. There waves materialized out of fog, chopping gently at the lowest stones, sloshing up between them. Here the air was thicker than ever with moisture. It was impossible to see for more than a few meters, either out over the water or along the shore.

"This chaste fog," George muttered. He checked his watch. "It's time. She's supposed to be waiting right around here somewhere. Look, we'd better separate, Art. You go south, along the rocks, and I'll go north. If you find her, give a whistle—can you whistle loud?"

"I can."

"Good. If you need help, yell out good and loud and keep on yelling. I'll be there as fast as I can."

"How far south do I go?"

George considered. "I'd say half a kilometer or less and you'll come to a harbor where a lot of private boats are tied up. Some fishermen will be around there too." The radio music was coming from that direction. "If you don't find her between here and the harbor, better turn back this way. I'll go north about the same distance and come back.

Whether we find her or not we'll meet again about here."

"Right."

Fred and Wolf came out of the park to stand beside the seawall amid the drifting billows of fog. There they paused uncertainly. At the moment there was no one else at all in sight—certainly no thin blond woman carrying a container.

Fred wished he had been able to find Lewandowski as well as Wolf, but there was no use wishing. He hadn't had time to wait and look around. He said: "This must be the place. I guess we better split up and look for her. How about if you go that way and I go this?"

"All right." Wolf and his neckpiece showed their double grin. "Watch out, man. They say there's a lot of apes hang out in these parks."

Fred laughed nervously, and with a tentative wave of his hand set off toward the south, walking parallel to the seawall. Wolf watched him go. Almost at once Fred's figure was swallowed by the fog.

Wolf turned and set out at a deliberate pace in the opposite direction. Despite having been awake all night, he felt alert and cheerful. It was fun to have a job of sorts, something exciting to do with his time. Also it was fun to help out a pal, and there might even be some money at the end of it, though he wasn't counting too much on that. Wolf didn't know what the whole thing was about—and didn't really care—except that it had something to do with illegal midwifing.

It was almost too easy. He hadn't walked a hundred steps and there she was, sitting on the second tier of stones down from the seawall's top. A young woman alone, thin and blond, and not even pretending to fish, doing nothing but waiting. There was a container with her, a white-handled red picnic cooler, and that nailed it down.

Her head swung around sharply when she heard a tiny scrape of stone under Wolf's sandal as he approached. At the sight of him she started to get up. She was wearing a translucent skirt, and open Cretan bodice.

Wolf grinned his knowledge at her, and came hopping along the stair of stone, down to the second step where she was. Conscious of being menacing, he watched her face, enjoying the little series of masks that she was trying on, masks of unconcern, defiance, even welcome, trying to hide the fear inside herself and throw him off stride and keep him away.

He came right up to her and reached out a hand and she recoiled. But he wasn't reaching out for her. Instead he scooped up the cooler, noting as he did so that it was surprisingly heavy. Not his job to wonder what it was. Wolf grinned at the woman once more, and turned and walked away from her, back the way he had come. Maybe she would be smart and simply let him go. But no, as soon as his back was turned to her she jumped him silently from behind.

The attack on his face and head was unskillful, but fierce. Wolf dropped the cooler and used both hands to fend her off. She went down on the rocks with a little cry of pain. "Wait!" she called to him then, seeing him pick up the cooler again. "Wait, can't we talk about this?"

He was already facing away from her, but he

turned his head enough to look back. He could feel the blood trickling down one side of his face from the place where her nails had raked him. But he only sighed. This was business, and Fred hadn't passed along any instructions that the woman was to be beaten up or injured in any way. People who hired this kind of business done usually spelled out just what they wanted, no more, no less.

Wolf shook his head, mocking and chiding. "Lady, lady. You know this thing don't really belong to you anyway." Not only was it heavy but also unusually cold. Well, he wasn't being paid to be curious.

The woman got to her feet, trying to smile again, wincing a little, pulling her bodice together, hiding her breasts provocatively. "Please," she called, first almost whispering, then again, louder. "Please, it *is* mine. Isn't there something you want more?"

Wolf gave a tiny laugh and turned away again, shaking his head. She wasn't bad, but this wasn't the time or place. He started off again, swinging the heavy cooler in one hand.

To his utter amazement, she jumped him again, this time screaming as she landed. This time the attack almost brought him down because it was so unexpected. Again he let the cooler fall on rocks, again he had to twist around and fend the clawing fingers from his eyes. Now he had a good grip on the woman's arms. Without much difficulty he avoided her clumsy attempt to knee him in the balls. This time he gave her a couple of violent shakes before he let her fly. At the last moment he avoided hurling her down the stairs of giant stone, and only cast her from him so that she fell on the same level. This time she went down harder, and lay there sobbing.

"Lady, you're pushin' your luck." Wolf almost wished she'd try it just once more. If she did . . .

Then there was the sound of running feet approaching. A little guy carrying a fishing pole and tackle box came dashing out of the fog along the stones, and came to a sudden stop a few steps off. A short guy with blond hair and a goatee, who looked enough like the woman to be her brother.

Wolf had fifteen kilos on him easily. He picked up the cooler yet once more, and, scowling, took a step in the way that he wanted to go. But the little guy only threw down his fishing gear, and took a step of his own, to stay in front of him on the same broad stair.

"Hey, it's a quin-tup-let," Wolf said easily. "And this one must be the runt of the litter." The little guy didn't back off, and Wolf reached into his pocket for his knife and switched it open.

"George," said the young woman behind Wolf, in a low, fainting voice. "It's my baby, stop him."

Wolf snarled and advanced, holding out the knife to make sure that little George got out of the way. But George came on at him instead, with a skip and a dart. Wolf, good with the knife, aimed at the oncoming flat belly. The body in front of him twisted away, somehow going down very low. Wolf never saw the upthrusting back-kick coming in under the knife, he only felt his breath driven out of him and his heart stop momentarily as the kick smashed into his ribs and broke them inward.

The world went dark. Knife and cooler dropped from his hands. He was aware of falling, a timeless, thoughtless moment in midair. And then impact came again.

*   *   *

Art Rodney, puffing and lumbering toward the sounds of distress and struggle, saw Fred Lohmann dash heedlessly past him through the fog, going in the same general direction that Art was. And then he saw Fred backing away, coming toward Art again along the huge stones of the seawall.

"George, I didn't know," Fred was saying. "George, I swear I didn't know." And then Fred turned and ran away, ran flat out, almost knocking Art down in his passage. Art could still hear the long strides pounding when Fred had vanished into the fog.

Advancing again, Art took in the scene before him with a glance. There was a knife lying on the rocks, and a man on the rocks below that, jammed headfirst into them down on the lowest tier of the wall where the crude stair turned into a jumble of blocks and boulders, amid which the lake thrust up its fists and splashed.

George, two tiers above, was looking down at the man and rubbing his knuckles nervously, or perhaps automatically. Not far from George there was a white-handled red picnic cooler, lying on its side, and beside the cooler sat Rita, sitting awkwardly, hugging herself as if she were in pain.

"Oh, darling, easy," she said into Art's ear as he descended on her. "Don't squeeze me. Oh, Art, you didn't bring the police down on us, did you?"

"No. No, I don't think so. I want to take you home."

"Our baby. We have to take care of our baby first." She was clutching at the cooler, and Art reached to set it right side up, as if that was going to make any difference to what was encapsulated inside.

Then he looked down at George, who had approached the fallen figure and was prodding it with a toe. Art asked: "What happened?" I got here as fast as I could when I heard a commotion. And I saw Fred run past me just now."

"Yeah. That was Fred." George shook his head and seemed to rouse himself. "Let's get out of here."

"And who's that?" Art moved a little, to where he could get a better look at the man with his head and shoulders jammed down into the seawall rocks. The man's eyes were open, blankly, over what looked like some kind of a fur collar. His face was lightly scratched, marked with little trickles of fresh blood. "Will he be all right if we just leave him?"

"He'll be dead," said George, in a voice that wavered once and came back strong again. "He's dead right now. He was after Rita. Let's get going." And he moved and picked up the cooler with one strong hand, and helped Rita to her feet with the other. "Art, get our fishpoles and stuff. I don't want to leave that here."

"Oh. Oh, chastity." Art looked once more at the dead man, and then pulled his eyes away from the sight. Somehow he gathered up all the fishing gear that he and George had carried here and dropped. Then he hurried on after his wife and her brother into the fog.

When Art caught up with them, he demanded: "Rita, did that fellow back there hurt you?"

"Not much. Not really. He only pushed me down ... and my ass is still sore from the parturition, and I have cramps. But they didn't have to make an incision or anything. I can walk. But I'm so tired I don't know how far."

Now she was clinging to Art's arm, leaning on

him, while George walked a little ahead of them carrying the cooler. They were moving through fog toward the sound of Orlando's voice on several radios.

SEVENTEEN

"Art. George. If anything happens to me, this is the situation. He's on the waiting list for a womb, but it may be months. The doctor says the safest place to take him in the meantime is the Loyola School of Medicine, Cryogenics Lab. They seem to have some safe depository, I don't know where. Loyola's on the north side of the city, Art. Somewhere. Ask for Gwen or Larry. I said we'd get him there. Oh, and he's been baptized . . . the doctor said he was afraid he was going to have to flee the city right away, or be arrested. Maybe there are worse things than that for us to fear." Rita looked over her shoulder, into thinning fog.

"Such as what?"

"That man back there. He was no policeman. And he wasn't really after me. Just my baby, not me. I'm sure of it."

Art felt a pang. Rizzo, somehow Rizzo. He patted his wife, hugged her, murmured soothing words.

She thought he didn't believe her. "I tell you, he was after the basket. He would have taken it and walked away if George hadn't stopped him."

Art, his head throbbing sickly now, the scalp wound burning, stared at George's back, moving three paces ahead of him through thinning mist. George said over his shoulder: "I'm glad he wasn't a cop. Hey, sis, what's your baby's name?" Art stared at the red cooler swinging in George's hand, seeing instead the dead body they had left behind them on the rocks. He and George both.

Rita said: "I haven't talked that over with his daddy yet. I think George Arthur. Or maybe Arthur George, though Art's always said he didn't want a junior."

They had been angling slightly inland, away from the seawall. Now, topping a little rise of grassy parkland, they encountered the wall ahead of them again. Almost directly ahead, amid thinning drifts of fog, several long, low piers extended out into the lake at right angles to the shoreline. Some boats were tied up to them, and the piers were thickly occupied by fisherfolk with their poles and nets and buckets. The sun was definitely up now, a fierce fog-veiled white entity above the watery horizon, visible between Great Lake-borne clouds of heavier stuff.

Here a gravel road ran just inland from the wall, and a few vehicles evidently belonging to the fisherfolk were parked along its edge. Just as the three people walking with the cooler reached the road, a police car appeared cruising in the middle distance, a face turned out of an open window in their direction.

"Alter course slightly," said George in a low voice. But it was no good. There was another car approaching along the road where it bent inland.

"Split up," said George succinctly. He thrust the picnic cooler into Art's hands and with the same movement took back his old tackle box. "Rita, take the bait jug," he added, and in the next instant was gone, sprinting into the fog toward the south. Now both police cars were accelerating, but the trio on which they had been closing in was vanishing three ways at once.

George went dashing around a clump of bushes, and then back onto the seawall, where he passed a group of fishermen. Then he slowed to a trot, and then to a walk. He looked back frequently, and cursed. Obviously neither of the cars had come after him, though he was deliberately staying near the road to lure them on.

But now at last there came a uniformed policeman running in pursuit of him on foot. "You there, halt!"

George was purposely deaf to the first yell, figuring they would give at least one more before they started shooting. If they were serious enough to shoot, which they probably weren't as yet, because the dead man could hardly have been found and reported to them so soon.

He heeded the second, closer shout, and looked round with polite surprise as an athletic policeman came running up.

"All right, hands in the air."

"What's the matter, officer?" George set the tackle box down and put his foot on it and raised his hands.

He was patted down, from behind, for weapons. Then the officer kicked the box. "What've you got in there?"

"Show me a search warrant and you can search me completely."

"I'm conducting a weapons search, mister, get your foot off that thing before I shoot it off."

The policeman's handgun was already drawn. George got, moving a few steps away and keeping his hands up. The policeman bent cautiously over the tackle box and peered into it. Then he looked up at George expressionlessly. "All right, come along. Bring this box of junk if you want it."

George picked up the box. The officer sheathed his pistol and with his left hand took a good grip on George's right sleeve, just above the elbow. It must be a technique they taught at the police academy, how to be ready to subdue resistance by the suspect. The grip was not bullying, and yet it was quite firm enough for business. Not bad for an amateur, not bad.

Fisherfolk looked up from their patient business to stare at the two of them as they passed. Now only one of the police cars was in sight. It was parked on the gravel road, with a scattering of the curious observing it from a little distance. Rita was sitting in the back seat, alone and apparently composed. A man in civvies sat in the front seat, twisted halfway around to face her. There was also a uniformed driver, who was busy right now on the radio.

The man in civilian clothes looked at George, and demanded of Rita: "Do you know this man?"

Her eyes turned neutrally to George, waiting for a signal.

"Of course she knows me. I'm her brother."

"George, this gentleman says he's Detective Simmons."

"What were you running off with, George? Empty tackle box, maybe? Don't you know it's against the law to interfere with police carrying out their duties?"

The box wasn't really empty, of course, but maybe

too close to empty to be convincing to a fisherman, and it certainly contained no fetal specimens. The patrolman was now giving his report. George held the box under his arm and remained silent; he saw that Rita still had the bait jug with her.

Presently Detective Simmons sighed and informed George that he was under arrest for conspiracy to violate the Population Control Laws, and made a little speech detailing his constitutional rights.

George was put into the back of the car, where he sat with Rita and one patrolman. With Detective Simmons up front beside the uniformed driver, the car began to move, cruising slowly north, going off the gravel road and over grass, following the shoreline of the lake. Then it turned and cruised the other way again. It stopping to let out one of the uniformed men, who stood looking out over the fishing piers, then walked off past them, talking on his hand radio.

Simmons turned to the people he had caged in the back seat. Through the intervening grillwork he said: "We're bringing along your tackle box and your empty bait-bucket, George and Rita, to show the judge what kind of tricks you try to pull. We're also going to bring that red picnic cooler and the fat man who's carrying it. We're going to pick that up in about a minute. Why don't you tell me something about it now, just to show you're willing to co-operate? Where were you taking it?"

"My sister and I want to see an attorney before we answer any more questions at all. This sounds like something serious."

"What do you think something serious is, George? What were you two and your sister's husband doing here today? No reason you can't tell me, if it wasn't anything wrong."

"Let us talk to an attorney," Rita said. "If you want us to answer questions."

Now a message was coming in on the car radio. Some police code words and a jargon of numbers had been found on the rocks near South Shore beach. More digit-laden jargon followed. The detective and the uniformed driver exchanged looks, but no more. George held his hands down so that the callus pads on his knuckles might not be noticed right away. Sooner or later somebody might make the connection. At the moment he felt no guilt, or fear; at the moment he was still as steady as a rock. Attorney, attorney, where will I find you? He had a couple of them among his students, but none in criminal law.

Now another message was coming in, this one on Simmons' little personal radio. From the back seat George couldn't quite make the message out, but abruptly the car was rolling again. It accelerated strongly, turned on its siren for a blast or two, then almost at once screeched rocking to a halt.

"That's Hall," Simmons in the front seat said, opening his door and getting out. Out of a small crowd, gathered as for an accident, a lean, stooped man was coming toward the police car, plodding with slow weariness as if he waded through mud. Actually his problem was not mud but water, George saw, for the man was wet as if he had just fallen into the lake. From the business socks inside his sandals little puddles were squeezed out at every step. Water plastered down his thinning hair and dripped from his translucent shorts and jacket.

Simmons, asking excited questions, hurried to meet him.

"That fat, fathering breeder!" was all Hall said at first. His voice was choked with anger as he stood there trying to press the water out of his clothing. "That quintuplet-siring crowder!" Some of the onlookers listening from a little distance smiled or snickered at the earnest vileness of the man's speech. One or two appeared sincerely shocked.

Simmons was holding his little radio ready. "If he shoved you in the water I can put in a call and charge him with assault and resisting arrest. That'll get us some more manpower out here. Which way did he go?"

"I don't know. Anyway, I don't care to press those charges." It seemed that a little strong language had served to discharge Hall's anger. He put up a hand now as if to ward off the detective's glare and exclamations of disgust. "He didn't hurt me. I don't think he even intended to knock me in the water. He was just determined to get away." Hall had taken his soggy jacket off, and now began to wave it like a distress signal, trying to dry it in the morning breeze. "I called out to him, when I saw that I had him cornered on a moored boat, I said just hand over the specimen and save yourself a lot of trouble. You and your wife and the whole world will be better off, I said. But then he came off the boat with this picnic cooler under his arm like a football. Just put down his head and charged, and he must weigh ninety kilos."

Hall during his speech had looked several times at Rita sitting in the car, but he had offered her no recognition until now. "Well, Mrs. Rodney, I suppose you and your husband and brother here are getting yourselves a lawyer. From the way you sit there looking so serenely into space, I suppose too that you've heard about the report."

Rita, her chin high, went on studying the horizon. George asked: "Report?"

"The new population forecast from the UN. The one we've all been afraid of. A real surprise. If the latest trends continue, world population is going to reach a peak of around ten billion in the next forty years, and then start down. Maybe even a rather sharp decline. Not that that will help the people who are going to go hungry in the next forty years, but it'll make it a little harder to convict people like yourselves before a jury." Mr. Hall was now standing completely nude in the dawn, shivering slightly but evidently not caring if they thought him rude or not. He was wringing out his shorts, his dripping codpiece slung over one shoulder.

"World population's going down?" asked the detective, sounding rather dumb. He couldn't seem to grasp it right away. George found he couldn't either.

Hall said: "Oh, we all knew it had to happen someday, one way or another. The only question was how and when. Still, when it does happen, we feel surprise."

Simmons was busy with his radio now. George asked: "But what is it? The Gay Leagues? They're growing fast."

"They were allowed for in previous forecasts. No, the thing that tipped the balance, that wasn't foreseen, was all this cultist celibacy. Half a dozen religions booming today, young people pulling themselves out of the reproductive pool by the tens of millions. People will think it will ease the population pressure right away, though of course it won't. It was hard enough before to get convictions, with bleeding-heart lawyers and frozen fetuses to cloud the issue. Now this. But we're going to try, sir, we're going to try. I'll see you in court, whether we manage to recover the specimen or not.''

George, riding north along the Outer Drive in the back of the police car, going to some police station where they would have to let him see a lawyer before he said a sublimatin' thing, held his sister's hand and looked out over the passing lake. The waves were coming in stronger now with a freshening breeze, starting to crest into whitecaps near the shore. The fog had gone. Get through, Art, get through. Loyola School of Medicine, Cryogenics Lab, ask for Gwen or Larry. You'd better not lose that kid now, I've killed a man to save him. I'd kill any other son of a bitch who tried to kill my nephew.

George smiled a little, for the new man born so strangely into the world, and at the same time he was very worried. The waves came in from the clear horizon, cresting into white. The crest of the wave has been reached. And now, to see which way the world slides down.

The Newest Adventure of the Galaxy's Only Two-Fisted Diplomat!

THE RETURN OF RETIEF

KEITH LAUMER

When the belligerent Ree decided they needed human space for their ever-increasing population, only Retief could cope.

$2.95

BAEN BOOKS

See next page for order information.

Coming in May 1985 from Baen Books—Poul Anderson's
first Terran Empire/Polesotechnic League novel in years!

THE GAME OF EMPIRE

Dominic Flandry has fought the good fight—but now
he is of an age more suited to deciding the fate of
empires from behind the throne. Others must take up
the challenge of courting danger on strange planets
filled with creatures stranger still . . . and such a one is
Diana Flandry, heir to all her father's adventures! Here
is an excerpt from THE GAME OF EMPIRE:

She sat on the tower of St. Barbara, kicking her heels
from the parapet, and looked across immensity. Overhead,
heaven was clear, deep blue save where the sun Patricius
stood small and fierce at midmorning. Two moons were
wanly aloft. A breeze blew cool. It would have been
deadly cold before Diana's people came to Imhotep; the
peak of Mt. Horn lifts a full twelve kilometers above sea
level.

"Who holds St. Barbara's holds the planet." That saying
was centuries obsolete, but the memory kept alive a
certain respect. Though ice bull herds no longer threatened to stampede through the original exploration base;
though the Troubles which left hostile bands marooned
and desperate, turning marauder, had ended when the
hand of the Terran Empire reached this far; though the
early defensive works would be useless in such upheav-
als as threatened the present age, and had long since
been demolished: still, one relic of them remained in
Olga's Landing, at the middle of what had become a
market square. Its guns had been taken away for scrap,
its chambers echoed hollow, sunseeker vine clambered
over the crumbling yellow stone of it, but St. Barbara's
stood yet; and it was a little audacious for a hoyden to
perch herself on top.

Diana often did. The neighborhood had stopped
minding—after all, she was everybody's friend—and to

strangers it meant nothing, except that human males were apt to shout and wave at the pretty girl. She grinned and waved back when she felt in the mood, but had learned to decline the invitations. Her aim was not always simply to enjoy the ever-shifting scenes. Sometimes she spied a chance to earn a credit or two, as when a newcomer seemed in want of a guide to the sights and amusements. At present she had no home of her own, unless you counted a ruinous temple where she kept hidden her meager possessions and, when nothing better was available, spread her sleeping bag.

Life spilled from narrow streets and surged between the walls enclosing the plaza. Pioneer buildings had run to brick, and never gone higher than three or four stories, under Imhotepan gravity. Booths huddled everywhere else against them. The wares were as multifarious as the sellers, anything from hinterland fruits and grains to ironware out of the smithies that made the air clangorous, from velvyl fabric and miniature computers of the inner Empire to jewels and skins and carvings off a hundred different worlds. A gundealer offered primitive home-produced chemical rifles, stunners of military type, and—illegally—several blasters, doubtless found in wrecked spacecraft after the Merseian onslaught was beaten back.

Folk were mainly human, but it was unlikely that many had seen Mother Terra. The planets where they were born and bred had marked them. Residents of Imhotep were necessarily muscular and never fat. Those whose families had lived here for generations, since Olga's Landing was a scientific base, and had thus melded into a type, tended to be dark-skinned and aquiline-featured.

A Navy man and a marine passed close by the tower. They were too intent on their talk to notice Diana, which was extraordinary. The harshness reached her: "—yeh, sure, they've grown it back for me." The spaceman waved his right arm. A short-sleeved undress shirt revealed it pallid and thin; regenerated tissue needs exercise to attain normal fitness. "But they said the budget doesn't allow repairing DNA throughout my body, after the radiation I took. I'll be dependent on biosupport the rest of my life, and I'll never dare father any kids."

"Merseian bastards," growled the marine. "I could damn near wish they had broken through and landed.

My unit had a warm welcome ready for 'em, I can tell you."

"Be glad they didn't," said his companion. "Did you really want nukes tearing up our planets? Wounds and all, I'll thank Admiral Magnusson every day I've got left to me, for turning them back the way he did, with that skeleton force the pinchfists on Terra allowed us." Bitterly: "*He* wouldn't begrudge the cost of fixing up entire a man that fought under him."

They disappeared into the throng. Diana shivered a bit and looked around for something cheerier than such a reminder of last year's events.

Nonhumans were on hand in fair number. Most were Tigeries, come from the lowlands on various business, their orange-black-white pelts vivid around skimpy garments. Generally they wore air helmets, with pressure pumps strapped to their backs, but on some, oxygills rose out of the shoulders, behind the heads, like elegant ruffs. Diana cried greetings to those she recognized. Otherwise she spied a centauroid Donarrian; the shiny integuments of three Irumclagians; a couple of tailed, green-skinned Shalmuans; and—and—

"What the flippin' fury!" She got to her feet—they were bare, and the stone felt warm beneath them—and stood precariously balanced, peering.

Around the corner of a Winged Smoke house had come a giant.